DEADMAN'S SWITCH

Also by BARBARA SERANELLA

THE MUNCH MANCINI CRIME NOVEL SERIES

BARBARA SERANELLA

DEADMAN'S SWITCH

THOMAS

DUNNE

BOOKS

ST. MARTIN'S MINOTAUR

NEW YORK

THOMAS DUNNE BOOKS.
An imprint of St. Martin's Press.

www.thomasdunnebooks.com
www.minotaurbooks.com

Book design by Jonathan Bennett

ISBN-13: 978-0-312-36170-9
ISBN-10: 0-312-36170-X

First Edition: April 2007

10   9   8   7   6   5   4   3   2   1

For all the wonderful people who prayed for me and sent their love in the summer of '05 and the long months since. The resulting miracles have been much appreciated.

And for Mom and Dad Shore, who have been nothing short of heroic.

DEADMAN'S SWITCH

PROLOGUE

Bob Peterson scanned the track before him. He'd been green-lit all the way to Beaumont and would easily make up the ten minutes he'd lost in Corona. Operating a passenger train was a series of races from one station to the next to maintain the schedule.

He notched the throttle up another position and settled in the worn engineer's chair. The surrounding hills looked as if they were painted on sheer sheets of billowing fabric. Like some movie backdrop. The locomotive's air-conditioning was on the blink, and the electric fan mounted under the sun visor was proving woefully inadequate to provide relief from the scorching summer sun.

His speed edged toward seventy as he scanned the rail ahead of his wheels. At first, his brain fought to dismiss what his eyes told him. How was it possible? He'd never seen anything like it in all his years. Fifty yards ahead of him, the tracks narrowed. What natural force could have nudged the tons of steel together and leave the concrete ties intact? None, was the answer.

He slammed the pneumatic brake handle forward, fighting resistance at the last notch. Resistance that also shouldn't have been there.

Instantly, the air reservoirs spewed their reserves. The roar of it filled his ears. He tried to turn his head, but couldn't. The train slowed with a mighty screech of protesting steel, and still he didn't move, not even to breathe. It was almost as if he were no longer connected to his body.

His head jerked back. He stared at the ceiling of the cab, as powerless over his body as he was over the tons of steel now slamming into itself. Cars piled up behind him. Kinetic energy built until one after another jumped the track. He watched the images in his mirrors, helpless to do anything but observe. The passenger coaches tumbled like dominoes down the hillsides to the left and right of him. He felt the tug from behind as the couplers and air lines wrenched loose.

The in-train phone rang, but he didn't reach for it. He couldn't even lift a leaden arm to shield his face.

My God, he thought, his body now screaming for the oxygen that his lungs refused to pump, *I'm going to die.*

A lone figure stood on the heat-scorched hillside. He was not aware of the heat, even though he wore full leather gear, boots, gloves, and a helmet. The dark visor was raised as he watched with a mixture of awe and fear the events he had put into motion.

The plan was working almost too well. He had no regrets about taking out his intended target, but the scope of the catastrophe was nearly more than he hoped for.

He had thought to derail only the first few cars. In the stillness following the crash, cries for help and moans of pain floated up to his position on the hill.

He felt bad for the innocents, but the clock couldn't be turned back. Derailing a train wasn't an exact science. What was done was done.

Now he had to act fast and efficiently. It wouldn't be long before others arrived. The job was not over, not until the final coup de grâce was delivered. Also essential was that he got away with it.

He lowered his visor and ran to the smoking ruin.

ACKNOWLEDGMENTS

I had a lot of help with this book and want to thank the many kind people who took the time to answer my many questions.

On the PR side there was Joan Gladstone, president and CEO of Gladstone International; Bob Roth; *Crisis Communications: A Casebook Approach* by Kathleen Fearn-Banks; Cheryl Pruett; Chuck Rossie of the CMR Group, Inc. (who sent me gobs of useful information as well as answering my questions in a very detailed manner); Tom Eichhorn, whose passion on the subject was very helpful.

On the train side: Jerry Hooten and his brother Dave Hooten, train master; Joseph Yannuzzi, general manager of Coaster Commuter Service; *Modern Diesel Locomotives* by Hans Halberstadt; Ted Leplack, NTSB investigator; Sue Phillips for an introduction to John Delgado, engineer; Robert Halstead, president of Ironwood Technologies, Inc. (who also took the time and interest to send me wonderful reams of information).

Readers: While this was still a work in progress I got lots of good feedback from my two critique groups: the Fictionaires of Orange County and "the Group who meet at Rachel's" in Coachella Valley;

Mari Lou Elders; April Henry (who wears many hats, including author, and PR person for Kaiser); Sarah Knight, who helped me believe in the book; Judith Anderson, who had the integrity to tell me the truth and not what I wanted to hear; Donna Moore, who helped in many ways; Jill Marsal and Sandy Dijkstra, who kept browbeating me to go back and make it better.

For forensic stuff: Dr. Joseph Cohen, Riverside coroner; Dr. Lou Boxer, friend and anesthesiologist; Dr. Doug Lyle, who knows almost everything about everything, and what he doesn't know, he'll look up for you; my dear brother, Dr. Larry Shore; my other, just as dear brother, David Shore, who helped me understand the business end of things. Take that any way you want.

Regarding OCD: my thanks to the many people who opened up to me.

And last, but never least, my husband, Ron. It's been a tough year and it would have been impossible without him. Did I get lucky or what?

TUESDAY

CHAPTER 1

In a crazy way, the train wreck had saved her.

"Crazy was her way," her husband used to say. It was a joke that died with him nine months ago.

As it was, the train wreck couldn't have come at a better time. Thirty-three-year-old Charlotte Lyon had been to the dentist the day before. There, she had had the bad luck to notice that the hygienist opened the door with the same hand she'd just had in a patient's mouth. The health worker's hand was still gloved, and she had put it right on the chrome knob with no regard for how many microbes and God knew what else she was releasing into the unsuspecting office. Had the woman never heard of blood- and saliva-born pathogens? What was she thinking?

Charlotte had been arguing with herself for the past eighteen hours over whether or not to report what she'd seen to the dentist. The problem was that after her appointment six months earlier, she had questioned him about the sterility of his instruments, and she didn't want him to think she was nuts.

Perish that thought, Char. The voice that spoke was the one she identified as being her saner self. Sanity was such a relative term. Compared with her mom, Charlotte was the picture of mental health. Compared with the average—or what she assumed was average—woman on the street, Char was not boring.

She pondered this dilemma as she sat in her North Laguna Beach home office. She'd bought her house in this section of Orange County because it was one of the few coastal communities in California that didn't sit on fault lines. Brad would have enjoyed the house's views of breaking waves, the barking of the seals, and the bracing salt air. She wiped a tear from her cheek. He was missing so much.

On clear nights, when the moon was bright, silvery highlights danced in the dark water. It was breathtaking, and the kind of thing that needed to be shared with another person. But that didn't seem to be in the cards for her. Not with her late husband anyway.

The house was built to give the ocean view to as many rooms as possible. Her home office was one of those rooms, although she kept it shuttered. When she was working, the only windows to the world she needed were provided by her computer screen and CNN. Bookshelves organized by topic gave the room color. A custom-built unit on the wall to her left incorporated filing cabinets and shelving for a combo TV-and-VCR.

By nature and avocation, Charlotte looked for trouble. She had a knack for it, plus it paid well. Enough to fill her closet with chic designer pantsuits and put a Mercedes in the driveway. The Mercedes sported a personalized license plate frame that summed up her life succinctly. It read, THINK NEGATIVELY.

Currently she was at work—or trying to be, the whole dentist thing was making it difficult to stay focused—on a crisis-preparedness plan for her newest client. Mercy Hospital in Newport Beach had signed on with her last week, and she was busy considering how many things could go wrong at a hospital. The list was staggering.

The television to her left flashed muted images as she faced her computer screen. A BREAKING NEWS banner fluttered across the television screen. Charlotte reached for the remote and turned up the volume.

The LIVE icon in the upper right of the screen didn't interfere with the vibrating image of a smoking ruin. The banner along the bottom of the screen read TRAIN DERAILMENT IN RIVERSIDE COUNTY. No, not smoke, she realized as she focused, but swirling dust. She pushed RECORD on the VCR as she studied the aerial footage. The locomotive had a yellow-and-silver cab. *Sunliner Express* in black script on a yellow background was clearly legible on the cars on their sides.

Charlotte looked for signs of death—tarped bodies, severed limbs. *Yeah, I'm the epitome of not boring,* she thought.

The derailment had happened on a stretch of track that ran parallel to a two-lane roadway on one side and the San Andreas fault line on the other. A deep fissure created by the 1857 Fort Tejon 8.0 earthquake cleaved the countryside. The low hills and surrounding countryside were brown and strung with power lines. She knew the area by its nickname: the Badlands. The V-shaped wedge of low desert was where the 60 and the 10 Freeways merged in Riverside County. The track was uninterrupted before and after the crash. There was no crossing or another wrecked vehicle, which would have been obvious reasons for the derailment. One of the passenger coaches had broken loose and slid down the embankment. The full scene of the crash was blocked from view by the drooping branches of several live oak trees, but from what she could see, the train twisted to either side of the rails, forming an S over the straight run of track.

She pressed SAVE for the Mercy Hospital document as the phone rang. The caller ID spelled out Dom. Dominic Cole was a corporate lawyer who often referred work to her. He was a decent guy, in his six-ties, married to the same woman for thirty-five years. If Charlotte could have picked her father, he would have been someone like Dom. Certainly not the loser drug-addict sperm donor her mother had found. Mom had dated a string of that type of man, each guy inter-changeable with the last. Long-haired, bearded zombies who passed the day drinking beer and smoking cigarettes—and those were the good ones. Char shook off the memories. That was then. This was now.

She hadn't taken on a big crisis job in nine months. Mostly she avoided face-to-face encounters with her clients as she adjusted to her widowhood. She never knew when she would burst into tears. Not only was that behavior unprofessional, but crying women tended to make people uncomfortable, as if they should be doing something to fix the situation. Lately, she had been regaining control over her emo-tions, managing most of the time to keep the tears inside. Maybe it was time to get back in the game.

She slid the earpiece of her wireless phone into place and posi-tioned the microphone to the right of her mouth so she could move and talk at the same time. "The train wreck?"

"You've been watching CNN?"

"I'm taping it. One of yours?"

"Yeah, Sun Rail. We're going to need your services."

"Is the company aware of my terms?" she asked. She liked to get that out in the open right away. Her fees were steep, but she earned them.

"I had them all read the *Forbes* profile. The CEO had already heard of you. We need you."

"Hazardous cargo?"

"No, just passengers."

"I saw the logo. The Sunliner is the new passenger line to the Indian casinos, right?" She went to her bedroom and selected a size 6, black

Armani pantsuit and a pair of black pumps that added two inches to her five-foot-five-inch frame.

"That's correct," he said. "It's been up and running for seven months, doing landmark business."

Unlike Amtrak's beleaguered Starliner service, she remembered reading in *The Wall Street Journal*, the Sunliner was hoping to revitalize the industry with elegant and punctual service.

"This is going to kill us . . . them," Dom said.

"Fatalities?"

"I can't say at this time," Dom said, doing his lawyer thing.

She ran a comb through her auburn hair and applied a fresh coat of lipstick. "Okay. I'm on my way." She felt herself shift into crisis mode. Energy coursed through her. She would require every bit of it in the next twenty-four hours. Speed was key. A plan needed to be devised, tough questions asked and answered, a statement and a press release composed, and a press conference scheduled. Her thoughts were focused and uncluttered, her hands steady. The worse the news, the calmer she became. Clients often couldn't believe how calm she was amidst chaos. The term *cold-blooded* had come up once or twice, though nothing could be further from the truth.

The real story was that the worse the disaster, the more at home she felt. Normal even, whatever that meant. Calamity and chaos were the world she was raised in, the waters where she swam. A train derailment was massive in terms of event crises, and it would challenge every one of her resources. She would have to remind herself not to grin. But so help her God, she lived for this shit. She didn't realize how much she had missed it.

An aunt in Charlotte's teen years had been first to spot her condition. It was that same aunt who encouraged her to embrace her neurosis and make it work for her.

Back then, in the eighties, the clinical term for her malady was impulse-control disorder. In more recent years—catering to the limited attention span of consumers—products, businesses, even diseases were labeled by their initials. Impulse control had evolved into being termed obsessive-compulsive disorder and finally OCD. Psychiatrists treated the illness with therapy and drugs that numbed the irrational urges.

She had lived with the needs that compelled her for enough years to be able to recognize when they had taken control. Her medication gave her a delay mechanism, a needed pause so she could reason with herself. She no longer had to spend half an hour making sure no water was running before she left her house. Fifteen minutes tops now. She had some tiny quirks involving counting and patterns, but she no longer washed her hands until they were raw.

On the bright side, her inherent hypervigilance gave her an almost psychic ability to predict catastrophe.

When she asked herself, *What's the worst that could happen?* her mind came up with scenarios that no one else had ever considered.

Charlotte didn't list her condition on her résumé, but anyone who dealt with her knew that she was the go-to girl for disaster-planning crisis management. Making the cover of *Forbes* magazine hadn't hurt either.

Her company, C. Lyon Communication Management, supplied several services. Her bread and butter was crisis response strategies, such as she was doing for Mercy Hospital. She also did media training for company spokespersons and litigation support, which was how she met Dom, who also understood the value of winning in the court of public opinion. All this had led to her supreme specialty. Crisis unwinding, for want of a better term. Her policy was open and honest disclosure of the facts, which meant identifying the cause of the problem, and when humanly possible, taking the measures necessary to ensure that the tragedy didn't repeat. But above all, her mission was to get to the truth. Without that, everything else was impossible.

"I'm pulling together a meeting with the board of directors," Dom told her now. "The corporate office is in Anaheim, the new building off of Disney Way."

"I know it well," she said. Disneyland had had its share of PR crises. "We're going to need bulletin boards, dry-erase boards, flip charts, maps of the crisis area as well as the whole route. Safety protocols, maintenance schedules, crew bios, and a fact sheet about the company. We'll issue a preliminary statement within the hour."

"So you're in?" he asked.

"Yes, I'm in. Were there fatalities?"

"Two," he said. "The engineer and a woman passenger."

She wanted to ask if either were married or had families, but stopped herself. She had to focus, not let her thoughts lead her back to the terrible day her own life had changed. "For now," she told Dom, "our thoughts and prayers are with the survivors and family members. Who, by the way, should be notified immediately. I don't want them hearing that their loved one died via television.

"Tell whoever's answering the phones that when the reporters call, we're still gathering information and preparing a statement."

The first statement was critical, she knew, and established the company's credibility or lack of it. And any delay would erode it. Lack of credibility, not knowing who to trust, put her on edge. And Charlotte always began by trusting no one. That rule had kept her alive this long.

CHAPTER 2

Thirty minutes later, Charlotte pulled into the guest parking of the sleek ten-story office building that was headquarters to Sun Rail. Several news vans were already there. Two reporters in the lobby pounced on her immediately. She took their cards and promised to let them know what was going on as soon as possible. Somewhat mollified, they backed off.

Charlotte showed her picture identification to the security guard.

What he saw was pleasing, or so his smile suggested as he gave her a visitor badge to affix to her lapel and buzzed her through to the bank of elevators. Sun Rail occupied the seventh and eighth floors. Charlotte would have preferred a lower level. She studied the fire exit routes while waiting for the car that would take her to her new client's boardroom.

Her jewelry was simple and understated, as were her shoes. She wore small diamond studs in her ears, a sleek Movado watch on her wrist, and a set of wedding rings on a gold chain around her neck. Years ago the PR business was thought of as a fluff job. Public relations professionals were mostly women and weren't taken seriously. Times had changed. Now women were sought after as spokespersons. Reporters and viewers, studies found, tended to trust a woman over a man. Still, no stiletto heels or low-cut blouses for her. Charlotte knew it was important to look professional, to be perceived as professional.

She entered the boardroom for her briefing. Ten grim-faced people were already there, waiting. She expected this. Usually by the time she was called in, her clients were pretty deep into the crisis, and the significance of their dilemma was freaking them out big-time.

Three of the attendees were women, a promising sign. Dominic slid a confidentiality agreement across the polished surface of the large square wooden table. The contract was pretty much boilerplate, written to protect all interested parties.

She scanned it quickly, signed it, and then placed a blank legal pad in front of her. Tape recorders tended to make executives nervous, and she was there to exert a calming influence, to be sympathetic, and to learn exactly what the hell had happened.

"Do you mind if I take notes?" she asked.

All eyes turned to the man in the navy blue Windbreaker. He was silver-haired in a way that would make a men's hair dye advertisement department shudder. He exuded power and confidence. A man in his prime. The fact that he was lean and tanned didn't hurt that overall impression. Charlotte figured he was probably in his late fifties or early sixties. She recognized the logo of the Balboa Yacht Club. Obviously, he was the big honcho. They would have to scare up a more somber outfit for him before he faced the cameras.

"Not at all, Ms. Lyon. I'm Bernard Rayney. Thank you for coming on such short notice." He licked his lips, but from where she was sitting, he was all out of saliva. As if noticing this, too, he slid his empty water glass to the young man hovering at his side. The assistant replenished his boss's drink from a crystal decanter. Charlotte noticed that the young man held the carafe with his thumb inside the lip. She envisioned his germs seeping into the room's water supply. As if they didn't have enough problems without a Typhoid Moron among them.

The other Sun Rail personnel around the table smiled and echoed their boss's sentiments. She hoped Rayney wasn't the kind of CEO who liked only good news. Most crises were not acts of God. Usually they were situations that erupted after a series of ignored signs. There were always people who knew what was going on, but who had waited or were afraid to speak up. Often, it was the innocent who suffered most, and that was intolerable.

"What do we know so far?" she asked.

Just then, a harried thin man who appeared to be in his forties hustled into the room, mumbling apologies for being late.

Raney waved his apology aside. "I'll let Stanley Mack answer that. He's our Train Master and VP in charge of operations. We brought him over from Amtrak. If you have questions about trains, specifically mechanical operation, Stan's your man."

Stan cleared his throat, made only a moment's eye contact with Charlotte, smiled nervously, and put on thick reading glasses. She felt a collective tension grip the room.

Stanley took a document from his pocket, unfolded it with shaking hands, and began reading. "The twelve fifteen p.m. run left Union Station on time, running a fifteen-car consist of one engine, eight passenger cars, five baggage and mail cars, and one flatbed car carrier. At three twenty this afternoon, for reasons unknown, six passenger cars jumped the track at mileage marker five-five-three, just east of Calimesa. The derailment threw three passenger cars on their sides."

Audible sighs of distress issued from the people surrounding her. Bernard Rayney remained collected. "Go on," he said.

"I'm not familiar with the term *consist*," Charlotte said.

"It's a grouping of train cars," Rayney said.

Charlotte made a note.

Stanley adjusted his glasses. Before speaking again, he inhaled through his nose with a wet slurping sound. He followed this with a gargling cough that dislodged mucus. She wondered if now he were going to spit it all out somewhere. Instead, he swallowed conspicuously, which was even worse. Charlotte hoped he wasn't the company's only train authority. She could always bring in an outside expert for the video-feed press updates.

"The locomotive remained on the track," he added.

"And the fatalities?" Charlotte asked.

"Still only two."

Only, Charlotte thought, forming a dislike for the man. Her expression never changed. Outwardly, she still appeared to be a sympathetic listener. She nodded for him to continue.

Stan cleared his throat again. "An elderly female passenger in the first car and the engineer, Bob Peterson."

Charlotte looked up from her notes. "And Bob Peterson was in the locomotive?"

"That's where the engineer rides."

She felt a wave of anger. She knew very well where the engineer was supposed to be. Stan was being a smart-ass or condescending. She stared at him until he started to blink uncontrollably. "Was he alone?" she asked.

"Yes, but that's all I know at the moment. The dead have been taken to the Riverside coroner's office for autopsy."

"Was he killed in the accident?" Charlotte asked. "On TV it didn't seem that the locomotive sustained any damage."

Stan looked at the door as if he would rather be anywhere but there. "That's what the autopsy should determine."

From the dropped eyes around the table, she knew she wasn't the only one who thought there was something hinky about the engineer's death. She turned to CEO Rayney. "What's being done to transport the passengers stranded on the tracks?"

"Mary?" he said, addressing a freckle-faced young woman who looked as if she was fresh from grad school.

"Hello, Ms. Lyon. I'm Mary Nightengale. I'm in charge of customer relations. The FBI asked us to keep everyone who wasn't injured at the accident site."

"Why was the FBI called in?" Charlotte asked.

"Post-9/11 policy. They have to make sure it wasn't an act of terrorism," Dom said.

"Do they have reason to believe that terrorists were responsible?" Charlotte asked.

"Not as far as we know," Mary said.

"Okay," Charlotte said. "Their concerns are understandable. So how many people are we talking about still at the scene?"

Mary consulted her notes. "According to the manifest, the train was carrying one hundred and sixty-one passengers and fifteen crew. Twelve of those passengers were taken by ambulance to Loma Linda Hospital. Ten were air-lifted to Eisenhower Hospital in Rancho Mirage."

"Were any of their injuries life-threatening?" Charlotte pictured a train coach pitching sideways, passengers screaming, falling in to each other. Hot coffee scalding flesh, bones cracking against metal bulkheads, bleeding from broken windows, the sheer claustrophobia of landing at the bottom of a heap of human debris with no way out.

"Not in the initial reports," Mary said.

"Someone from the company should go to the hospitals." *Not me,* Charlotte thought. She hated hospitals; they were way too depressing. "The media will be all over. The hospital staff will be aware of confidentiality and secrecy laws, so reporters will be looking for statements from ambulance drivers, families of other patients, whoever might have been walking by when the casualties arrived. We need a rep from the company there to set themselves up as the primary news resource."

"I'm on it," Mary said.

"Do you have someone for both hospitals?" Charlotte asked.

"I have an intern from Pepperdine," Mary volunteered. "He's very sharp."

"All right." Charlotte liked this girl's attitude and willingness to jump in to a potentially difficult situation with both feet. "I'll need each of you to coordinate with the hospitals' public relations staff. I'm sure they'll welcome your help. And let's get the remaining people at the crash site into some air-conditioned buses, at least. Call a livery service or sightseeing business. Pay whatever you have to. The people and their comfort are our first concern. I'll need copies of the manifest."

Mary looked at her boss for confirmation.

He nodded. "Do it."

Mary had already made copies, as well as prepared all the other documents Charlotte had told Dom she would need. They were nicely presented in a press kit folder, complete with Mary's card.

Charlotte accepted the folder with a grateful smile. Then she scratched herself a cryptic note on her notepad in the shorthand only she could decipher. She was thinking subpoena, especially now that she knew the FBI was involved. She had no love for the Feds nor did she feel any compulsion to work with them on anything. The Feds had divided her family, promised protection, then thrown them out in the cold when the case her mother had helped to make was over with and the tiny family of three was no longer useful. Charlotte had been fourteen. Jill, ten.

"What other agencies have been contacted?" Charlotte asked.

Dom spoke up. "The National Transportation Safety Board, the union, the Federal Railroad Administration, the Red Cross, local fire and police."

"Get rid of the Red Cross unless we absolutely need them," she said. The Red Cross communicated *disaster.* It was her job to keep those kinds of words disassociated from her client's name. "Have the families of the deceased been notified?"

"Dorothy Peterson, the engineer's wife, knows," Rayney said. "The coroner's office said they would handle the other one as soon as they confirm her identity."

As always, another human being's lack of sensitivity appalled Charlotte. When her own husband was killed, the news had been delivered to her by a stranger. It had felt very wrong that some previously unknown man arrived in her life only to change it so drastically. She had invited him in for coffee. After he left, she threw away the cup he had used, knowing she would never be able to wash it enough times and that it would forever turn any drink bitter. She wondered again if Engineer Bob had kids, and if the elderly female passenger was a wife, mother, or grandmother.

She opened her BlackBerry and looked up the names of several grief counselors she had worked with on other jobs. On a fresh piece of paper, she copied their names and phone numbers. She tacked the list to the bulletin board she had requested. "We care," she reiterated. "We send in our own people to help the bereaved. We don't leave them alone, even if it means flying in friends and family members to be at their sides." She crossed the room to stand before the white board.

She felt the shift of their trust. It was in their eyes and posture. Even CEO Rayney leaned forward in his chair to listen. She wrote *passengers, employees, board members* and then stopped.

"Is this company publicly traded?"

Rayney looked uncomfortable for a moment and then answered, "No."

"How about financial partners or investors?" It was important to discover who stood to win or lose by this crash, and of those publics, who had the very most at stake.

"I don't see what this has to do with anything," the CEO said.

Charlotte wondered if his avoidance was motivated by arrogance or something darker. Business schools taught CEOs to be self-reliant problem solvers and to exude confidence. This training had the adverse effect of making them resistant to advice. "I need all the facts at my disposal if I am to do my best for your company. We need to look beyond the immediate crisis and consider the long term. I want to help you avoid shortcuts now that will come back to haunt you in the future."

Dominic spoke. "Bernard, we can trust her. She's legally bound to keep our confidences."

Rayney didn't look happy as he fixed her with a look that sent a small thrill of fear through her, almost like an electrical shock. The potential for ruthlessness in his expression left her fingertips tingling with adrenaline. She hoped he never used that look on camera. He needed to shave, too.

She put on her sympathetic face and waited for him to speak.

"In three months," he finally said, "we are planning to announce an initial public stock offering."

Ahh, she thought, this certainly upped the stakes. Bad timing for an image-damaging blow, but even more reason for him to be forthright. She couldn't contain the way the story was going to be reported if she didn't have the facts.

The worst thing that could happen to her was to get blindsided by a client who supplied her with incomplete information. She had her own reputation to consider. No one customer was worth being caught in an embarrassing, even dangerous situation because of his or her cowardice or unwillingness to face the truth. That's why she made it a personal rule never to rely on just one source for her information.

"Bernard," she said. "You don't mind if I call you Bernard, do you?" Without waiting for his answer, she plowed on. "I'll go the distance with you, but you gotta do the same with me. I need complete access if I'm going to help you get through this. You don't have the time to waste."

Rayney gave her a gritted-teeth smile. "What else do you need?"

"I need to find out exactly how and why that train derailed, and when and how the engineer died. We need to communicate to all interested parties as well as the public at large that we suited up, showed up, and won't rest until we have the answers. That we'll do everything we can to ensure it doesn't happen again. We need to get the top experts in derailment analysis on it immediately. If the NTSB hasn't sent us their best, find out who it is, and get him or her here."

Rayney pointed a finger at the young man who had stuck his thumb in the water pitcher. "Andrew, make it happen."

"We need a war room with five telephones, all networked to an eight-hundred number for a 24-7 hot line. Mary, have your intern contact his classmates. We need intelligent bodies to man the phones. They need to write down all the questions being asked and by whom, then promise the caller a call back with the answers later on. I'll write up a script. Does the company have a Web site?"

"Yes," Rayney said.

"Can we immediately update it from here?"

"Andrew?" Rayney asked.

The assistant made a note. "I'll find out."

Charlotte turned to the CEO. "Bernard, you need to shave and look presentable for the cameras. You're about to have your fifteen minutes of fame."

"Great," he said. "Just fucking great."

"I'll get my laptop from my car so I can get to work on a statement and press release." Charlotte reached into her satchel and removed a list of her local and national press contacts, highlighting in yellow those she wanted invited to the initial press conference. "Let's also stock up on bottled water and energy bars. We have a long night ahead."

Nobody asked her what they would do if the accident was the company's fault. She wouldn't have hesitated with her answer. She never shied from the truth, no matter who found it inconvenient. Sometimes that was a dangerous position to take.

CHAPTER 3

Charlotte went down to her car and retrieved her laptop as well as her small Walkman TV. The trunk of her car was always packed with her various "go kits." She kept clothing suitable for any type of weather, toiletries, and changes of underwear. In a sealed plastic box with separate compartments were plenty of batteries, flashlights, and extension cords, also pills to purify water, pills to minimize radiation exposure, and pills to keep her awake. She had cameras—digital, disposable, and movie. Phone cards, walkie-talkies, flares, blankets, an emergency stash of cash, and MREs.

She wondered if she still had a spare tire under all that.

The only thing she wasn't prepared for was no crisis at all. Then she would have too much time to dwell on all the tragedies-waiting-to-happen surrounding her. The rituals would take over, everything done in multiples of ten, whether it was brushing her teeth or loading the washing machine. The furniture wouldn't align correctly.

She knew very well when she was having an OCD moment and perhaps overreacting, but self-awareness and force of will weren't always enough to stop her. Didn't smokers know how bad cigarettes were for their health every time they lit up? Weren't overeaters aware when they were chewing again? At least with her condition, the outward signs of her obsession were a meticulously clean house and a well-organized desk. She wasn't counting the times she couldn't leave the house for fear of forgetting some crucial detail. At times like that, all the tools her therapist suggested and the drugs meant to dull her impulses were little help. Only total absorption in real crisis set her free.

"Ms. Lyon?"

Charlotte turned. "Andrew, isn't it? Call me Charlotte."

"Do you need some help?" he asked.

So Mary Nightengale wasn't the only go-getter in the company. She unfolded a wheeled trolley and started filling a plastic crate with supplies. She included a printer/fax machine, name badge blanks, and extra ink cartridges.

"Thanks," she told him, "you can bring the box of stuff on the dolly." She slung her laptop in its carrying case over her shoulder and let him lead the way. Two satellite vans, one from MSNBC and the other from FOX News, had already begun setting up in the parking lot. CNN wouldn't be far behind. The high-speed, low-density media would want a new wrinkle every half hour. The major media would be content with morning, evening, and late-night updates for their scheduled shows.

Dominic was waiting in the conference room that would serve as her operation base. "I've been going over our contract with Union Pacific," he said.

"Let me get wired up so I don't miss any of this," she said. They stood against the wall so as not to be in the way of workers plugging in telephones and bringing in cases of bottled water.

She set up her laptop and printer on an empty table, pleased to find a T3 outlet for her modem. She booted up her computer, and it opened to a word processing program. She went online and set her search engines to seek out articles with the key words *Sun Rail* and *Sunliner* and *Derailment* in them and to notify her with an audible alarm when they got a hit.

"All right," she said. "I'm ready."

Dom spoke slowly. "The good news is that the maintenance and inspection of the track is Union Pacific's responsibility. Sun Rail pays for the use of the track by the mile. We provide our own engineers, conductors, and cars."

"So our responsibility is the rolling equipment and the crew."

He looked troubled. "Yes, but there is also an indemnification clause written into the contract. Sun Rail is liable for any lawsuits or claims that arise from any problem we cause on the line. Union Pacific is already wanting to know how soon the track will be open again."

"Is it a well-traveled route?" She saw Andrew and gestured for him to come over.

"Freight runs through every three hours," Dom said. "This track stretches all the way to New Orleans. The freight runners already grouse about the deal we struck and how our passenger trains clog up their rails. They will assess penalties for every hour the track is closed."

"I understand their needs," she said calmly. "But the investigation must be thorough."

Andrew was now standing attentively at her side. "What can I get you?"

"Stationery with the company logo on it, and a podium."

"You want it miked?"

She smiled at him. "You read my mind."

After Andrew left, Charlotte turned back to Dom. "Bernard Rayney needs to get out to the hospital and get his picture taken. I want Train Master Stan at the crash site for background information, but I don't want him in front of any cameras alone."

"Stan's already on his way to the site," Dom said, "and I'll accompany Rayney to the hospital."

"Good. Use Mary Nightengale for live updates. The cameras will love her." Mary also didn't seem to be the type who would giggle or fidget with her hair. Charlotte couldn't have a company spokesperson who looked or acted too young. Mary was an articulate and intelligent young woman. She'd do fine.

Dom shook out his cuffs and straightened his tie, the attorney's equivalent to girding his loins. "NTSB is sending a ten-man team. One guy is coming from the Gardena office. His name is . . ." Dom consulted the notes he'd scribbled on an envelope. "Here it is. Todd Hannigan. Union Pacific is also sending a team of supervisors, and we'll have people from the Federal Railroad Administration."

"I'll join them there after I draft a press release." She typed as she spoke.

"Hannigan is stopping here first. Maybe you two could ride out there together."

"Sure," she said. "But we'll need to take my car."

Dom smiled. "I'm glad you're here, Charlotte."

"Me too." She already felt the vise releasing. As the panic level around her increased, her own emotional state leveled to a cruising altitude. She had even managed to go a whole hour without thinking about Brad.

His cell phone rang. When he saw that the caller was Lorrin, he wanted to scream. The guy shouldn't be calling him, especially not now. Phone records could be checked.

"What's up?" he asked, keeping his tone light.

"The company hired a troubleshooter. A really good one," Lorrin said.

He could practically hear his accomplice sweating. "Don't worry. I'm on it."

"I've heard of this Charlotte Lyon. She has a one hundred percent success record. She's going to figure it out and find us. I know it."

"Only if you freak out. Just stick to the script. They won't have any reason to believe that the wreck wasn't an accident. Evidence will show it was avoidable, and that will satisfy her." He hoped he was speaking the truth. Charlotte Lyon's involvement in the investigation was going to be a problem. Just one more complication he hadn't really counted on.

"This isn't just murder. It's murder with special circumstances," Lorrin said, the panic clear in his voice. "We could get the needle for this."

"No one's getting the needle. Maybe you should take a few days off."

"Won't that look suspicious?" Lorrin asked.

"No more so than you sweating bullets. Relax, will you? I'm on this. If I think she's even close to figuring it out, I'll give you plenty of time to split the country. Don't call me again unless it's from a pay phone."

To be fair, some of Lorrin's concerns were legitimate. He had gone online to check Charlotte out as soon as he learned of her hire. It was important to know thine enemy. Her Web site didn't explain her nine-month hiatus from crises investigation, but he knew about her husband dying. Too bad she didn't have a baby or something. That would be a good thing. Something to use as leverage against her. Her Web site didn't list whom she loved. He'd have to figure that out other ways.

Maybe he'd be so bold as to just come out and ask her.

Once he had a handle on her vulnerabilities, he knew he could slow her down. It remained to be seen if he could stop her. For her sake, he hoped he could.

If she got too close, if it came down to the choice of her or him, she would have to be eliminated. What was one more person's blood on his hands?

He had to act fast. Things were threatening to spin out of control. Lorrin was completely losing it. He hadn't had that big a conscience when he took the money for the job. But then again, he wasn't the brightest guy in the universe.

Charlotte concentrated on the facts as they came in. She compiled a list of tidbits to feed to the press when they asked for hourly updates. All the better to reinforce that Sun Rail was the best source for news of the event.

Charlotte caught up with Mary Nightengale in the hallway. "I need you to contact the media and let them know when and where the press conference will be held. CEO Rayney will be reading a statement and taking some questions. You'll be the contact person here when I'm not available. Just stay professional."

"You got it," Mary said. "We're doing everything we can to take care of our customers and will be working closely with investigators to get at the cause of the crash."

"That's it," Charlotte said, "and what you don't know, you don't know."

"I can handle that."

"And before you head out to Loma Linda," Charlotte said, "I'll need a copy of all the key Sun Rail employees' office and cell numbers."

Mary reached into her holdall. "I have them here."

Charlotte was impressed once more. "Okay, so get going." She found a quiet corner and programmed the numbers into her BlackBerry.

As the deadline loomed, she wrote a tentative press release and printed exactly ten copies. She would wait for approval from the board before she printed the final draft on the company letterhead or posted it on the company Web site after Rayney made his statement for the camera.

CONTACT: Charlotte Lyon

(949) 555-1212

FOR IMMEDIATE RELEASE

4 P.M., JULY 13, 2004

SUN RAIL RUSHES AID TO PASSENGERS IN DERAILMENT

Sun Rail announced today it is dispatching grief counselors and other aid to passengers and crew on its Sunliner Express train, which derailed today with 176 aboard.

"The safety and comfort of our passengers is Sun Rail's highest priority," said CEO Bernard Rayney. "We will devote all our resources to assist the passengers and support the investigation into the cause."

Rayney noted this was the first accident in the nine months since the company began its operation to the Palm Springs area, which carries 500 passengers daily.

The derailment of the 15-car Sunliner Express occurred at 3:20 P.M. today near Yucaipa. It carried 161 passengers and a crew of 15.

A passenger and a crew member died. Twenty-two others suffered non-life-threatening injuries and were transported to nearby hospitals, Loma Linda and Eisenhower near Palm Springs.

Three passenger coaches overturned, Sun Rail said. All others remained upright.

CEO Raney said Sun Rail plans to cover the medical expenses of those injured in the accident and make arrangements for family members to visit loved ones, including overnight lodging if required.

29

Grief counselors will be available to all those aboard, Raney said, and buses were dispatched to transport the remaining passengers to their destinations.

Sun Rail will work closely with and assist investigators from Union Pacific, the National Transportation Safety Board, the Federal Railroad Administration, local law enforcement, and the FBI. Friends and family members seeking information about loved ones can call Sun Rail's toll-free hotline: 1-800-555-6214. Updates will be posted on the company Web site: *www. sunrail.org*

She handed the copies to Andrew. "Take these to each of the people present at our meeting. Have them read it, suggest changes they deem appropriate, and then sign the bottom. Bring them back to me as soon as you can. We're having a press conference in twenty minutes." She consulted her notes. "Wait a minute—I'll go with you to CEO Rayney's office." She needed to prep him.

Rayney's office door was open. She was pleased to see that he had changed into a suit and shaved without cutting himself. "Are you ready to meet the press?" she asked.

He ran his fingers through his hair, brushing it back. "If you think it's absolutely necessary."

"I do. I've prepared a statement stating the facts as we know them. We need you to put a face on the company, to humanize it. Stress that all is being done to look after the comfort and safety of employees and customers. We will issue updates when we have them. We need all the information about this situation to come in the front door. We need to get ahead of the story so we can define the story with the facts. It's my job to direct reporters to the sources. Sources that are fair and accurate."

"How about a one-on-one interview? Couldn't we control that a bit more?"

"We'll schedule those later. Right now we need to tell what happened, what it means, and what we're doing. This needs to come from us."

He put on his glasses and read the statement.

She waited until he looked up again. "The media will want to ask individual questions. Just stick to the facts. You'll be fine. I know this is nerve-racking, but don't try to make a joke. You'll be quoted out of context. Remember that. And be honest. A lie will screw you forever."

"Should I smile?"

"Do you feel like smiling?" she asked.

"No, I guess not," he admitted.

"Go with that instinct." She straightened his tie and plucked a loose thread from his shoulder. "Drink some water before you take the first question. Listen to the whole question before you answer it. If you don't know an answer, say that. Don't speculate. Say *we* often. *We* care, *we* are investigating, *we* will do whatever we can to find out how this happened. Never say 'no comment.' It makes you look shifty. Just tell the story like you would explain it to a teenage babysitter."

CHAPTER 4

They opened the door to the pressroom, and once again Charlotte knew how it must feel to be an A-list actor at the premiere of a blockbuster movie. She didn't think she'd like it one bit. Well, maybe with an A-list hunk on her arm, it wouldn't be so bad.

Cameras pointed their way, cables attaching videocams to microphones draped the reporters' arms, a bouquet of foam-covered microphones sprouted in front of Rayney's face. He hesitated, momentarily overwhelmed. Charlotte tightened her grip on his arm and steered him to the podium.

"Thank you for coming," she began. "My name is Charlotte Lyon, and I am the press liaison for Sun Rail. Charles Rayney, the CEO of Sun Rail, will now give you the facts as we know them. Copies of his statement will be made available to you following the conference. Please hold your questions until after the statement."

The room quieted.

Rayney took a sip of water and read the statement.

"Mr. Rayney, Mr. Rayney," the reporters clamored, and hands shot up.

Charlotte called on the reporter from the *L.A. Times*, promising herself that she would lead with the *OC Register* reporter next time.

"Has the FBI ruled out terrorism?"

"They are on the site now," Rayney said, "but so far we've had no indications of terrorism. The investigation will be thorough. As soon as we know, we'll let you know."

Charlotte called on the *OC Register* reporter; now the network people looked miffed. "If terrorism is found, will you shut down your passenger service?"

"We would never put our guests or employees at risk."

Charlotte nodded approvingly. Questions that began with *if* were often traps to elicit a guess or speculation. She would be in deep caca if Rayney made a mistake this soon into the crisis. He was the highest-ranking executive; there was no one left to bat cleanup.

CEO Rayney continued to hold his own with the reporters, taking multiple-part questions, separating them, and rephrasing the parts he wanted to answer to suit the answer he wanted to give. She stepped in when the questions got repetitive.

"Thank you, ladies and gentlemen, for your thoughtful concern at such a sad time. Mr. Rayney has to leave us now to visit the injured passengers at Loma Linda. Please be sure to get a copy of the press release. We appreciate your help in getting the eight-hundred phone number out there for those who need it."

Dom nodded to her as she threaded through the crowd of reporters. His expression revealed nothing, but she knew they had done as well as could be hoped. Dom had a man with him she didn't know. The guy was in his early forties, with an outdoorsman-type face that was creased and tanned from wind and sun. His sunglasses were on top of his head, taming only part of his curly brown hair and revealing eyes shining with enthusiasm. A laminated badge hanging around his neck identified him as Todd Hannigan with the NTSB. He had a leather carryall in his left hand and held out his right as Dom made the introductions.

"If it's all right, I'd like to ride out to the site with you," Charlotte said. She offered her hand, realizing in sudden horror that she was playing with her hair with the other and had unwittingly sucked in her stomach. Professionalism be damned, Hannigan was a hottie. As she shook his hand, she noted the strength of his grip, and the lack of a wedding ring. "It would help me to learn how the investigation is conducted so I can facilitate the NTSB's needs on our end."

"Fine by me," he said, "but I came on my motorcycle."

"Ahh, that would explain the outfit." She had wondered if leather jackets, Levi's, and boots were approved office wear. "If you don't mind, we'll take my car. I'm sure we can secure you a parking space in the company's garage."

"Works for me as long as we get going." He bounced on the balls of his feet as he spoke, not quite with impatience, more like anticipation, like a racehorse at the starting gate.

Twenty minutes later they were on the freeway heading east. Hannigan had agreed to slip on disposable surgical booties over his boots, accepting her explanation about just having her car detailed, and he had barely lifted an eyebrow when she spread plastic on the backseat before he threw his grip back there.

"So what will happen first?" she asked now.

"We'll divide into teams to look for causal factors. One team would be Operations, which would cover the actual driving of the train. Normally we would interview the engineer, but since that's not possible, we'll have to rely on the information we download from the event recorder."

"You mean like a black box?"

"Yeah, exactly. The event recorder will tell us how fast the train was going, if the engineer was throttling or braking or sounding his horn. What kind of brakes he was using."

She cut in. "The engineer who died was named Bob Peterson."

"I was just speaking in general," he said.

"And I was being specific." She realized she had come off curt. She didn't want to alienate Mr. Hannigan, even if it seemed he had forgotten that two people had died. "You were telling me about brakes?"

He drummed his fingers on his knee. "Yeah, right. Trains have three kinds of brakes, especially the bigger ones. The first set is the independent brakes that act on all wheels of the locomotive, much like a car's brakes except that they're pneumatically actuated rather than hydraulically. The second set is the dynamic brakes. They're more helpful for a freight train hauling a mile of cars. The dynamic brakes apply braking force to the drive wheels by turning the traction motors into generators. This conversion of power pits the momentum of the train against the resistance of the magnetic fields and this slows the train."

"Slow down, cowboy," Charlotte said. "You're making my head hurt."

He grinned. "I'm simplifying the process, of course."

"And I appreciate that," she said dryly. She couldn't picture herself writing any of what he had just said into a press release. "Explain it to me like I'm a ten-year-old writing a school paper."

"The third set of brakes are the train-line brakes, which are also air-actuated, but the air pressure releases them."

"So," Charlotte cut in to make sure she had it right, "if the cars separate and the air pipes rupture or lose pressure, then those brakes automatically engage."

His eyes positively glowed. He hunched his body toward her, straining against his seat belt, and clearly in his element. "That's right. Now, if there was an EIE . . . an engineer-initiated emergency, some say an engineer-induced emergency—anyhow, the recorder will tell us that, too."

"Is human error a likely cause?"

"Oh yeah. We've had cases where the engineer fell asleep and blew through a signal or didn't follow the track warrants. One time an eastbound train took a siding to await the passage of a westbound train—"

Charlotte interrupted. "How is it determined which trains have the right of way?"

"Trains are assigned priority. We have traffic controllers, just like airports. The case I was talking about, the train order instructed the engineer to wait for a specific locomotive on the head end of the passing train. Only he must not have paid too good attention, because he mistook one passing train for the other and got back on the track too soon. Five miles later—" Hannigan slammed his fists together to demonstrate. "—he collided head-on with the westbound train he was supposed to avoid. That was a nasty one." He bobbed his head as if he were keeping time to a rock-and-roll song.

"I'll bet," she said, signaling to get over to the fast lane so she could use the car pool lane. Normally she stuck to the middle lane, which was statistically the safest, but it was rush hour, and they needed to take advantage of every time-saving option.

Hannigan twisted in his seat to help her gauge the oncoming traffic. "You got it. Just punch it."

Charlotte ignored his advice, waiting until she could see both headlights of the car she hoped to overcome in her rearview mirror. And this guy called himself a safety professional? When was the last time *he* had read a Department of Motor Vehicles manual?

Hannigan looked longingly at her stereo system, but didn't ask her to switch it on. "Anyhow, on that wreck I was talking about? I don't think it would have gone down like that if the main line had been signaled."

"Huh?"

He slammed his palm into his forehead. "Didn't I mention that it happened in unsignaled territory? That was a big part of the story."

"You're going to have to be gentle with me until I get up to speed."

His mouth twisted into a half smile, and he made a self-depreciating shrug. "Sorry, I guess I do go off a bit. I just love everything about trains."

"Yeah, I got that."

They were quiet for a few miles. Charlotte wondered if the engineer's death had preceded the accident. How he died had yet to be determined. All she knew was that his death didn't appear to be from the physical trauma of the derailment and that he was the only guy at the helm when it happened. Part of her job was to anticipate the tough questions and make sure everyone who spoke to the press was ready for them. She took a deep breath and unleashed the genie beside her from his bottle. "Why was the engineer alone in the cab?"

"On a trip less than six hours long, he was well within the rules."

A Ford Explorer came up behind her and flashed his high beams. She checked her speedometer and saw she was doing exactly the speed limit.

"I think he wants you to speed up," Hannigan said.

"You think?" She checked her mirrors and increased her speed by five miles an hour. "How long is a typical shift?"

"It varies. Engineers work on rotation. They work all hours. If they aren't rested, they're supposed to tell the dispatcher. We'll be reviewing the engineer's last forty-eight hours. You're welcome to be there when we conduct our interviews."

"Thank you." The driver of the Explorer had a disgusted look on his young face. He made a palm-up hand gesture as if to ask *What are you doing?* The sun glinted on his eyebrow studs. She ignored the teenager's histrionics (for his own good) and focused on the matter at hand. "Is a passenger train more difficult to drive than a freight train?"

"Not at all. Any engineer who's driven freight can drive a baby train like the Sunliner."

"What constitutes a baby train?"

Hannigan twisted his lips as he thought. "Thirty-five cars and under. Piece of cake for any engineer with any kind of experience. Let me put it this way, it's like the difference between driving an eighteen-wheeler and a Miata."

The Explorer exited the car pool lane. The young driver seemed to be shouting something at her as he passed. Most of the words appeared to begin with an *F* sound. His body language indicated the same. She smiled sweetly at him. "What if the engineer has a heart attack or something and he's all alone up there?"

"Trains have devices called crew alerters. If the engineer doesn't make any control adjustments for fifteen seconds, the alerter flashes a light over the control board. There's a button the engineer pushes to reset it. If he doesn't, the light blinks faster and then makes an audible alarm. If the engineer doesn't react to the alarm, the alerter puts on the brakes."

"A deadman's switch?"

He shook his head. "I haven't seen a train with a deadman's switch for about twenty years." He looked up and to his left, focusing on the memory. "The deadman's switch was a foot control. The engineer had to keep standing on it or the brakes would engage."

"I guess two guys had to be in the cab at all times."

He laughed. "Guys used to weight it down with toolboxes, rocks, all sorts of things so they could go to the bathroom."

She smiled back. "Kind of defeated the purpose, then, didn't it?"

"The newer equipment is much more sophisticated."

But not foolproof, she thought without taking her eyes off the road. In her experience, the terms *foolproof* and *failsafe* were oxymorons. Shit happened. Terrible, tragic shit.

"Would putting on the brakes suddenly make the train derail?" she asked.

"It shouldn't."

Well, yeah, duh, Charlotte thought to herself, *or why would trains have them?*

"But they could be a contributing factor," he added.

She checked her mirrors and noticed he was staring at her hands. He was probably noticing her death grip on the steering wheel. The car pool lane put her next to the concrete barriers, and she found it unnerving. Todd Hannigan was probably one of those motorcyclists who liked to weave in and out of traffic. "What will the other investigators be looking at?"

"We'll have a team inspecting the track. Another will check out the mechanical: the train truck, the wheels, the brakes, dragging equipment. Any of those things could cause a derail. The fourth team will cover the signaling system. We'll get to the bottom of this. Trains leave big clues when something goes wrong."

"Why did the locomotive stay on the track when the cars behind it didn't?"

He looked at her with surprised interest, as if she had hit on something important. "That's something we'll be looking at very closely. In fact, that's one of the reasons I was so anxious to get in on this one."

"Let's hope we solve the puzzle soon."

He grinned. "Now where's the fun in that?"

CHAPTER 5

"You mind if we stop at the strip mall here?" Charlotte asked as she signaled to get off the freeway.

"Probably a good idea to use the restrooms and stock up on water," Hannigan said.

"I want to top off my gas, too," Charlotte said.

Hannigan checked her gauge and saw that it still registered three-quarters full. She was a quirky one, all right. He supposed that made her good at her job, but still it must be exhausting being her.

She opened the trunk and retrieved a flight bag full of clothes.

"What's all this?" he asked.

"Just some stuff I won't mind getting dirty or throwing away if they get contaminated."

He scratched his head. "The train wasn't carrying any chemicals."

"I know," she said, "but there could be blood or polluted water or animal feces out there. The tennis shoes will make it easier to negotiate the countryside."

He nodded as if all that were completely reasonable. He slipped off the booties and doubted her I-just-got-the-car-detailed excuse. Not that the car wasn't as clean as it was the day it rolled off the assembly line. She was worried that he was contaminated. He supposed she'd seen a lot of shit in her job that made her so cautious.

Charlotte put the gas nozzle in her tank and set the mechanism on the auto-fill mode.

"I'll watch it," he volunteered.

"Thanks. I'm going to change in that Denny's. I won't be long."

He smiled, picturing her in the Denny's restroom, carefully changing her clothes without touching anything except her garments and the flight bag she kept them in. He'd dated an architect once who perfected the art of peeing without touching the seat at the job site's Porta Pottis. Or so she said.

Hannigan pulled two orange safety vests from his kit and put one of them on. The gas nozzle clicked off. He put everything back where it went, tightened the gas cap, and went into the convenience store. The air-conditioning was on full bore, and it felt great. He cruised the snack aisle, selecting bags of chips, granola bars, and packages of trail mix. Charlotte still hadn't returned, so he collected her change and got the receipt. He bought a case of bottled water to go with the food and paid for it all with a government credit card.

Charlotte was exiting the Denny's at the same he came out the store. She was wearing Levi's, a T-shirt, and white tennis shoes. Her hair was tied back into a ponytail. She looked ten years younger. The jeans fit well, too, especially in the ass.

"There you are." He lifted up the case of water. The plastic bottles had already begun to sweat. "Want to open the trunk for me?"

"I don't think there's room in there."

"How about in the backseat?"

"Sure. Nice vest."

"It has a certain sense of style." That got a smile out of her.

42

"I like it," she said. "It suits you."

"I have one for you, too." What he was thinking was how vulnerable she looked when she smiled. She probably hated that. The woman definitely needed to loosen up. When they got through at the accident site, maybe he could talk her into having a few drinks with him.

She folded the passenger seat forward so he could put the water on the backseat. He was treated to another look at her backside and wondered if she knew what she was doing. He put the water and snacks on the plastic spread over the backseat.

"All set?" she asked.

"Almost." He presented her with the other vest. "Don't worry. It's clean."

"Speaking of clean." She handed him a tube of waterless antibacterial soap. "Help yourself."

Amused, he squeezed some of the solution on his hands. It spread like lotion.

She shook out the vest with a look of distaste on her face. "Yeah, well there's clean and there is *clean*."

"It's been washed and decontaminated and no one has worn it since," he lied.

"And just my size. How thoughtful."

His cell phone rang and he answered with a curt "Hannigan..." What Charlotte heard next was, "I'm about a mile out. We stopped at the convenience store. Anybody need anything? ... All right. We're on our way."

"I hope I'm not getting you in any trouble," she said.

"Not to worry." He had her turn left off the 60 Freeway on Redlands Boulevard, then a right on San Timoteo Canyon Road. This took them past big, sprawling horse estates and several stock farms. As they got closer to the wreck, the homes seen from the road grew sparser. Just before the wreck, the land on the right of them was strung with ancient rusty barbed wire. Mailboxes of different vintages and sizes clustered at the bases of dirt driveways.

Police cruisers were parked broadside to close the road. Even from fifty yards away, it looked as if a bomb had gone off on the railroad tracks. The Mercedes's thermometer registered the outside temperature at 104 degrees. She pulled onto the dirt shoulder, behind the line of vehicles from all the different agencies. Dirt swirled around them. She stared at the film of grit settling on her windshield.

"So much for your wax job," Hannigan said.

"Not to worry," she said.

Charlotte could see that they would have their hands full.

The media was there in full-blown swarm. Enough time had elapsed since the wreck that all the major networks were there as well as local media. Several helicopters hovered overhead. What she saw was the expense the press had gone through and their motivation to amortize those costs. They needed the story to be big enough to fill a lot of airtime and newsprint, whatever that took.

Hannigan grabbed the water, she retrieved her leather twin-pocket portfolio which did double duty as a clipboard and a shield to ward off outstretched hands. She clipped her phone-integrated BlackBerry to her belt and slung her digital camera around her neck. Hannigan's NTSB badge got them through the police barricade. Using the zoom lens, she took pictures of the train cars on their sides, the twisted rails, a tree reduced to kindling, and scattered gravel—what she soon learned was called ballast—from the track bed.

She also documented the twenty or so rescue workers, including cops, firemen, and Caltrans road crews who were sifting through the wreckage. A group of misplaced passengers sought shade under what trees there were.

The passenger cars on their sides had ladders propped against them. Another man wearing an orange vest like the one Hannigan had lent her was spray-painting a large X in yellow paint on the side facing up. Baggage and personal items littered the hillside. Dirt and sand kicked up from the wreck colored the scene in sepia tones. A fireman knelt beside a young girl so that they could be eye to eye as he spoke to her. The little girl looked frightened, and the firefighter's face was a mask of gentle patience and concern.

Too bad she wasn't working for the fire department, Charlotte thought, talk about your "money shot."

Yellow caution tape strung from sawhorses isolated the wreckage. Five other NTSB employees inspected the track behind the still-standing locomotive. They spotted Hannigan and Charlotte and picked their way carefully through the twisted rail and spilled ballast to get to them. Tiny thorned plants pricked at her ankles; at least she hoped they were plants and not insects. Visions of Lyme disease and West Nile virus swirled in her head like so many macabre sugarplums. She noticed gopher holes in the hard-pack and was reminded that it was snake season.

"What you got?" Hannigan asked.

"It's a weird one, boss." The guy who spoke had a shaved head and was sweating profusely.

Boss? Charlotte thought.

"Yeah," Hannigan said to the bald guy. "This one's gonna be tricky."

She turned to Hannigan. Now that they were on the site, he seemed taller, more substantial. "What exactly is your job title?"

"I used to be an operations investigator. Now I'm the Supervisor of

Investigations. The NTSB has primary jurisdiction, so I guess that makes me the boss of bosses unless tampering is found."

"And then what?" she asked.

"If this crash turns out to be intentional, the FBI will take over and we'll assist them."

Charlotte looked over the wreckage surrounding them. "Do you think this was intentional?"

"It's too soon to rule anything out." He took her arm and guided her out of the way of two men wheeling a large butane tank and cutting torch on a dolly. "Excuse me, I have to get to work."

Hannigan turned back to the waiting NTSB team, pointing to different members as he issued orders. "I need printouts from the signal boxes going back ten miles. Patricia, how long before the crane gets here?"

"Two hours if we can get a Caltrans escort," the woman he'd called Patricia said with a cell phone pressed to her ear.

"Coordinate with Jay Liffey on that," Hannigan said. "He's over there." He pointed and when Patricia turned, Charlotte noticed a thick blond braid running halfway down the woman's back. Patricia spoke into her phone as she headed off to confer with the Caltrans guy.

Hannigan walked toward the chewed-up track, his team at his heels. Charlotte followed, but had to keep her eyes on the ground to avoid tripping. Hannigan, she decided, was part mountain goat.

"Where are the Feds?" Hannigan asked a lean black guy on his left.

"Interviewing passengers," the guy said. "Waiting for you."

Hannigan swept his hand behind him, pointing at Charlotte without breaking stride. "Charlotte Lyon, meet CJ Post. Charlotte is the PR rep for Sun Rail. CJ is our track man."

"What does CJ stand for?" she asked, pen poised over her legal pad.

"Casey Jones."

She looked up. "You're kidding, right?"

"No, ma'am. I come from a long line of railroaders."

They arrived at the mess of twisted steel. Men with gas-powered saws were there already, positioned at a point where the track was still intact.

"How will you make sense out of this?" she asked.

CJ smiled. "We start by determining the POD." In answer to her quizzical look, he clarified. "Point of derailment. We'll be looking for ding marks, secondary tracks on the ties and in the ballast where the first wheel climbed the rail. We have a state-of-the-art metallurgical lab. We'll pull the rails off, get them back to the labs, and get a look and see whether there was any signs of heat fatigue, whether they were worn, whether they had a flattened head that might have contributed to the accident."

"So you think this was an accident?" she asked.

He looked momentarily perplexed. "Accidents are what we investigate."

She let that go, but made a note to herself. Professionals were often unaware of their preconceptions. That's why they called them blind spots and why it often took an outsider such as herself to see clearly.

"What else could have caused this?" she asked.

"As far as the tracks?" He squinted as sunlight bounced off the up-rooted steel around him. "We'll be looking at the rail fasteners for stress. How they're bent, whether they were fitted properly. If I were a guessing man, I'd say we were dealing with a heat buckle. We'll start at the POD and look back two to three hundred feet for sun kinks."

"Sun kinks?" she asked, having to shout over the sound of the disc saws grinding through steel.

"Warpage of the rail due to high temperatures," CJ shouted back. "Widens the gauge and the truck wheels drop off the rails. Anything else, usually the locomotive would have derailed first. But with a sun kink, the train gets to rocking and bumping as each car hits the buckle. It could take a few hundred feet before the first car jumps the track. Like I say, we'll cut this whole section out and take it back to our lab for analysis."

"How long will all this take?"

"We should have all the answers within eight to ten months."

"That long?" This was terrible news. Charlotte couldn't work in limbo. Customers as well as potential investors needed to be reassured. She couldn't do that without being able to explain why it happened, and more important, why it wouldn't happen again.

"We're very thorough."

"Couldn't you be thorough and fast?" she asked, but was drowned out by the sound of jackhammers and men shouting.

CHAPTER 6

Charlotte brought water over to the crowd of bewildered passengers who were standing and sitting in the shade of a fire engine. They looked dirty and hot. She walked among them, distributing water and listening.

"Was it terrorists?" someone asked.

"Did we hit something?"

"Was it an earthquake?"

"Who died?"

She listened to all the questions. The one most commonly asked was, "What happened?"

She got on her cell phone and called Mary Nightengale. "When are we getting some transportation in here for our passengers?"

"Amtrak is sending two buses. You should see the first one in about ten minutes."

Charlotte looked at her watch. "How many people will it hold?"

"They said about fifty."

"Okay, good. Good job. What about the rest?"

"I found a livery service in Moreno Valley. We've got some vans coming and two limos. That should accommodate whoever's left."

"Are you at the hospital?"

"Yeah, it's a total circus," Mary said.

"Here, too. Do what you can."

Charlotte approached one of the FBI agents and identified herself. "I have the passenger manifest." She handed him a copy. "And transportation is on the way. Can we get these people their personal belongings before they leave?"

"Not until the dogs get through," he said, "and we get the go-ahead from NTSB that it's safe."

She watched the handlers put their animals through their paces. Something in the dogs' attitudes reminded her a little of Todd Hannigan, all that enthusiastic sniffing. "Are they looking for explosives?"

"Yes, ma'am."

She thanked him, hiding her dislike of FBI agents, especially one who called her *ma'am* and made it sound as if he were doing her a favor.

The locomotive had come to a stop on a straight stretch of track. Uprooted Russian thistle and black-eyed Susans traced a path where the passenger coaches had skidded on their sides. She felt the pall of death emanating from the train cars. If death had a color and shape, it would be a black fog. Those unlucky enough to inhale it felt the weight of it in their chest and around their heart. It took forever to dissipate.

The last car in the consist was a two-tiered automobile carrier with four new Range Rovers on the upper level. It had remained on the tracks, just as the locomotive had. She found a neutral smile for the FBI agent. "Would it be possible to string a second perimeter? I'd like to set up a dedicated media access area."

"Sure," he said, "as long as it's outside our investigation scene quarantine."

"Oh, absolutely," Charlotte said. She saw Stan had arrived. He and another man were studying the undercarriage of the trains on the ground. She turned back to the Fed. "Now, about the passengers."

"Where are you going to take these people?" the agent asked.

"That's up to them. I'm going to ask each of them where they want to go and we'll work it out."

"Need some help?" a woman with short white hair asked. She was wearing a light Windbreaker with a Red Cross patch sewn on the sleeve and a name tag that read PHOEBE HOWARD. Charlotte realized she had been hasty in wanting to shun the Red Cross's help. Phoebe struck her as one of those tough old birds who would be up to any challenge.

"That would be great. I have one hundred and twenty-two people to sort out. We've got buses coming to take them to their destinations or starting points, their preference. When possible, check their name against their picture ID, get a phone number, and find out where they want to go."

"We should triage them according to special needs, too," Phoebe said. "Medical conditions and handicaps."

"Good thinking." Charlotte handed copies of the manifest to Phoebe and another woman who could have been her sister. This left Charlotte free to mingle with the passengers and listen.

Phoebe had one of those bullhorn voices that could cut through cold rolled steel. "Okay, people," she said, "we're going to get you all somewhere where you can get comfortable. I need last names starting with *A* through *L* over here, the rest over there. Please have your picture identifications out, people with small children or special needs to the front, and we'll get this show back on the road."

There were appreciative murmurings and even a few scattered laughs as people sorted themselves out. Charlotte moved with the larger group.

The mood was surprisingly upbeat. People letting off excited giggles. Generally expressing amazement and relief that the accident hadn't been worse.

"What was it like?" she asked a man in shorts and a polo shirt. The guy looked like he was heading to Palm Springs to play some golf. In fact, he looked like he still wanted to make his tee time. Other than having dust on his shoes and a few smudges on his clothes, he was tanned, kempt, and relaxed.

"One minute we were barreling along," the golfer said, "then I see the conductor brace himself and there was this huge whooshing sound." He demonstrated, spreading his hands as he blew out. "Then there was a jolt and then a rattling vibration like we'd hit some bad road." Now the golfer shook his shoulders and bobbed his head to simulate the bumps and rattling. "I was looking out the window and all these bushes start passing by, then everything tilts and we go into this slow roll. I mean it was unreal. Everyone's hanging on now, to the seats, each other. If people were screaming, I didn't hear them. It was loud, like an earthquake. Then it was over. We stopped. There was silence, absolute silence, then people started moaning and calling for help. Some of the windows had blown out, and we helped each other climb out. There was another guy helping, too, but I don't think he'd been on the train. He was wearing off-road motorcycle gear."

Charlotte wondered what happened to the biker; he might have witnessed something. She handed the golfer a business card. "How would you like to be on television?"

"I don't know."

"I'm sure your family would be relieved to see you're all right." She gave him her most winning smile. She knew gold when she heard it. The guy was calm, articulate, and unscathed.

"Well, you put it that way, sure. I'm not married, by the way."

She felt her smile freezing. She didn't remember asking.

He ran a finger over the top edge of her portfolio. "Maybe we could have a drink later."

She couldn't believe it. The guy was hitting on her. Talk about unflappable. She saw the reporter for Channel 9 News and waved to her. "Kelly, I've got an exclusive interview for you." Out of the side of her mouth she added, "Kelly's a sweetheart. Single, too." Kelly was also a narcissistic barracuda, but Charlotte figured this guy could handle himself.

She turned too quickly and ran solidly into the chest of Todd Hannigan. "I'm going to check out the locomotive cab now," he said. "You want to tag along?"

"Absolutely." She walked quickly to keep up with him and in her haste tripped over a rock. He caught her arm. Charlotte caught herself feeling jealous at how at ease he seemed with his body.

"You okay?"

"Sure," she said, not wanting to be perceived as some girly girl. "I really appreciate you keeping me in the loop. It makes my job a lot easier."

"I have a confession to make," he said, looking a little sheepish. "I checked you out."

"You did?"

"I thought your name sounded familiar, so I Googled you before I left Gardena. Then it all came back. I read about your involvement in that outbreak of salmonella poisoning on the Mexican cruise ship last summer. I can't remember the name of the cruise line."

She smiled. "Then I did my job. What do you remember of that story?"

"That the passengers who got sick were all part of a group celebrating someone's fiftieth wedding anniversary and that you discovered that the salmonella came from a roadside stand. Strawberries, wasn't it?"

She nodded.

"And what and how you figured it out was an amazing bit of detective work. I was impressed. The strawberry fields had been fertilized with contaminated manure, right?"

"Wash your fruit." For some unholy Freudian reason, her eyes chose that moment to stray to his crotch. She was horrified to feel herself blush, and it wasn't just a glow in her cheeks. She was one of those people whose ears turned bright red. She struggled to change the subject. "I didn't necessarily want my name in the story. That was the reporter's doing."

"The headline caught my eye," he said. "Master of Disaster."

She had the story framed in her office and included it in her company press kits. The salmonella strawberries had not been the first or the only crisis she had unwound, but it had given her business a big boost. Especially the fact that the cruise line's name was never readily associated with the poisonings.

There were two cases that public relations experts referenced as the textbook models of dos and don'ts. Johnson & Johnson set the example for what to do right in the infamous Tylenol-tampering case. Most people remembered that the poisoning of over-the-counter medication led to the invention of tamper-proof packaging. Fewer recalled that the original killer, a would-be extortionist, was never found or identified. She would have liked to catch the bastard.

The hallmark of badly handled crisis turned catastrophe was the case of the *Exxon Valdez*. Bad enough that the oil tanker crashed into a reef and dumped eleven million gallons of crude oil into the pristine waters of Prince William Sound. The name of the ship compounded the disaster. Would the damage to Exxon's reputation have been as severe if the ship had been named simply the *Valdez*? An interesting thought, but there were many other problems with how the crisis was handled.

Exxon CEO Rawl declined to go to the site of the tragedy or speak at press conferences. The president of Exxon shipping did go before cameras, but wasn't briefed by public relations personnel beforehand and was slaughtered by the press. Critical days passed before Rawl issued a statement via television telling the public what chemicals would be used to clean up the spill, but he made no apologies nor showed any emotion.

The court of public opinion, not to be underrated, was irate. Customers canceled their credit cards. Environmentalists, fishermen, and the press continued their high-profile assaults on the company's perceived sluggish response to the disaster. Exxon became the villain.

Charlotte often dreamed of what would have happened if she had been the one handling the PR. Or better yet, if she had created a policy for the company beforehand that prevented the tragedy from happening. She sure wouldn't have allowed Captain Hazelwood to smoke as he was found doing when the Coast Guard arrived just after the spill. The oil fumes were so thick that helicopters couldn't fly through it, and the guy was smoking. Made her shudder to think of it.

Sometimes, in Charlotte's more spiritual moments, she thought maybe that all her hardships, all her suffering, had been God's way to prepare her to serve the greater good. In less spiritual moments, she thought the whole thing was a pretty lousy trade-off. Whichever way she was feeling didn't stop her from doing the best job she could. Lives depended on it. That was first.

They arrived at the cab of the locomotive. The wheels had been chocked. A mechanic in overalls inserted one end of a red hose into an outlet labeled DUMMY.

"He's capping the locomotive's air and electrical systems, isolating them from the rest of the system," Hannigan explained. To the mechanic he said, "All set?"

The guy stared at Charlotte a moment before answering. "We'll know better when you start her up."

Hannigan pointed out a miniature octagonal red stop sign attached to a lever and sticking out from the engine casing. "Pushing this shuts off the fuel supply to the diesel motor. Whoever got here first would have done that. You can see it's down now."

"One of the crew?"

"Probably."

Hannigan climbed up the ladder leading to the front platform and opened the narrow metal door. She followed him into the nose of the cab and then up another short flight of steel stairs. At the top of the stairs, he opened a second door and held it ajar for her. She entered first. The engineer must have been very dead by the time the paramedics arrived. There were no discarded syringe wrappers or any other evidence of a last-ditch effort to keep the man alive. In fact (thank God), there was no blood at all. Just a chrome coffee thermos that had ended up beneath the empty chair.

Hannigan bagged the thermos and set it by the door.

She took pictures of the controls and the view from the windows. The engineer's station was on the right of the cab. The side window was open, and a fine patina of brown dust had settled on everything. The driver's gauges, buttons, and levers were spread across an open L-shaped desktop. Yellow sponge foam protruded from the seat of the swiveling engineer's chair where constant use had worn away the fabric on the left side.

The control buttons were labeled according to function: horn, bell, lights, sand. Gauges with dual needles, one red, the other white, were positioned vertically to the driver's left. The speedometer was a large round analog type mounted near the top center of the wide windshield.

On the desktop directly in front of the engineer's chair and to the left of the three square buttons, sheets of nine-by-eleven paper hung crookedly from a one-inch binder clip. To the right were four separate levers that looked like the console transmission shifter on her Mercedes.

She leaned forward for a closer look at the dark specks on the control panel and saw that they were small dead flies, at least twenty of them, as if a swarm had all suddenly perished at once.

"Look at this," she said.

"That's odd," he agreed.

"What do you make of it?" She ripped a piece of paper from her notebook and scooped up a few of the dead insects.

Hannigan shrugged and then pointed to a lever with a red handle. "Looks like he holed it, all right."

"What do you mean?" she asked.

"You see how the lever is all the way forward? The engineer was the only one who could have put it there. Two things happen when the lever is positioned to the last notch. First, all the air that holds all the brakes off the wheels vents very quickly."

He pointed to the button marked SAND next to the brake lever. "And plugging it also dumps sand on the wheels for added traction."

"I was wondering," she said.

She noted the disturbance of the powdered dirt on the floor of the cab and the relative cleanliness of the red-handled lever. Engineer Bob must have been gripping it when he died.

The radio microphone was still in its cradle as was the black telephone handset that she assumed was part of an in-train intercom system. Charlotte would have to find out if anyone was able to reach the engineer before or after the derail. That would narrow down the time of his death and perhaps provide more clues as to what had happened just prior to the event.

The cab door opened and Stan joined them in the cockpit, carrying a laptop computer. Charlotte moved over to the left and out of the way, but not before noticing the train master's surprise at seeing her there.

"You here to give me a download?" Hannigan asked.

"Yes, sir," Stan said as he opened a panel at the rear of the cab.

The sign outside warned of high voltage. Charlotte started looking around for a piece of wood or plastic with which to rescue Hannigan if and when he was electrocuted. She could already picture him flopping on the corrugated steel floor, smoke rising from his burnt flesh.

As if reading her mind, Hanningan turned to Charlotte and said, "There's no big juice here now with the engine off. The battery backup is sufficient for a download."

Stan plugged a multiprong adapter into a socket labeled EVENT RECORDER. Charlotte wondered how he managed with the tremors in his hands. She wondered if he was nervous or a drinker or if he suffered from some medical condition.

Both men viewed the laptop screen as Stan followed the prompts. Stan wiped his nose on his dirty sleeve several times during the process and coughed his phlegm-rich cough. She cringed and took a step away from him.

Hanningan pulled an envelope from his pocket and extracted what looked like one of those credit-card-size hotel room keys. She knew it by its technical name. It was a computer SRAM card and, according to the designation under the directional arrows, was capable of holding four megabytes of data. He slipped the SRAM card in a slot on the side of the computer. "Now I'm transferring the information we just collected."

"And we'll have our own copies," she said.

Stan nodded. "If you're all done with me."

"Sure, thanks," Hannigan said.

"Am I being paranoid, or did I suddenly grow a second head?" she asked after Stan was gone.

Hannigan chuckled as he pulled the card and put it back in its envelope. "These old-timers probably never saw a woman in the cab before. They're having trouble processing it."

"Oh, jeez, welcome to the new millennium already."

Hannigan put the throttle in idle position and flipped a series of switches and knobs. The engine responded sluggishly at first, or so it seemed to her, and then began chugging noisily. He kept an eye on the display of gauges monitoring fuel and oil pressures.

She watched the needle on the air pressure dial stutter toward the 100 psi mark. The amp gauge stayed at zero. She hoped that it was all good. The radio squawked, and then an electric fan positioned to blow air on the driver's face whirred to life. She instinctively shielded her camera lens as she closed her eyes and turned away from the dirt the fan kicked up. Hannigan turned it off, and when she opened her eyes again, all that had been shielded from the first onslaught of desert chaff: the red brake handle, the engineer's chair, and the stack of papers clipped to the console were as filthy as the rest. The dead insects had also been scattered.

"Sorry about that," he said, brushing dirt and sand from his hair. He freed the sheaf of papers clipped to the control station and dumped the dirt off them.

"What are those?" she asked, wondering if Hannigan had noticed that they were free from dirt prior to the fan starting up again.

"Special orders, track conditions. When the engineer begins his run, he's issued the day's bulletins to go over with his crew. What special speed limits are in effect, where maintenance gangs will be working, that sort of thing." He folded the papers twice and stuck them in his vest's inside pocket.

"Will I get copies of those?"

"Your train master can print you a set."

The dust acted like fingerprint powder on the chrome and smooth plastic surfaces which made the absence of palm prints on the brake lever all the more noticeable. "Do engineers wear gloves?"

He shrugged. "Most don't. Some do, but they're considered dandies."

Boys.

She coughed into her hand to hide her smile. "How long will you be working here?"

"We'll have investigators out here for at least a week going over everything. Right now, the push is on to get the track back into operation. First we need to examine the wheels and brakes; then the railroad mechanics will rerail the cars they can and tow them back to the yard. They'll set the ones with damaged trucks out of the way and get to them later."

"How long will it take to fix the track?"

"We'll get some replacement panels out here pretty quick. Big dozers will shove all the old stuff out of the way, cranes will set the new tracks in place, and CAT crews will come in with new ballast. They'll work through the night to have this stretch patched by morning and approved for reduced-speed traffic."

"So what's next?" she asked.

"The crew."

"I'll help with that. I asked for the personnel files first thing. As soon as we get all the passengers on their way, I'll drive you back to Anaheim and make you copies."

"Hold that thought," Hannigan said as his cell rang. "Hannigan." He held up a finger to her as if to say, *one moment,* and nodded as he listened. "I'm in the engine, send him over . . . I've got the engineer's thermos. I'm going to need a tox on it."

"These, too," Charlotte said, handing over the packet of dead flies.

Hannigan put them in a separate bag.

A moment later, someone whistled from beneath the window. Hannigan tossed down the thermos and bag of dead insects. "Ready?" he asked her, but didn't wait for an answer. He pulled two paper towels from a clip on the back wall and said, "Let me go first."

They went back down the few stairs to the front compartment. It was dark and humid and hot in the nose of the locomotive, like a steel cave. "Where's the bathroom?" she asked.

"There isn't one."

"Bummer." Add train engineer, Charlotte decided, to the list of jobs she'd never do.

Hannigan stopped on the platform and fitted a paper towel in each hand so he could wipe the hand rails as he descended the steep vertical stairs. "Exhaust soot," he explained.

She checked her hands, but didn't see any black soot from the climb up.

There was a two-foot drop to the ground at the bottom of the ladder. He waited to assist her if she needed it. She realized she wouldn't mind his hands on her again, but she waved aside his help and bent her knees as she hit the dirt. Charlotte was about to ask him about the lack of soot as well as the lack of dirt on the reports, but a man in a short-sleeved white shirt and jeans was waiting for them.

"Todd Hannigan?" the man asked.

Hannigan turned. "You got 'im."

The man held out a hand. "I'm Bill McBride. I was the assistant engineer on this run, and I'm goddamned happy to be alive."

CHAPTER 7

Hannigan shook McBride's hand and introduced Charlotte as the Sun Rail rep.

"Ma'am," McBride said with a tip of his cap. "Begging your pardon, for the cussing and all."

Charlotte heard the Deep South in his vowels. "No apology necessary. I'm sure it's been a traumatic day."

"Did you work with Bob Peterson often?" Hannigan asked.

"The engineer who died?" McBride mopped sweat off his forehead with a red bandanna. "No. This was the first time. In fact, I hadn't made this run before. I thought this would be a good opportunity to familiarize myself with this route." He laughed at the irony. "Some introduction, huh?"

"How did you happen to take this run?" Hannigan asked.

"I was next up in the rotation. The regular man had to leave at the last minute. His wife was having a baby."

"What was his name?" Hannigan asked.

"You know, sir, I don't even remember," McBride admitted.

"That's all right," Hannigan said. "I can find out easily enough."

Charlotte's phone rang as Hannigan asked, "Who shut down the engine?"

She excused herself and took the call. It was from Dom.

"How is it looking out there?" he asked.

"We're getting it all sorted out," she said. "Where are you?"

"I'm with Bernard Rayney at the hospital. We've got four passengers with injuries serious enough to warrant admission, and the rest will probably be released by the end of the day."

"That's great. Offer to put them up in a nice hotel if they want, and communicate that to the main office. We'll add that to the stack of tidbits I put together for hourly updates. How's Rayney holding up?"

"Understandably upset and looking to put a lid on all this. Plus, we're getting pressure to get the track clear. Time is money."

She smiled into the phone. *God save us from nonbillable, wasted hours.* "They're still inspecting it, but I believe the locomotive is salvageable. Cranes are on their way to clear the track, and repair crews should have the line back in operation by morning." She took a few more steps away from Hannigan and his interviewee. "I'm going to need the personnel records on Bill McBride. He's the guy who subbed today for the regular assistant engineer. The regular guy's wife went into labor. Supposedly. I'll make sure that was really the case, and if so, how she's doing. Might make for a good human interest story. This Todd Hannigan guy from the NTSB seems pretty competent. I'll update the company Web site when we get through here."

She returned in time to hear Hannigan schedule an appointment at the NTSB office with McBride for tomorrow at eleven in the morning. Hannigan gave McBride a business card as his phone rang. He told whoever it was that he'd be right there.

Charlotte hung back so that she could have a moment alone with McBride.

"Bill, how are you feeling? Do you need to see a doctor?" She opened her portfolio, turned to a fresh page on her legal pad, made a note of the time, and wrote down his name.

"No, ma'am," he said. "I'll be fine. Just a mite shaken, to tell you the truth."

She noticed his trembling hands out of her peripheral vision, seemed to be an epidemic of that around here. "Is this your first derailment?"

"I hope it's my only one."

"I'm sure. What were your impressions of Bob Peterson?"

"Ma'am?"

"Please, call me Charlotte." She smiled to show him she was his friend, perhaps even an ally. "I'm new here myself. How would you characterize the engineer prior to the run? Annoyed, relaxed, friendly? Sober?"

"I only saw him a minute, and I'd never put any train in the hands of a drunk."

"Did he complain of an upset stomach? Or did he seem to be in pain or out of sorts?"

"Not that I noticed. All's he really said to me was that it was a pretty routine run."

"Aren't y'all supposed to go over the day's route together before you leave?" She heard herself say *y'all* and hoped he didn't think she was mocking his accent. It was truly an unpremeditated slip of the tongue. She'd always found Southern drawls contagious.

He looked uncomfortable. "They'd done that already. I had a copy of the bulletins, but I missed the briefing. I did think that ... well, I mean, I wasn't completely sure and ..."

She closed her notebook and put away her pen. "Sure about what?"

"Well, it's pretty hot out here, and there were some slow orders issued for certain parts of the route. The rails have a tendency to want to buckle in hot weather. We used to get that a lot in Mississippi in the summer months. I didn't have any bulletins about this mileage marker, and I knew he made this run all the time."

"What were you thinking?" She lowered her volume so that he had to lean in close to her to catch her words. "What were your instincts?"

McBride made another pass with his bandanna, this time at the sweat on his upper lip. "He seemed to be going a mite fast into the turns is all."

"Did you attempt to call him on that?" Charlotte asked, remembering the black telephone receiver she'd seen hanging from a hook at the end of the engineer's work station.

"I didn't want to be rude."

She nodded, understanding his position as the new guy wanting to make a good first impression. There had been a plane crash in Portland, Oregon, in the late seventies. The investigation later showed that nobody wanted to point out to the pilot that he was running out of gas. Everyone assumed that he knew, and thought it would be rude to point it out.

"I don't know why he didn't want me in the cab with him. Maybe things would have turned out differently if I had pushed."

"You're saying you wanted to ride in the cab and the engineer said no?" Charlotte asked.

"Maybe that's how they work it with the new guy. The conductor told me to stay in the passenger section until we got to Palm Springs."

"Sounds like you didn't have much of a choice in the matter," Charlotte said, but her mind was already elsewhere, spinning out conspiracy theories.

McBride shook his head, unconvinced, perhaps unwilling to be let off the hook so easily. "Maybe he was testing me, seeing if I would insist. Hell, I don't know. I just feel like I let everyone down."

"We don't know anything for sure yet," Charlotte said. "Hold off booking that guilt trip until all the facts are in."

Past McBride, Charlotte saw the roving reporter from CBS News, Cal Morton.

"Excuse me, Mr. McBride, I need to go talk to this reporter."

Cal Morton's wireless mike was at his side as his cameraman wiped down the lens on his shoulder cam. She liked Cal. He was intelligent and mostly ethical. She waved to him and pointed to an empty place at the far edge of the press perimeter. Cal motioned for his cameraman to follow him, and they met at the spot she'd indicated.

"Aren't you that cover girl?" he asked with a grin. "Where have you been?"

"Around. Treat me nice," she said, "and I'll autograph your copy."

"Another time, for sure. What you got for me?"

"Would you like a comment from an authority on train wrecks?" she asked.

"That would be great."

"I'll set it up," she said.

"What do they think happened here?" Cal asked.

"That's what we're all working to discover," she said. Cal knew better than to use the bogus promise of keeping it off the record. With reporters, nothing should ever be regarded as off the record. She'd learned that the hard way.

While still in college, she had interned at the mayor's office. She was young, eager, naive, and enjoyed the newfound popularity that arose from being in the know. She had hoped to practice a little quid pro quo with a charismatic reporter named Dennis O'Connor. One of the party's major contributors was about to be indicted by a federal grand jury. Charlotte had called her supposed good friend Dennis and confided the coming news on the condition he wait one day before breaking the story.

The news hit the wire that evening with Dennis O'Connor's byline. Charlotte was fired and told never to expect to work in politics again. When she confronted Dennis the next day, his apology consisted of five words: "It was just too good."

She really had no one to blame but herself. It was a valuable lesson, and one day she intended to thank Dennis properly.

She smiled at Cal. "I'm going to let the expert explain it to you and your viewers. You'll like this guy. His name is CJ Post. The CJ stands for Casey Jones, and the guy knows railroads. He's an investigator with NTSB. His specialty is tracks."

"Thanks, Charlotte. I owe you one."

"Just don't waste his time. He's got an important job here."

She found CJ supervising the loading of railroad track into a flatbed truck. "You got a minute?"

CJ smiled knowingly. "He had a girlfriend, but they broke up. She didn't like him traveling so much."

"What?" Charlotte felt another blush coming on. "No, that's not what I wanted. I mean, that's not what I was going to ask you."

"Oh, sorry. My mistake. Whatcha need?"

"Would you mind repeating for the news camera exactly what you told me? I've got the reporter all prepped. I asked him to respect your time. It will take two minutes tops. Try to keep it easy on the jargon. You got kids, CJ?"

"No."

"Okay, pretend you're explaining the situation to the pizza delivery guy. Easy on the jargon, don't confuse him with big dumps of technical information. Just keep it simple."

"Yeah, okay." He tried to sound reluctant, but he was already straightening his collar and slicking back his short hair.

CJ came across knowledgeable, if a tiny bit wooden. She waited until the interview was over and then walked him back to where he had been working. "You be sure to let me know if there's anything you need help with. If anyone from Sun Rail isn't getting back to you quickly enough or anything like that, give me a call." She handed him her business card with her cell number and e-mail address. "I'd also like to kept in the loop of your investigation."

"As soon as we're ready to publish a report, I'll let you know."

The first bus arrived. The Red Cross volunteers had put together a group of fifty who wanted to continue on to the Palm Springs area. Many of those people were older, retired types who couldn't wait to drop their money in the popular Coachella Valley Indian casinos.

Charlotte took the list of those passengers, and of the hotels where they would be staying. She would send staff to tape statements tomorrow while the facts were still fresh in everyone's minds. She'd also set up trauma assessments with the psych counselors.

She noticed a man in a navy blue uniform sitting off by himself with his head in his hands. Sorrow radiated from his shoulders like an aura. She ran through the manifest until she came upon the name of the crew member listed as the conductor.

She grabbed a couple bottles of water and approached him. "Sam? Sam Ricketts?"

He raised his head, and she saw tears streaking his cheeks. "Who are you?"

She handed him a water. "Charlotte Lyon. Sun Rail hired me to help out here. Did you know Bob Peterson well?"

He cracked open the water and took a long pull. "Only twenty-five years. He was a good man. The best."

"Did he seem ill before you took off for today's run?"

"Hell no. He was the same as always. God, I can't believe he's gone." Ricketts brushed roughly at his face. She gave him a moment to compose himself.

"Was it unusual for him to ride solo in the cab?" she asked.

"He wasn't much for small talk. I figured the new guy would be yakking his head off. So to give Bob a break, I kept the kid with me. If he'd been up front with Bob, he might've been able to do something."

She looked at him with true sympathy. "We're all haunted by what-ifs. Let's hold off judgment until we figure out the when, why, and how of it all."

She was thinking that this was going to be a case of a lot of little wrong actions adding up. Each by itself could have been absorbed, but cascading one after another created a catastrophe. A good example of that had been the most recent East Coast blackout. The power grid failure had been traced to many factors: an overloaded system, misinterpretation of existing regulations, a malfunctioning alarm that might have alerted engineers. Put it all together at the height of summer, stir in a little human error and bad timing, and the result was eight states and parts of eastern Canada without power for thirty hours.

She was also open to the idea that the cause of the wreck was more sinister than that. A few things were already making her Spidey senses tingle. Not that she would communicate her suspicions to the Feds. The sooner they got uninvolved, the better.

Charlotte would give what evidence she gathered to the NTSB and let them collect the credit. And if there was a crime involved, she would leave it to them to contact the proper authorities.

The second bus arrived, followed shortly by several limousines and a van. Charlotte oversaw the loading of the last of the passengers. It had gotten dark and Caltrans brought in a portable plant light to illuminate the investigation. The chug of the generator drowned out the buzz of night insects.

The Red Cross people had set up tables with sandwiches and drinks. She found Todd Hannigan having an impromptu picnic.

He patted the ground next to him. "Pull up a patch."

She removed her safety vest, spread it back down next to him, and then sat on it cross-legged. "I noticed that the FBI left."

"Yeah, there really wasn't much more for them to do here." He took a large bite of his sandwich and chewed with gusto.

"Tasty?" she asked.

He thrust the half missing a bite toward her. "Want some?"

She held up her own sandwich. "No, I'm good." She took a sip of her bottled water and scooted the sandwich free of the plastic wrap. "So they didn't find signs of sabotage?"

"The Feds were satisfied."

"Great." She realized she'd put more enthusiasm into her response than she had intended. Hannigan didn't seem to notice. "And you?"

"We're all just gathering data at this point," he said. "We'll know more in a few weeks."

"How long before we get some answers as to what caused the engineer's death?"

He scratched at his sideburn, and a piece of lettuce dropped on his pant leg. "A few days probably. Same as the toxicology reports on the crew."

"They all seemed sober to me," she said, trying not to notice the bit of roast beef that had joined the lettuce. If he put either back in his mouth, she was out of there.

He cast his hand before him to encompass the scene. "Something like this can be pretty sobering." He finished off his sandwich. "It's one of an engineer's worst fears."

"I would think it would be *the* worst."

"Seeing the face of a person before your trains hits them. That's the worst."

"Is that common?" she asked. "Having someone die under your wheels?"

He picked up a twig and started breaking it into little pieces. "Any engineer with any length of experience will have some stories. People don't realize that the train is twice as wide as the track. You get drunks walking the line, or kids playing near the rails, they don't have any idea of the danger. Ninety-nine percent of the time, though, it's a suicide. The worst time is around the holidays." He threw the bits of branch into the dirt in front of him, one piece at a time, but with vehemence. She wondered what demons he had to exorcize.

"It must be awful," she said.

"Not something you forget. I know it might be hard to believe, engines being so big and all, but an engineer feels everything between his wheels and the rail. He feels it all through the seat of his pants. He can even tell when he runs over a penny."

He looked at her as if expecting her to challenge him. "Wow," she said without a shred of skepticism.

"When your train clobbers someone, you see it happen in your head over and over again. It happens fast, but it seems like slow motion. The thud of a body is unmistakable."

"I don't know how you would get over a thing like that," she said.

He shrugged. "Some guys take it in stride. I know one engineer who has eighteen stick figures on his travel mug. He says he's assisted in more suicides than Dr. Kevorkian."

She laughed and instantly felt ashamed for being amused. Her therapist assured her that gallows humor was a perfectly acceptable coping method. And what about the people who flocked to disaster scenes as if they were free concerts in the park? she'd ask. Her shrink explained that this appeal of the macabre was nothing more sinister than basic human curiosity, but that was hard for Charlotte to buy.

Then 9/11 happened. All those supposedly normal people were glued to their televisions, repeatedly watching the Twin Towers collapse or imagining what it must have been like to have been aboard one of those planes. Another side effect was the mass paralysis of business. Her shrink said most people were completely unprepared for a worst-case scenario. Score another one for OCD.

She turned to Todd Hannigan as an obvious conclusion caught up with her. "You think Bob Peterson saw someone on the tracks?"

"Only he would know, and he ain't saying."

She considered that and all its ramifications. Who speaks for a dead man? "Does it go in an engineer's record, when they hit someone?"

"I wouldn't put it in a guy's file, and I don't know any train masters who would. What would be the point? It's not like it's intentional."

"You can't swerve to avoid them."

"All you can do is look away and wait." He stared ahead of him. "My first one was a teenage boy with girlfriend problems. He jumped right in front of me. I lost him from my range of vision. Then I felt the thud. He stayed hooked to the engine for a half mile, locked onto the scoop. I still hear the body dragging."

"I can imagine," she said truthfully.

"When you hit someone, when there's a fatality, you don't get off the engine. You wait until the investigators arrive. So you don't actually see the body, but it doesn't matter. Your imagination fills in the rest. Those images stick with you forever."

She noticed his switch to plural, but before she could frame her next question, he stood abruptly and wiped his hands against his pants. A clear signal that the discussion was over.

"I'm going to be here another couple hours. I'll catch a ride back with someone or ferry back with the salvaged cars. Either way, you don't have to wait for me."

She stood also. "I'll get those personnel records and have them on call for you at the Sun Rail offices."

Before she left, she gathered the annotated passenger manifests from the Red Cross ladies. First thing tomorrow, she would begin interviewing the passengers who opted to return to Orange County and Los Angeles. She called Mary Nightengale, who was still at the hospital.

"What's the status of the injured passengers?"

Mary sounded tired. "The most serious injury was a broken leg. The other hospitalized passengers suffered mostly bumps and bruises and are being held overnight as a precautionary measure."

"Treat them like family," Charlotte said. "Anything they need."

"The lady with the broken leg says some guy on a motorcycle helped her to safety."

"Not one of the passengers or crew? Did she get his name?"

"No, and now she wants to find out who he was so she can thank him."

"What did he look like?" Charlotte asked.

"That's the thing. The guy never took off his helmet. She has no idea."

"I'd like to find this guy, too," Charlotte said. "Maybe he witnessed something that will help with the investigation."

"At the very least, we should publicly thank him."

"You read my mind. Ever consider a career in public relations?"

Mary laughed, and Charlotte was glad to hear it. "I'm heading back to Orange County. Call me if you need me." Secretly she hoped that she wouldn't. The last thing any of them needed was any more surprises, especially newsworthy ones.

WEDNESDAY

CHAPTER 8

Hannigan wanted to beat his head against the dashboard. "She must think I'm the biggest wuss in the world."

"The PR woman?" CJ asked. "Why would she think that?" He was at the wheel of the company truck that was taking him back to NTSB headquarters.

"I all but cried telling her about the first fatality I was a part of."

"Relax. Women like that kind of thing. And what do you care what she thinks anyway?"

"I know what you're saying." Hannigan rolled down his window a few inches to let the cooler evening air caress his face. "She's kind of a wack job."

"And some guys like that in a woman," CJ said knowingly.

Hannigan looked at his friend for a moment, and then they both busted out laughing. Hannigan raised both hands in surrender. "Guilty."

When Charlotte got home, it was close to midnight. She was still jacked up from the day's events, so she began creating a safety comparison of train travel versus other modes of transportation. If the derailment continued making news, she would be ready with a tie-in angle.

One way to address a crisis was to divert the media's attention. The publicist representing the Philadelphia hotel where all those legionnaires died was a good example. Hell, they'd even named the disease after the victims. The airborne contagion might just as easily have been known by the name of the hotel, but the PR people were smart and made the story about the American Legion, the hospital, WHO, and the CDC.

Another ploy was to find a sacrificial lamb. The dead train engineer was a good candidate for that position, but only if the derailment was his fault. If it were something else, then that would have to be addressed. Taking the easy way out was not an option. She had to live with herself, and she wasn't going to make that job any harder than it already was.

She vowed long ago never to feed the blame culture. The world was sick with it. (That and spurious lawsuits.) Her husband's company had been all about finger-pointing. The staff was always on the lookout for someone else to hold accountable for any misstep that impacted the company. She would never participate in an investigation geared toward finding the easiest way out. Not at the cost of finding the real reasons and possibly preventing future tragedy. She owed that to Brad's memory.

She returned to her other data on train derailments. In the past year, 150 of those wrecks were attributed to human error. Seventy-three were written off to miscellaneous (as in extreme weather conditions). Signal failure accounted for only ten. Track problems were the leading cause of 210.

She made a note to herself to learn about what safety measures were already in place and how much time and effort the railroad spent on maintenance and inspection.

Her online research also found an exposé that made the front page of *The New York Times*. The article's thesis was well documented, at least to the untrained eye. Apparently, according to the stats presented, it was much safer to be riding inside a train than crossing in front of one. No surprise there. What was shocking (and made for above-the-fold headlines) was the purported custom of the railroads to sidestep blame for those fatalities.

The article insinuated a widespread conspiracy by every rail company in America. In one case, the maintenance guys repaired a faulty signal before the body was cold and while the local cop was busy elsewhere. Now really, Charlotte thought, what midlevel employee would risk a felony charge of impeding a police investigation for the sake of the company ducking a lawsuit? And how would the repair crew get the order to do such a thing within hours of the accident? The exposé felt like a blatant case of "gotcha" journalism. Although she had to ask herself if she would be so quick to champion the country's rail system before she met Todd Hannigan.

She thought about his abrupt shift of attitude after telling her about the kid he hit. It obviously still got to him. That wasn't a bad thing at all. She liked it when a guy had a sensitive side to him. Hannigan seemed to have quite a number of sides. Up until the moment when he talked about his first assisted suicide, there had been something infectious about his enthusiasm. If a person were going to catch something, why couldn't it be a good thing?

She smiled at her uncharacteristic optimism, worked for an hour, and then went to bed.

At 1:15 A.M., Charlotte's cell phone rang. She glanced at the caller ID screen as she picked up the call. "What is it, Mary?"

"The name on the manifest was her assistant's." Mary seemed to be out of breath.

"Whose name?" Charlotte asked.

"The passenger who died was Rachel Priest. The actress."

Actress, environmentalist, philanthropist. Rachel Priest had worn many hats. She was also one of the most beloved public figures since Mother Teresa. "What was she doing on the train?" Charlotte asked, wondering what was making a slow ticking noise. She was holding one of her hands out in front of her, fingers spread and palm out as if to stop the charge of a mad beast.

"She was bringing back a group of underprivileged kids from the desert. She had developed a scholarship to expose farmworker children to the arts. She booked an entire car to bring those kids back to Los Angeles with plans to visit the Getty Museum, see live stage productions, and go to the museums. But her assistant made the arrangements and Ms. Priest was alone in the front car, so nobody realized who she was."

"Breathe." Charlotte identified the ticking noise. It was the sound of her own tears hitting the papers on her desk. Rachael Priest had been one of the good ones. "Does the media know yet?"

"The coroner is trying to contact her son in Switzerland. He's hiking or something."

"So, no?" Charlotte asked.

"Yes, no. To the best of my knowledge, the media doesn't know."

"How about CEO Rayney?"

"Should I call him?" Mary seemed to have gained control over her hyperventilating. Charlotte knew that passing the burden had helped her.

"I'll take care of that." Charlotte swung her legs out of bed and walked toward her office. "All right, here's what I want you to do, Mary. This thing isn't going to go away anytime soon. You need to get some rest. I'll need you sharp tomorrow. You did the right thing to call me. Be glad this didn't happen on the return trip."

"I thought of that," Mary said.

Charlotte said good night as she booted up her computer and flicked on CNN. She Googled "Rachel Priest" and clicked on the link to the actress's Web site. There, she studied the well-known star's face. Good bones, straight teeth, those trademark blue eyes that had earned her the roles of the world's most legendary beauties. She'd played Helen of Troy and, rumor had it, was offered Cleopatra before Elizabeth Taylor. She also created memorable roles as a lovable con artist, the first woman president of the United States, and a lady gunslinger with a weakness for orphans. At seventy-plus, she still worked regularly and donated the lion's share of her earnings to her many causes. The woman had an elegance about her that transcended age barriers. Critics admitted that they would pay money to watch her walk a dog.

Even her final charitable act of paying for an entire empty train car to ensure that all the Coachella Valley kids would be able to ride together to Los Angeles had possibly saved lives.

There was not a whisper about her untimely death. Yet.

The world, Charlotte included, had lost a champion; a mother/ sister/friend figure. She could imagine the commemorative plates being sold on the home shopping networks as early as next week. The accident site was going to sprout more dead flowers than the Rose Parade. People would come from all over to hold candlelight vigils for their fallen icon.

The shit storm was coming, Charlotte thought. "Sun Rail," she said out loud, "Welcome to my world."

CHAPTER 9

Charlotte's alarm woke her at 4 A.M. The birds outside her window were chirping. She wondered what sort of clock they answered to. The impact of Rachel Priest's death hit her all over again. This was how it had been in the weeks and months after Brad was killed. The first waking moments were her only freedom. That first stir to consciousness, the befuddled state as the brain sorts dream from reality, nightmare from tragedy. She had a few seconds of sleepy bliss before the wrenching realization that always followed too quickly. Then she'd be fully awake and cognizant that all the nightmares were true and that it was happiness that was just a dream.

Work and routine had been the only things that carried her through those dark days.

"Up and at 'em," she said out loud as she threw off her bedcovers.

Along those lines, she also wondered if Todd Hannigan was up yet and how late he had stayed at the scene.

She'd call him when the hour got a little more civilized. She knew he was going to be conducting interviews of the crew this morning at his office in Gardena. She wanted to get some B-rolls of the NTSB's metallurgical lab so the public would be reassured at the science applied to the investigation. He was the logical guy to go to for that request.

She went through her morning grooming and dressing rituals. The pattern she followed was two articles of clothing followed by a non-clothing item. Panties, bra, deodorant; nylons, pants, sunscreen; top, shoes, hair. The last portion, which she saved until just before she was ready to leave the house, was shoes, jacket, makeup. Brad hadn't noticed the ritual until they'd been dating for six months; of course, he wasn't a trained investigator.

She turned on CNN and checked e-mail while she had her coffee and cereal. Dispensing quickly with those correspondences, she clicked on the chat page on Rachel Priest's Web site. The news still hadn't broken. It was a matter of hours, perhaps minutes.

She would have liked to wait until six before she called Bernard Rayney, but that would be a mistake. It was three hours later in New York, and the morning network news-interview shows would be airing soon.

"There's been a new wrinkle," she said when he answered his phone.

"What now?" he asked, the stress clearly audible in his voice.

"The deceased passenger has been identified. As of one this morning, the coroner had not released her name pending the location of her son. He's in Switzerland."

"Switzerland," Rayney repeated.

"Yes. The dead passenger was Rachel Priest."

"Oh, God."

"We're trying to locate her son. I need to draft a news release, and I would like to make sure he knows and is comfortable with what I'd like to say."

"What else?" Rayney asked.

"I'd like the green light from you to set up a Good Samaritan fund in her honor. The company could pitch in the first ten thousand and offer to match funds that are donated in Rachel's name. The money will then be bestowed to one of Rachel's favorite causes. Perhaps the youth-to-art program." Charlotte briefly described the reason Rachel had chartered the Sunliner train in the first place. "I'd like you to make the announcement."

"All right, if you think this best," he said.

"I do. I would also like to recognize a hero of yesterday's tragedy. There was a man on a motorcycle who was first on the scene. This person helped people out of the cars after the crash. I'd like to thank him publicly and draw attention to his selfless actions."

"Who was this guy? Did you meet him?"

"That's the thing. He was wearing a helmet and in protective gear. Most likely he had been dirt-biking over the hill when the accident occurred. The De Anza Motorcycle Park is a few miles from the crash site. Whoever the guy was, he didn't stick around after the other help arrived."

"How will we identify him, then?" Rayney asked, sounding more confident for having been given a solvable problem.

"We'll announce that we're looking for him at our press conference this morning as well as post it on the company Web site. I'll set up a dedicated phone line to take tips and pledges for the fund. We'll set up the press conference at ten. I'd like to have it near the crash site. Her fans will congregate there as soon as the news of her death gets out and create some sort of memorial. I'm going to have some open tents erected and a platform built with a podium. We don't need the reporters or mourners to get sunstroke. I also don't want anyone interfering with the investigator's work."

"How bad is this?"

"This is going to be front-page material all over the world," she said.

"This isn't going away anytime soon, is it?"

"I'll do my best, but I'm not going to make you any promises I can't keep."

"Fair enough," Rayney said. "I'll see you out there." He sounded numb, even resigned.

"Don't give up hope. I've only just begun. And drive safely. Better still, take a train."

The news of Rachel Priest's death came out at a few minutes after 5 A.M., PST. The talk shows preempted scheduled guests to show footage of the derailment, followed by film clips and file footage of some of her fund-raising events. The only stations that didn't interrupt their programming were one cooking show and the Sci-Fi Channel. The Internet providers made it their top story. Radio stations reacted by playing no music. Instead, the disc jockeys took calls and expressed their own reactions. Rachel Priest's fan Web site couldn't handle the flow of posts. It didn't matter who or how the news leaked out. The dam had burst.

Charlotte ordered a large wreath of white roses with a black bow and charged the arrangement to Sun Rail. She monitored the radio stations as she drove to the depot in Corona. She was against the main going-to-work traffic flow, but her median speed was still in the forty mph range. Rayney and his entourage arrived before her on the company's private rail car, and she ferried the rest of the way with them.

Rayney looked as if he had aged ten years since yesterday. Andrew, his assistant, hovered nearby, an anxious expression on his young face. Stan obviously hadn't bathed, but he had sweated. Copiously. He seemed to be wearing the same clothes as when she had met him.

The executive coach was equipped with sleeping quarters, a full bathroom, and galley. Cushioned, swiveling armchairs lined both walls. Downwind wasn't possible, so she settled for a chair as far away from Stan as possible. Andrew played steward. The rest of them swung their chairs so that they were facing each other. Dom was probably going for dapper, but his hands shook as he sipped his coffee, and his cuff was misbuttoned.

While Andrew was mixing the drinks and putting them on a tray, Charlotte opened the folder on her lap. "I've written a statement for you, and I'd like to go over it." She passed copies to each of the men. "If you would read it out loud."

Rayney rubbed his eyes and then donned dark-rimmed reading glasses. "Yesterday, the world lost a friend and bright light, Rachel Priest. She had a wonderful talent. Via the screen, we welcomed her into our homes and hearts. Her face was as familiar to us as our own family members'. She will be missed.

"Sun Rail also lost one of its family members yesterday. Engineer Bob Peterson. Bob wasn't a celebrity, but he was a husband and a father and a friend. He leaves behind a wife, a daughter, a son-in-law, and two grandchildren.

"Our investigators, as well as teams from Union Pacific, the NTSB, and the Federal Rail Association will work around the clock to bring you answers of how this tragic event came to pass. Information as it is verified and confirmed will be available on our Web site at www. sunrail.org. These answers will not fill the void these untimely deaths have created. Nothing will."

Charlotte interrupted. "Pause here and look at the faces around you."

He looked at her for a moment, showing the full weight of his burden in his eyes. His expression was that of a man whose family was being held for ransom in an unfriendly country.

"That's exactly what I want," she said. "Please continue."

Rayney scooted his glasses a fraction of an inch closer to his eyes and began reading again. He crossed his legs, and she noticed he was wearing two unmatched socks. "But we as humans and Americans often feel the need to do something concrete, to speak with our actions. Such a person was the unidentified Good Samaritan who acted anonymously and heroically to help several injured passengers to safety. All we know is that he was wearing off-road motorcycle gear and that he labored alone to do what he could before the rescue workers arrived. I would like to shake his hand and thank him personally.

"We have also created a Good Samaritan fund and will match all donations contributed in the next month. Proceeds will go directly to the Rachel Priest foundation, which services the many causes she so tirelessly championed. I think Ms. Priest would have wanted her work to continue.

"We've established several toll-free hotlines."

Charlotte handed Rayney a printed placard. On it was the company Web site address and the 800 numbers. "Hold this up in front of you and keep it there while you field questions."

Rayney nodded. "I like it. Straightforward. Clean. To the point." He turned to the attorney. "Dom? What do you think?"

Dom didn't answer immediately, taking his time to read through the statement again to himself. "The question of culpability is bound to be raised."

"We'll have to await the outcome of the investigation," Rayney said.

"That's right," Charlotte said. "We're doing all that we can. Remember: We showed up, we suited up, and we won't rest until we have the answers."

"And hope to God it wasn't our fault," Rayney said. Rayney and Dom exchanged intense heartfelt looks, and Charlotte wondered how much of their personal wealth was tied up in this venture.

When they arrived at the news conference, the number of media had swelled threefold with the addition of the international press.

Charlotte kicked things off. She stood on the small wooden dais they had erected with the tracks in the background. The gigantic memorial mound of flowers, candles, stuffed animals, and written messages was fifty yards to her left. Not a satisfying shot for the media cameras to record them both simultaneously. The track behind her was back in operation, but the area surrounding the POD was still restricted to investigators only. She stood tall as she faced the press, and her voice was steady. It was hot as hell. She figured this would be to their advantage and keep the conference short.

"As you all know, Rachel Priest died yesterday. The coroner has not released his findings, but should have a preliminary report ready for publication by this evening. Please remember that though this is a media event because of Ms. Priest's high visibility and popularity, two people have died, and their survivors deserve their privacy and our consideration.

"Now the CEO of Sun Rail, Bernard Rayney, has a few words."

Bernard Rayney then took the podium and read his statement. He had no sooner finished than the questions flew at him like birdshot.

"Did she die at the scene?"

"How soon was it before medical help arrived?"

"What were her injuries?"

"Was she able to say any last words?"

"Who was with her?"

"What safety precautions were taken in the event of a derail, and why didn't they work?"

Charlotte returned to the stage and nodded sympathetically at every reporter who posed a question. She knew they were doing their jobs. Just as she was doing hers. As her head bobbed yes, her oft-repeated response was, "I don't know yet" and "The family is my number-one priority, and it will have to be up to them what details are made public."

As prearranged, Dom handed her a folded piece of paper. She opened it and read it, nodding as she did so as if reassured by what she was seeing. The reporter's questions hushed as their curiosity piqued. Bernard Rayney stepped down from the podium to allow Charlotte center stage.

She held the note open and announced, "The FBI has determined that this was not an act of terrorism and have pulled out from the investigation."

"What do they think caused it?" a UPI stringer asked. "Could anyone see it coming?"

"That's up to the NTSB to determine. They're the experts and we'll continue working closely with them. Thank you all for being here. Please check our Web site for updates."

Rayney and Dom were already back on the train when she joined them there.

"What can we expect now?" Rayney asked. He had removed his jacket, and his shirt was soaked through with sweat.

She passed the men bottles of water and opened one for herself. "There's a phenomenon in emergencies. At first, everyone, including the media, act as if they're part of the rescue team." She waved with her bottle to the scene outside the window. The celebrity newscasters were posed dramatically as they taped their reports. The message being that they were risking life and limb to bring the story to their viewers.

The train made a small lurch as it got under way.

"Then a subtle shift takes place from rescue to analysis," she continued. "Eventually the crisis will peak, hard to predict when, but we'll know. Elected officials will start visiting the scene. The story is really on its last legs when the press start attacking each other, accusing each other of sensationalism. We've already made it to the second stage. The questions have turned from who, what, when, and where to wanting to know how and why. We need to stay ahead of the story as it breaks, to anticipate. That's why it's imperative that we have the answers first. My husband used to play pickup basketball. He called it getting the jump on the ball."

Rayney made a small grimace of a smile, then put his head back and closed his eyes. The movement of the railcar rocked his head gently from side to side as if even in sleep he was saying, *No, no, no.* Dom stared out the window. His eyes didn't move. It was obvious he wasn't enjoying the landscape or whatever he was thinking.

She thought about what she hadn't told them. Once the politicians showed up, the only remaining juicy tidbit was finding who to blame. This would come in the form of attacks on the railroad or the dead engineer or even the project itself. Then the story would die until the lawsuits began.

So they were calling him a Good Samaritan. They were almost right. Yes, he had done a criminal thing, but he wasn't a bad person. What he did had been a sacrifice, and now it was too late for regrets. He had left no evidence tying himself to the derailment. He'd been very careful about that.

Lorrin had nothing to worry about as long as he held his mud and stuck to his script. He used a prepaid phone card and a public pay phone to call Lorrin. He wasn't at work. He'd called in sick, they said.

The Samaritan hung up and called Lorrin's home number.

"We should turn ourselves in," Lorrin said.

"And do what? Spend the rest of our lives in jail?" His tone implied what a stupid choice that would be. They had talked about prison and how tough it would be.

"I never meant for anyone to die. I'll explain."

"And how will you explain the sudden appearance of nine thousand dollars in your checking account? On your salary?"

"Listen, I can't sleep. I can't eat. I don't know what to do."

"You go back to work," the Samaritan said. "If you break your pattern, it will only make you look suspicious. What's done is done. We're going to have to ride it out."

"I wish I'd never met you," the guy said.

The Samaritan was beginning to feel the same way. The guy had definitely moved out of accomplice territory and onto the endangered species list.

CHAPTER 10

When Charlotte got back to her car, she called Dorothy Peterson and asked if she could come pay her respects. The grief counselor that she had sent to the Peterson home had stayed with the new widow until ten in the evening. The daughter was driving in from San Francisco and had refused the company's offer to fly her down.

The Petersons' house was in Fullerton. Charlotte knew from the company's records that Bob's yearly salary was $110,000 and that his benefit package included health and dental. Dorothy Peterson was a homemaker.

Sam Ricketts answered the door. Charlotte shouldn't have been surprised. The conductor had mentioned his long friendship with Engineer Bob.

Dorothy Peterson offered Charlotte something to drink before they sat down in her living room. Ricketts hovered over her protectively. Charlotte wondered if he had spent the night. Nobody should have to face that first night alone.

Charlotte knew how the woman felt, or more precisely what she didn't feel. Dorothy Peterson was probably at the disbelief stage. Her husband's dirty laundry still filled half the hamper; perhaps there were glasses and spoons in the dishwasher still bearing the imprints of his touch.

Brad never finished reading the novel by his side of the bed, and nine months later, Charlotte still hadn't removed his bookmark. For a week after he died, the hole he hadn't finished digging in the yard still had the shovel stuck in the ground beside it. Rain and wind had since restored the dirt. It had taken her a month to put away the shovel.

Dorothy Peterson was still surrounded by evidence of her husband's life, and none yet of his death. Proof, for a few brief delusional moments yet, that he wasn't gone. If his job took him away from home for days at a time, he might yet return. The permanence of her new reality wouldn't take hold until after the funeral. And then there would still be moments when she would lift the phone to call him or think she heard his car in the driveway. It was six months before Charlotte stopped calling out, "I'm home," to the empty house. She'd finally had to move.

She was doing this woman no favors by being here, shattering the hope that this was all some terrible mix-up, but better her than someone else.

"I'm sorry I never met your husband," Charlotte said.

Dorothy wiped at her eyes. "He was a good man, a good father."

Ricketts patted her shoulder. Dorothy grabbed his hand and didn't let go. Ricketts didn't seem as guilt ridden as he had been right after the derailment. The only vibe Charlotte was getting now was something close to contentment.

Charlotte took a sip of the iced tea Dorothy had brewed. Uneven wedges of lemons bobbed in the pitcher. Charlotte had seen the tree in the front yard on the way in. "Your yard is beautiful. It shows a lot of love."

"That was Bob. You should see his vegetables. Remind me to give you some tomatoes that we preserved."

Charlotte knew she would politely forget. Botulism and *E. coli* were only a couple of the reasons. "Did he love his work?"

Dorothy looked at the clock over her mantel and then at the front door. "Why do you ask?"

"The train people I've been meeting all seem to have a huge passion for trains."

Dorothy smiled faintly. "They call them foamers. Because when the subject of trains comes up, they foam at the mouth. To Bob, it was a job. He left his work at work. We're counting the days to his retirement. Were."

Charlotte glanced at a picture on the table beside the sofa. The Petersons were dressed in waders, floppy hats, and plaid flannel shirts. Each of them was holding a dead salmon and smiling proudly. Dorothy twisted at her wedding ring.

Without realizing what she was doing, Charlotte reached for the chain around her throat and patted her own set of rings. She drew her hand away quickly. This was not about her or Brad, and she didn't want to confuse the two cases.

Charlotte focused on the newer widow. "I already asked Mr. Ricketts if he noticed anything out of the ordinary about Bob's behavior yesterday morning. Did you?"

"Well, no, not really. But when Bob has a run, he gets up early. He sleeps in the guest room so's not to disturb me. I didn't even hear him go."

Charlotte felt pain for the woman. No good-bye kiss. No final *I love you* or *Be careful* or *Pick up some fried chicken on your way home.* "How was his health?"

"Well, we're all feeling our years."

"Any heart condition or chronic illness?"

Dorothy shook her head. "Arthritis, but that doesn't kill a person."

"No, ma'am, it sure doesn't."

"Maybe I shouldn't be talking to you. The man from the union said not to say or sign anything."

Charlotte looked sincerely into Dorothy's eyes, hoping to convey that her intentions were honorable. She believed that all people came equipped with bullshit detectors, and she had nothing to hide. Her conscience was clear. "I agree that you shouldn't sign anything. I haven't brought anything with me. We're all just trying to figure out how this happened."

The phone rang. Dorothy rose heavily and crossed the room to answer it.

Charlotte watched the woman's face blanch after her initial hello.

Dorothy's voice had a strange croak to it as she asked, "How did you get this number?"

Charlotte was already on her feet when Dorothy dropped the phone, made a small cry of pain, and faltered. Fearing the woman would crack her head open, Charlotte rushed to her aid, but Ricketts beat her to the woman's side. Dorothy gripped the small table where the telephone sat, causing several framed family photos to fall face-down with loud slaps. With Charlotte's and Rickett's support, Dorothy dragged herself to a nearby armchair as if she were pulling herself against the current in an unfriendly sea.

Charlotte picked up the phone. "Who is this?"

"He murdered Rachel," the caller said. "I hope he rots in hell."

Charlotte hung up.

"How did they find us so fast?" Dorothy asked.

The phone rang again. Charlotte answered.

"Monster," a different voice said.

"We have a trace on this phone," Charlotte said. "And we will press charges."

The caller hung up after making a rude suggestion.

Charlotte turned back to Dorothy. "Do you have an answering machine?"

"In the kitchen."

"Do you mind if I change the message?"

"It won't help. Nothing does."

"Do I have your permission to try?"

Dorothy jumped when the phone rang again. "Yes. Please. Yes."

Charlotte turned off the ringer and went into the kitchen. On the third ring, the machine picked up. The outgoing message began with Dorothy clearing her throat and then saying slowly and carefully, "You have reached the residence of Bob and Dottie Peterson. If you leave a message, we'll call you back." Charlotte was glad it wasn't Bob's voice she was erasing. Dorothy might regret that later. She set the machine to answer on the first ring with a fifteen-second cutoff on incoming messages. She pushed record and said, "Leave your name. This line is monitored by the police. We prosecute any form of slander or harassment."

Charlotte returned to the living room. Dorothy sat with her head down and her hands pressed over her eyes and forehead.

Charlotte rested her own hand ever so gently on the woman's shoulder. "Is there anything else I can do for you?"

"My daughter Stacy is on her way. Stacy and Eric. Her husband. They have a son and a daughter. My grandson plays soccer. My granddaughter is taking piano lessons." She put her hands down for a second and laughed at herself. "I don't know why I'm telling you all this."

Charlotte righted the pictures that had fallen. "How old are they?"

"My grandson, Sean, is eight. Little Tracy is seven. Would you like something to eat?"

"Dottie," Ricketts said, "you don't need to be fussing over everyone."

"I'm fine," Charlotte said.

Charlotte sat down across from Dorothy, giving her a view out the front window. "This is a terrible time," she told them both. "Fans of celebrities with Rachel Priest's status can be quite rabid. There is no evidence that your husband was to blame. We still don't know, and we won't know for a while, exactly what happened."

"That doesn't matter. Of course it was an accident. Bob would never hurt someone on purpose. You ask anyone who knows him... knew him. Sam?"

"That's right, Dottie." Ricketts glared at Charlotte. "The man was a saint."

Charlotte had a moment of sympathy for Ricketts. Sainthood was a tough act to follow. She should know. Since Brad died, she couldn't remember a single bad thing about him.

A Volvo station wagon pulled into the driveway. A man and a woman got out. The woman was a younger version of Dorothy and looked bereft.

"Does your daughter drive a Volvo?" Charlotte asked.

Dorothy sat up straight and wiped the tears from her face. "Is she here?"

The door opened and Charlotte was spared from having to respond. The two women embraced and sobbed on each other's shoulders. Ricketts surrounded both women with his arms.

"Are you from the church?" Eric asked Charlotte.

"No." She offered him a business card. "I'm here on behalf of Sun Rail. We're all terribly grief stricken by this tragedy."

Eric motioned for Charlotte to follow him into the kitchen. "We saw the train on the news. Was Bob in the locomotive? It didn't seem to be damaged. How did he die?"

"That's one of many questions we still have. What do you think?"

96

"What do I think? We're in shock. He was sixty-one, a hearty sixty-one. He's dead. Are you saying that it was his fault?" The temperature in the kitchen seemed to drop thirty degrees.

"I'm not looking to assign blame. I'm only interested in the truth. Obviously this whole thing is going to be very high profile." She told him about the calls and how she had altered the answering machine.

"How did they find her so fast?" Eric said.

"Your mother-in-law wondered the same thing. I have to assume that they went through every Bob Peterson in the phone book."

"They weren't listed."

"Really? Why is that?"

Eric looked at the door. "You'd have to ask my mother-in-law, but not today."

She wondered what he was holding back and why. "May I—?"

"No," Eric said, cutting her off. "No more right now, please. Listen, I don't mean to be rude. Give us some time alone, as a family."

"I was just going to say that if you had any questions, please don't hesitate to call me. The company has hired grief counselors. You all should avail yourselves of their services."

"It's coming a little late for some of us, but thanks. Now please, leave."

Charlotte's phone rang on her way to the Anaheim offices of Sun Rail. It was Andrew. "Sherwood Priest is here. Rachel's son. You better get here ASAP."

CHAPTER 11

Andrew met Charlotte at the elevator. "I put Mr. Priest in Mr. Rayney's office."

"Where's Mr. Rayney?" Charlotte asked.

"I don't know." Andrew twisted his lip nervously. "His cell phone is either off or he's out of range. Should I try him again?"

"Is Mr. Priest by himself?"

"Yes. He wants to meet with someone in charge, and he doesn't look happy."

"He *is* mourning his mother," Charlotte said.

"He's not sad so much as angry. He's demanding a public apology from the company."

"I'll go speak to him." Charlotte knocked on the door to CEO Rayney's office, waited a moment, and then entered.

The smell of cigar smoke was the first thing to assault her.

Sherwood Priest was seated behind Rayney's desk and had made himself at home. He held up a hand to hush her, and she saw that he was on the phone. Sun Rail's phone, to be precise. She wondered if he were calling Switzerland.

Where Rachel Priest had been tall and elegant, her son was short and porky. His hair was impossibly dark for a man his age. He had to be in his late forties. He was dressed in the best clothes money could buy, right down to argyle socks and Italian loafers, all of which she got a view of as he pushed back in the CEO's chair and put his feet on the desk.

There were no ashtrays in the office, so she brought him a water glass for his cigar.

He flicked his ashes with a practiced flourish.

"You wanted to see me?" she asked.

"Hold on a minute," he said into the phone, and then to Charlotte, "Coffee, honey. Cream and whatever sweetener you have."

"Mr. Priest, I'm Charlotte Lyon. I'm representing Sun Rail until CEO Rayney can get here. I would really like to talk to you."

"I'll call you back," he said into the phone.

"If you need to smoke, we can go outside."

"You're going to bust my balls about smoking?" He looked at her as if she had suggested he should hold his breath.

"I'm terribly sorry for your loss," she said.

Andrew entered the room looking nervous. She turned to him. "Would you get Mr. Priest some coffee, please? Cream and sweetener."

Andrew was out the door already when Priest said, "Fuck the coffee."

Charlotte blinked. His shift to hostility was so quick, she was stunned.

He glared at her. His eyes were dark, crafty, rodentlike, scanning continuously as if looking for an angle. "What were you thinking?"

"About what?" Now she was sorry that Andrew was gone. She would have liked a witness.

"You know. You're going to make me spell it out? You fucking people are all alike. Don't think I'm going to be all nicey-nicey because they sent in a broad. That don't begin to cut it."

"Mr. Priest, I know this is a difficult time for you. We are here to help any way we can. What exactly have I done to reduce you to swearing?"

"It's what you haven't done. I had to fly commercial, for starters."

Charlotte had known people who bypassed shock and denial in the grief process and jumped straight to anger, but this guy was in a league of his own.

"Sun Rail doesn't own a private jet," she said. "If we did, we would have put it at your disposal. We're extremely sorry for your loss."

"Yeah, you said so." He waved the hand holding the cigar, leaving a stinking trail of his disbelief.

"We made every effort to contact you as soon as possible, and we will continue to keep you updated as we learn more."

"I wanted an apology an hour ago." He stabbed his fat brown cigar in her direction. "Too little, too late, honey."

"What do you want now?" she asked.

"To shut you down. I want you all out of a job. I'm hiring my own investigators, and I've instructed my attorney to sue Sun Rail out of existence. You all haven't begun to feel sorry."

The last thing she was going to do was try to talk this blowhard out of anything. She kept her face neutral and her voice steady. "The firm that represents Sun Rail is Dominic Cole and Associates. The NTSB is investigating and will publish their results in about eight months."

"And wouldn't you all just love all that extra time to hide the company's assets and who knows what else? No way in hell, lady." He threw his cigar in the wastepaper basket without bothering to extinguish it and charged from the room.

At some point in Priest's tirade, Andrew had returned. He flattened himself against the wall as Priest swept past on his way out the door; then he ran to the wastebasket and retrieved the smoldering cigar.

101

Charlotte handed him a dry water glass. "Don't douse it with water or we'll never get the smell out of here."

Andrew took the glass to his desk in the anteroom and sealed it shut with plastic packing tape.

Charlotte followed after him. "Is your mother still alive, Andrew?"

"Yes." He set the glass full of smoke on his desk and eyed it warily.

"Do you love her?"

"Of course. My mother is a saint."

Another one, Charlotte mused.

Andrew blushed. "I mean, you know how it is, sometimes she can be a little high maintenance, but she's my mom. I'd do anything for her."

Charlotte nodded. Her own mother was a mess, but you only got one. It was a special relationship, no matter what the circumstances.

"Do you think if she died suddenly that you would take the time to shower, shave, and dress to the nines before you confronted the people you believed were responsible for her death?"

"I'd probably forget to open the garage door before I backed my car out," he said. "But that's just me. Should I try to reach Mr. Rayney again?"

She was already dialing Dom's cell number. "Yes, please. Let me know when you get through."

Charlotte went down to the press room and checked the fan Web site of Rachel Priest. Posts were pouring in on the chat page. Expressions of sorrow mostly. She was on the lookout for a PR professional's worst foe: the word-of-mouth rumor that had no regard for facts or truth. These urban myths were made powerful by being linked to so-called reliable sources such as a relative of a friend who was in position to know the "real" truth. Impossible to verify, difficult to dispute. This disastrous game of telephone was magnified exponentially by the Internet. All she could do was hope to keep up with the yarns being spun and have the real facts to counter them.

She joined the ongoing chat. According to the list, there were forty-five people in the chat room. She posed the question, "What do you all think of Sherwood Priest?" She signed her post "Serenity."

—He caused Rachel nothing but heartache.

Such as??? Charlotte typed back.

The answers popped up immediately, coming faster than she could read them and making the page scroll at three times its former speed.

—I met the Jerk in Aspen. He promised he would introduce me to his mother. I made reservations for dinner at a really nice and expensive restaurant. He showed up, but said his mother had been detained. I found out the next day that his mother was in Wisconsin shooting a movie. And I still got stuck paying for dinner.

A second example soon appeared.

—He stiffed my brother for a huge repair bill on his car. I wrote Rachel, and she sent my brother a check. I'll always love her for that.

Thirty more stories punctuated by expressions of extreme dislike were posted before the board moderator sent a private pop-up message suggesting Charlotte visit the archives. There she would find countless testimonials to Sherwood's sleaziness. Charlotte bookmarked the page. She hadn't really learned anything she hadn't figured out for herself.

She called the Riverside coroner and spoke to the head pathologist, Dr. Patrick Donavon. She'd had occasion to consult with him before and found him brilliant. He told her that his office had scheduled the autopsies of the train fatalities for early the next morning and suggested lunch.

They agreed on noon at the Mission Inn in downtown Riverside.

"I'll meet you in the parking lot. The press is all over this place," Dr. Donavon said.

"I'll bet. Famous Dead People attract them like flies. They'll be trying to get pictures."

"I have uniformed deputies at the doors. The reporters have even been trying to get statements from them. My Public Information Officers are swamped with calls. It's all very disruptive."

"The son is in town now. I assume he'll be making the funeral arrangements. I hope you have an easier time with him than I did."

"Believe me, I've seen the spectrum of family reactions," he said. "I'm looking forward to seeing you, but drive safely. Don't rush on my account."

"I'll leave myself plenty of time," she assured him.

"And buckle up," he said.

"I always do." She hung up the phone smiling. She liked the way his mind worked.

"Good news?" Andrew asked.

"Not yet. I need you to do something for me."

He was at her heels instantly with his pad out. She could get used to this personal assistant thing.

"The assistant engineer who was supposed to work the run. Find out if his wife delivered and tell him I want to ask him some questions. In person."

Andrew looked up after he finished writing. "Anything else?"

"Did you find a private railroad investigator?"

"Yes, there's a firm in Irvine. Iron Horse Technologies. They're litigation experts, and they specialize in virtual recreations of accidents. They're not cheap, but they're supposed to be the best."

"Hire them."

She called Todd Hannigan, but he was out. When asked if she wanted his voice mail, she was momentarily stymied. She hadn't been rehearsing to speak to an answering machine. She told the operator she would call back.

She sent him an e-mail asking him to call her and left her cell number in case he had misplaced her card. Her phone rang ten seconds after she hit SEND. Her caller ID showed her that it was her sister, Jill.

"Mom's dying," Jill said without preamble.

Speak of the devil. Charlotte made an exasperated sigh. The woman had incredible timing. "Again?"

"She might really mean it this time," Jill said. "She said she had to take an ambulance to the emergency room."

"Where are you?" Charlotte asked.

"New York. I have an audition."

"Don't you dare cancel it. I'll check on Mom and let you know if it's the big one."

"She's at USC."

"Probably trying to score drugs," Charlotte said.

"Now, now," Jill said, "be nice."

"Believe me," Charlotte said. "I was."

To call her mother a drama queen would be a gross oversimplification. Hypochondriac didn't begin to cover it either, because some of her health problems were real, others exaggerated, and the rest ignored. Lisa Slokum simply didn't buy into any reality that didn't work for her. Over the years, Charlotte had learned what she could ignore and what she had to pay attention to. Jill faced the same struggles. Being the big sister by four years, Charlotte tried to spare Jill when she could. Charlotte had a therapist once who tried to break her out of her role as family savior, but Charlotte felt it made her a nicer person and didn't see the need to change. Besides, if she got selfishly "healthy," their small family really would fall apart, and she wasn't willing to let that happen.

"I'll take care of it," Charlotte told Jill. "Let me know how the audition goes." She spent the next ten minutes circulating around the war room, making sure the interns were returning calls, and feeding updates to the press. Then she visited the ladies' room and washed her hands with the lotion-enhanced antiseptic soap that she never left home without.

The fact that Mom hadn't called Charlotte already meant that it wasn't time to rally the troops. Still, a hospital stay was hovering toward serious.

She called the USC Medical Center and discovered her mother had been admitted and was in a ward on the fifth floor. At her request, the operator transferred Charlotte to the nurse's desk. Charlotte identified herself as Lisa Slokum's daughter. She purposely didn't ask to speak to her mother. In her experience, it was the floor nurses who really knew what was going on.

"Your mother is being treated for severe anemia," the nurse said. "She's having a transfusion now."

Charlotte shuddered. Having a stranger's blood pumped into her veins was one of her worst fears. "Will she be all right?"

"Oh, yes. This is very treatable."

"What causes this?"

"A variety of things. Her doctor will explain it to you. For now we'll treat the symptoms. She should have come in when she first started passing black stool. From what we can gather, she's been bleeding for nine weeks."

Charlotte heard the hint of disapproval in the nurse's voice. Surely she didn't think Charlotte had been negligent in not inspecting her mother's feces. "How long will she need to stay in the hospital?"

"We're hoping to stabilize her by tomorrow."

"Thank you. Please tell her I'll call her later."

"We'll call you if there is any change, Jill," the nurse said.

"No, I'm the other daughter. Charlotte. Charlotte Lyon."

"Her chart doesn't mention you. Your mother told admitting that she only had one daughter."

"I'm sure it was just an oversight," Charlotte said. She left her phone number with the nurse and wished her mother didn't have the power to wound her without even speaking to her.

CHAPTER 12

Hannigan finally returned her call. He was heading out to the crash site in the afternoon. She told him she would join him there after stopping to visit the passenger with the broken leg. It wasn't yet noon, and she already felt like she had put in a full day. She doubled up on caffeine and hit the road.

Donna Moore, formerly of England, had been released from the hospital early that morning. The company had sent a car to drive her home.

Charlotte saw her through the front window as she reached over to ring the bell. The patient was sitting on a small couch in her living room. A long gypsy skirt covered her legs. Her long and wildly curly cinnamon-colored hair was only partially tamed by a bright green scrunchie. Books were stacked three high on the table in front of her.

"Come in," Donna yelled. "It's open. Mind the cat, though."

Charlotte let herself in. The Clash were pondering loudly if they should stay or should they split. Charlotte approved the Brit's taste in music. She had brought flowers and a box of chocolates. Both were well received.

Charlotte set the vase of flowers near the stereo system and studied

Donna's impressive punk collection. "Don't get up," Charlotte said as she handed over the chocolates.

Donna laughed as she turned down the volume with a remote control.

"Did you find my angel yet?" she asked, opening the See's box with relish. "Oh goody, Nuts and Chews, my favorites." She offered Charlotte the first pick.

"You mean our Good Samaritan?" Charlotte went for the rectangles she knew had hard toffee in the center. "Sadly, no. He's either in a news blackout or prefers anonymity."

"Pity. Here, have a look at this." Donna raised her long skirt to show off the signatures she'd collected on her cast. "I stopped by the firehouse to thank all those lovely firemen. They signed my cast, a few of them wrote their phone numbers as well." She winked.

"Hmm," Charlotte said. "I don't see the Red Cross ladies' signatures anywhere."

"No, them I'll send biscuits."

Charlotte laughed. "I'm glad to see you're getting on so well. Do you ride trains a lot?"

"All over Europe and the UK, now here. It was lovely until, you know."

"I see that your seat was on the right side, near the window. This gave you a view of the road just before the wreck."

"Yes," she said, rummaging around for another chocolate. "We were coming into a lovely horseshoe curve. You could see the whole train at once."

"Were there any cars on the road?"

"Not a soul besides us."

"Did you notice anything out of order?"

"You mean before I went arse over tits?"

"Yes."

She pondered for a moment. "The horn didn't sound. Usually when the train makes a sudden unexpected stop, it's because some poor bloke has wandered too close to the tracks, or a bloody car is trying to beat the signal. There was plenty of noise as the cars fell over, but no warning before." Donna picked up a straightened wire coat hanger and stuck it between cast and skin. The look on her face was almost orgasmic as she found and satisfied an itch.

Charlotte checked her watch, thinking of Hannigan. "How are your food supplies? Do you have anyone coming over to help you? We could arrange a nurse, if you want."

"Not to worry, I've got loads of friends. I've been meaning to catch up on my reading. You're very sweet to care, but really, I'm getting along. I'm chuffed for the holiday."

Charlotte left her card. "No mosh pits for a while."

"Too right." She wiggled her toes and sighed. "And I do miss my shoes."

Charlotte smiled. The Violent Femmes were playing before she reached the walkway.

She had been sporting a multihued Mohawk and dark green lipstick when she saw them in Hollywood, opening for the Pretenders. Before that Charlotte's look had been lanky strands of ink-black hair that fell down her back and covered half of her white powdered face. Then everyone was doing that, and the overriding illogic of all of them seeking identities and their place in the world as individuals while all sounding and dressing exactly alike struck her for the folly it was.

Once, Charlotte had done a complete shaving of all her body hair. She'd paid for that in many ways, especially as it grew back.

Even at the height of her punk days, she hadn't gone the piercing or tattoo route. In fact, the only reason that her ears were pierced was because her mom had done it herself when Char was a baby. The AIDS virus had been identified in her teenage years, and leprosy was a known risk of tattooing. Now there was hepatitis C and who knew how many blood-borne pathogens yet to be discovered. So nothing involving needles for her. However, if someone were to look closely, he or she might find a few small bald patches where the hair had refused to grow back. No one had been allowed to look that closely in a long time.

Charlotte's next stop, after a quick call to confirm he was there, was the home of Sam Ricketts. Sam lived in North Orange County, near the San Bernardino County line in Yorba Linda. It was a pleasant bedroom community, whose claim to fame was the Richard Milhous Nixon presidential library, birthplace, and farmhouse. Sam Ricketts was watering his lawn when she pulled up in front.

"You want to come in?" There was a distinct lack of enthusiasm in his voice.

"If that's all right," she said. Surely he didn't expect to stand out in the heat to talk to her.

He shut off the hose and made a low whistle. An arthritic golden retriever sunning himself on the driveway lifted his head groggily. "C'mon, Buddy, we're going in for a minute."

Buddy ambled to his feet, yawned mightily, and shook himself. Tail wagging, and trailing a flurry of dog hair, he followed the people inside.

Ricketts indicated a kitchen chair and offered Charlotte a cold drink. She accepted a bottled iced tea as Buddy settled with a contented sigh on a dog cushion by the back door. His tail never quit its metronome beat.

"All dogs are Buddhists," Ricketts said. "Always happy to be just where they are. Guess that's why I favor them over people."

"I can't argue with that," Charlotte said.

There were no cookbooks or fanciful spoon holders in his kitchen counters, or plants in the garden window over the kitchen sink. Even the refrigerator was devoid of magnets. According to Sam Ricketts's personnel file, he was a bachelor. It appeared that he had intended to stay that way. Or maybe he was waiting for the right woman to become available.

"How are you?" she asked.

"Taking a few days off, but I'll be back to work by Friday. They don't pay me to sit around and watch the grass grow."

"How's Dottie holding up?"

"Her daughter and son-in-law are staying with her." He threw the dog a small square biscuit from a jar of doggy treats. The dog missed catching it, but soon found it between his front paws.

"But they can only stay so long," he continued. "With Bob gone, she's going to need help getting around. She quit driving after her stroke."

"I wasn't aware of that. Maybe she'll move closer to her daughter now."

He looked slightly perplexed. "You think?"

"Taking care of sick or elderly parents often seems to fall on the daughter." Especially the older one.

"She's not that sick," Ricketts said.

"And she has you," Charlotte added.

Ricketts scowled at her. "If you have something to say, just come out and say it."

Not yet, Charlotte thought. "Have you been interviewed by the NTSB?"

"Yeah, they talked to me last night after I saw you, and then they had me come over there this morning."

"How did it go?"

"About how I expected. That fellow, Hannigan, walked me through the morning of the crash."

"Would you mind going over it again for me?"

His face said he minded very much, but he was smart enough to know that her polite request carried the full authority of Sun Rail. "I told him we reported for duty at five A.M., signed in, and collected our paperwork."

"That would be the track bulletins?"

"Yeah, everything: our route, our train, our schedule. Bob, Ed Muller, and I got engine eight sixty-two. We went over the trip. Hannigan asked me several times about any slow orders. We had a few high track-temp indicators from some readers east of the Palm Springs depot, and a road crew to watch out for in Corona, but that was it. I told him it was all in our printed orders, but he made me go through a couple times from memory."

Ricketts lit a cigarette. "I hope you don't mind. I've been trying to quit."

"It's your house," she said. His lungs, as well, but she wasn't there to preach. "Is that unusual for an investigator to spend so much time on your slow orders?"

"I don't know. Nothing about the last twenty-four hours has been usual."

She made a note of Hannigan's line of questioning. Later, she would ask Iron Horse Technologies, the company's outside investigators, what they made of it. "So then after you got your paperwork and assignment?"

"We hauled our grips to the train and went through our air brake checks. Everything was fine. Had a good set and release. Ready to highball, then Muller's beeper went off."

"Telling him his wife was in labor?"

"That's right, and then the new guy, McBride, took over as assistant engineer."

Charlotte consulted her notes. "One of the passengers said he saw you brace yourself just before the accident. Did you feel something?"

"We were coming into a turn at full speed." He hit on his cigarette defiantly, as if there was nothing more to say on the subject.

She nodded as if that answer was perfectly satisfactory, but put an asterisk next to her notes. This was her own shorthand, reminding her to revisit the point. "And then did you go over the track orders again with the new guy?"

Ricketts looked uncomfortable. "It was a routine run, and we really didn't have time. Besides, I was keeping him with me."

"Did you circumvent safety protocols?"

"Not exactly."

She nodded again and added another asterisk. "The person who called Dottie's house when we were there accused Bob of being a murderer."

"What an asshole."

"I agree," she said. "If the calls continue, we'll have the police put a tap on her line. I got the impression that this sort of thing had happened before."

Ricketts's expression, while never friendly, now dropped all pretense of warmth. "Why do you say that?"

"Is it true? Why was their number unlisted? She seemed to think that nothing would make the callers stop. She sounded as if she were drawing on previous experience."

"Lady," Ricketts said, "do us all a favor and stick to doing what you do. Dottie don't need any extra trouble from anyone."

"Make no mistake, Mr. Ricketts," Charlotte said. "I am very much doing exactly what I do, and I'm very good at it. You do not want to cross swords with me."

Buddy chose that moment to whine.

"It's okay, boy," Ricketts told the dog, "she's leaving." He opened the door and waited for her to use it. "You got any more questions for me, contact the union rep. I don't need any more harassment."

On her way out the door, Charlotte spotted a framed photo on the mantel that almost made her stumble. It was Sam and Dottie sans Bob. Judging by their haircuts, clothing, and age at the time they had posed for this shot, it was taken in the eighties. In a home with not many personal touches, the picture wouldn't have been more noticeable if it were lit by klieg lights.

She had an hour in traffic to ponder the interview. Maybe Sam Ricketts knew that Bob Peterson's autopsy was tomorrow, and that there wouldn't be any new information until then. Still, it seemed odd that he hadn't speculated out loud as to what exactly killed his good friend.

She arrived at the crash site and parked behind Hannigan's company truck. The heat and bright sunlight assailed her as she left her air-conditioned Mercedes, but she was ready for it with fifty SPF sunblock, a hat, and dark sunglasses. She'd also worn a pair of high-top hiking shoes to discourage ankle-biting varmints and had sprayed even her outer clothing with insect repellent.

Police were still restricting traffic to the scene of the crash. Even at that, the spontaneous memorial of flowers, candles, stuffed animals, and notes from fans to Rachel Priest ran the length of a city block. Charlotte took a minute to compartmentalize her personal grief before she called out a hello and slipped under the yellow tape guarding the scene of the accident.

Hannigan waved her over. He was standing on the raised rail bed beside the now repaired POD and scanning the surrounding hillsides. A coil of electrical cable was looped over one shoulder, and he was wearing a cap that had CAPTAIN KANGAROO stitched in red across the front. The silliness of his cap had the odd effect of making him appear more manly somehow. Maybe it was the confidence with which he wore it.

"Whatcha looking for?" Charlotte asked.

"Witnesses." He offered her a hand up the slope. "I was just about to walk the track, if you care to join me."

She let him help her, then looked both ways up and down the twin rails of track.

"Don't worry," he said. "There isn't a scheduled train for another hour."

"If you say so."

"And we've got a ten-mile-per-hour limit in effect until the new ballast gets properly tamped."

She kicked at the rocks underfoot, and one went skidding into the underbrush. "How long does that take?"

"However long it takes to move fifty thousand gross tons over the new surface."

"It's hard for me to think in terms of all that weight." She looked down at the two sets of rails. "These seem very close together. Is there enough room for one train to pass the other?"

"The center-to-center distance between the two sets is thirteen to fifteen feet. I know it doesn't seem like a lot, but it really is."

They walked as they talked. Hannigan kept his eyes panning left to right, with occasional glances up the hillsides. Charlotte kept looking up and down the track in case some train had missed the memo that there were people here.

"What if the trains are rocking side to side?" she asked. "Wouldn't they scrape against each other?"

"I suppose it's possible if there's a preexisting track problem. Remember, this is a well-traveled line, so there are frequent inspections. The condition of the rails is monitored very closely."

"How?"

"By rail detector cars that travel along the track looking for defects. They're equipped with laser beams." He chuckled. "We used to hate getting stuck behind them because they always seemed to find something wrong and then put out slow orders."

"Still," she said, "better to be safe, right?"

"Oh, absolutely." They reached the base of a signal. He pointed at the coned lens. "See how it's green?"

Charlotte looked up. The light was indeed glowing green.

"The rails are charged. If the continuity breaks, the light would turn red on both sides of the interrupt. A train on the track also completes the side-to-side circuit and turns the light red in both directions."

The concrete base of the lightpole had a locked metal panel on the side facing away from the tracks. "Every signal has its own event recorder. We came out here yesterday with signalmen and gathered data from every light back three miles."

"Did you find anything wrong?"

"Not yet." He showed her the C-clamps on either end of the cable looped over his shoulder. "This is a shunt. If I want to test the light or an engineer's compliance to the light, I— Well, here, I'll show you." He unwound the cable and stretched it across the tracks. "Hoboes used to throw pieces of metal across the track to trigger the light, and then jump on when the train slowed." He fastened the clamp to each rail.

She looked up at the light. "It's red now."

Hannigan disconnected the shunt, and after some seconds, the light changed back to green. He studied the hills around him as he rewound the cable. The only animal visible was a circling hawk, and even it seemed to be flying at half speed.

She watched Hannigan work for a moment, then decided that the best way to deliver her news was through the front door. "The company is hiring a private investigation company that specializes in train crashes. I hope that won't be a problem." She watched his reaction closely, waiting for signs of jurisdictional territoriality.

He didn't look up right away, and when he did, he seemed a bit cooler. "They can start nosing around as soon as we're through here."

"Look, it's nothing against your ability or competence. Rachel Priest's son is hiring his own experts with the express purpose of finding Sun Rail at fault. I'm not looking to affect the outcome of the investigation, but I don't want to get caught flatfooted either. I also want to be able to counter any unfair or untrue accusations."

"Yeah, I get all that." He didn't look very happy. "But right now we have ultimate authority here, and that doesn't change, no matter *who* asks."

"Okay, fair enough." At least she knew Sherwood's people weren't going to get any further than her own. So why were her feelings hurt?

"Pretty desolate out here," she said. "Especially at midday in this heat."

"Yeah," Hannigan said. "Great time and place to have a train wreck if you didn't want any witnesses."

This thought had crossed her mind as well.

CHAPTER 13

Charlotte waited at the crash site until her hired guns arrived. The lead man from Iron Horse Technologies was a thirty-something, dark-complexioned man named Hank Nunzio who favored turquoise and silver jewelry. She wondered if Nunzio was a Native American name. She made introductions and then decided her talents would be put to better use elsewhere. The furor over Rachel Priest's death had grown to global proportions. Three different television stations were running marathons of every movie she'd ever appeared in. Charlotte didn't want to come off cynical, but somebody was making a lot on residuals.

On her way back to Laguna Beach, just before she turned off the Riverside Freeway to the southbound toll road, her cell rang. She put the caller on speaker.

"Is this Charlotte Lyon?"

"Speaking."

"I'm Dr. Dee Trenbeth. Your mother has been in my care. The nurse gave me your number as the contact person."

Her ears rang a familiar warning knell. "Is something wrong?"

"She's checked herself out of the hospital, against my advice. I tried calling her at home, but she hung up on me."

"Did she have a fight with somebody?"

"Have you spoken to her?" Dr. Trenbeth asked.

"No, I just know my mother." Charlotte felt an Excedrin headache coming on.

"I don't mean to alarm you unduly, but she has a potentially life-threatening condition. If we get her back into treatment in the next twelve hours, I have every confidence that she'll recover. But without it—"

"I hear you, Doctor, and I appreciate the call. I'll take care of it." Charlotte disconnected and took a few moments to practice some primal scream therapy. Her mother had a history of biopsies, phantom pain, and deep tissue injuries requiring lawsuits. Now it looked as if she finally had a real condition, and she refused treatment.

Charlotte pushed the speed dial and got her mother's answering machine. The outgoing message was delivered in her mother's deceptively reasonable voice giving all the usual spiel.

"I know you're there, Mom. Please talk to me."

"What?"

"You tell me. I just got a call from a very nice doctor who said you had acted against her advice. Mom, you have to go back to the hospital."

"They wouldn't let me smoke. Where's the compassion in that?"

The trick to dealing with her mother was bypassing logic and seeing the world through her eyes. "Smoke a bunch right now, and I'll get you some of that gum. I can meet you at the hospital in about forty minutes."

"How am I supposed to get there?"

"How did you get home?"

"I took the bus. I'm a sick woman. You don't expect me to take public transportation on the way back, do you?"

"Call a cab. I'll pay for it."

"And I want my old bed back." Charlotte heard her mother inhale as she considered what else to add to her list of demands. "I don't want to have to go through all that bullshit registration again."

"No, Mother, I understand." Those sorts of things were for normal people. "I'll call the hospital and get it all set up. Just please get yourself there."

"I thought you didn't do hospitals."

There was a hint of smugness in her mother's tone, as if Charlotte were the difficult one. "I'll see you there," Charlotte said, holding back a sigh.

Charlotte called the hospital and spoke to admitting. Dr. Trenbeth had already called, and the woman in admitting promised to do what she could to get the doctor's wayward patient's bed back. That was more easily promised than done, as it turned out. Charlotte met her mother's taxi at the entrance to the lobby. She had obviously worked her charm on the cabdriver. As Charlotte paid the fare, the guy fixed her with a baleful gaze and said, "You're the daughter? You have my sympathies."

Charlotte was torn between laughing, crying, and feeling offended. She settled for a tight smile and a five-dollar tip. "Thank you for sharing."

Her mother squeezed out of the cab, rendering herself breathless with the effort. A small blessing.

"Did you pack a bag?" Charlotte asked.

"It was all I could do to get here."

Back here, Charlotte wanted to say, annoyed that her mother hadn't even brought a toilet kit. Charlotte would buy a toothbrush and comb in the gift shop. No way did she have the time or inclination to shuttle back and forth between her mother's apartment and the medical facility tonight.

Getting her mother rechecked in took another two hours in the emergency room. Which meant two hours of keeping her mother from throwing a fit while filling out forms and trying to ignore the pain and suffering around her. She had her mother's policy and social security numbers stored in her BlackBerry, but the hospital also wanted to see a picture ID. Of course, there was no picture ID. That would have required some foresight and conformity on her mother's part.

Charlotte had to explain this with her mother swearing loudly in the background, further endearing herself to the overworked staff.

Every time a new sick person entered through the pneumatic doors, Lisa would say loudly, "Now what?" Her tone suggested that the new arrivals were choosing now to suffer their broken bones, bleeding wounds, and life-threatening diseases with the sole and selfish purpose of keeping Lisa from her bed.

The upside was that after the first hour and a half, Charlotte no longer felt the germs crawling on her clothes. She paged Dr. Trenbeth several times. The good and harried doctor finally responded and helped get her mother squared away. Charlotte had just finished saying good-bye to her mother and was walking across the lobby when her phone rang. She answered with a weary, "Charlotte Lyon." As she did so, she glanced up at the overhead television and read the teaser banner for the lead story of the eleven o'clock news.

DEATH TRAIN ENGINEER HAD NERVOUS BREAKDOWN

"Are you seeing this?" Dom asked.

"Is it true?" she asked.

"Could they broadcast it if it wasn't?"

She responded with a weary chuckle. "Thanks, Dom, I needed a little levity." She rubbed her eyes with a freshly disinfected hand. "I'll get back to you as soon as I know more."

She checked her watch. She was an hour away from home. She would just make it there in time for the bad news. Though in truth, this wasn't completely unexpected. Crises had a way of escalating. Her job was to stay focused on the core issue.

She pulled into her garage at 10:55 and entered the house through her laundry room. This always presented a small challenge when she got home after dark. There was a light switch immediately to her left when she entered the back door, and then a second switch on the other side of the room at the door leading to the hall. She could handle one switch in the ON position when the lights were on, but when the lights were off, both switches had to be down or she didn't feel certain she could trust her eyes. So whatever switch she used to turn on the light had to be used to turn off the light. Weird, she knew, but a small concession to the imp in her mind. As in any war, you needed to pick your battles. She kept meaning to get the switch rewired by some nonjudgmental electrician.

Because she was in a hurry to get to the television, she used the switch closest to the garage. She would sort it out after the news.

She went to her office so she could go online while waiting for the segment to run. She didn't have to wait long. It was the top story on every network station. She turned to the channel with the worst reputation for exploitation. The anchor was a heavy-jowled white man. She'd seen him in person and knew that he looked better on camera than off. He gave the news as if it had been delivered to him personally on gold tablets from on high. When in truth, he did none of his own investigating. Without a teleprompter, he'd be just another blowhard.

"Bob Peterson, our sources disclosed today, was in frail mental health." A picture of Bob Peterson appeared above the newscaster's right shoulder. It was not the smiling image she had seen in his living room. Peterson's hair was disheveled and his expression grim. It looked more like a celebrity mug shot after a drunk-driving arrest.

"Last year," the anchor continued, "emotional trauma caused this sixty-one-year-old grandfather to voluntarily commit himself to a mental hospital for treatment." Viewers would assume, she knew, that the photo was taken at the nuthouse.

"Health officials wouldn't comment, but sources close to the family have told reporters that Mr. Peterson suffered from depression and posttraumatic stress. The condition was work-related after the train Peterson engineered cut through a car trying to beat the train and killed the driver. NTSB and the National Railroad Association both ruled that Peterson was not at fault." He paused to look down his glasses and veer from his script. The derailment footage played behind him, then switched to a press photo of Rachel Priest feeding a bottle of formula to an undernourished African baby. This was replaced by a head shot of Rachel alone with a banner that read: IN MEMORIAM.

"Nice job of oversight, guys," the anchor quipped.

The scene of the newsroom was supplanted by a shot of a white-haired man in a faded denim jacket who was identified as Russell Grannis, friend and neighbor. "Killing that girl took all the fun out of his job," Grannis told the camera. "Especially this last time."

An optimist might think that things could only get better from this point. Charlotte wasn't an optimist. Someone was feeding this information to the press. She needed to get to them first.

She scrolled through her e-mails, finding one from Andrew. The assistant engineer, Ed Muller, and his wife, Megan, were the proud parents of a healthy baby girl. Andrew included Ed's home and cell phone numbers. Yawning, Charlotte printed the information.

She went through the house, checking locks, watering her houseplants, and making sure nothing had been left on. One of her last stops was the laundry room. She flipped the switch near the hallway up, which turned the lights off; then she took ten toe-to-heel steps across the floor to the switch by the door leading to the garage and flipped it down. Now the lights were on again. She crossed the floor again, flipped the hallway switch down and felt a slight relief as order was restored to her universe. Both switches down. Lights off. Time for a nice long shower and bed.

THURSDAY

CHAPTER 14

On Thursday morning, Charlotte made the time to go visit Ed Muller and his new baby. She loved babies. It never ceased to amaze her what small sizes people came in or how she and her sister had survived to adulthood. Between the rough crowd her mother ran with, the frequent bouts of homelessness, and the drug binges, that alone was a small miracle. Yet somehow she and Jill had lived to adulthood and enjoyed success. Jill had a small cult following on the off-Broadway circuit. The smaller venues she played didn't quite pay the bills, but she was doing what she loved, and at least she had goals.

Maybe someday Charlotte would experience the wonder of having her own child. Of course, first she needed a date. Single parenthood didn't appeal to her. She did enough on her own as it was.

The Mullers lived in a quiet suburban section of Tustin. Their two-story town house was in one of those developments that offered three floor plans and one color scheme. What the units lacked in imagination was compensated for with affordability. The streets—most of them culs de sac—had names like Avocado, Orange Blossom, and Grove, harkening back to a time when Orange County was more about agriculture and less about strip malls.

She parked in visitor parking and followed a winding concrete path to the Mullers's condominium. There was a mezuzah on the doorpost and the sounds of children screaming happily in one of the association pools. An air-conditioning unit hung silently from an upstairs window. Charlotte wondered if it were broken or if the Mullers were saving money.

When Ed Muller answered the door, Charlotte introduced herself.

"Oh sure," Ed Muller said. "Come in. Sorry about the mess."

"No bother," Charlotte said, presenting them with a box of chocolate cigars. "I hear you've been busy."

"You can say that," Muller said, a smile creasing the stubble on his jaw.

She was wearing business attire and found herself stepping high to avoid wads of Kleenex on the carpet. Ed cleared a path before her, scooping the offending tissue into a wastepaper basket. It was clear that the family had been spending their time on the street-level floor. The baby's bassinet and changing table occupied one corner. Packages of disposable diapers, a pram with more storage pockets than a herd of kangaroos, and a stack of baby clothes and accessories—most of which were still half-wrapped in gift paper—were piled against adjoining walls. Blankets and pillows adorned the couch.

Mother and baby rocked gently in an old-fashioned wooden rocking chair. Megan smiled warmly and parted the blanket covering the baby's sleeping face. Charlotte again wondered how her mother had managed. Twice. With no help or money. She wondered how, but, after turning thirty she no longer questioned the why.

"She's beautiful." Charlotte felt tears welling up behind her eyes. They were tears of happiness that something so pure and innocent could exist in this world.

130

"And smart," Megan said, sharing a chuckle with her husband.

"She knows exactly the moment when we both fall asleep," Ed explained.

The Mullers yawned, laughed, and apologized simultaneously.

Charlotte missed being married just then, missed it with an intensity that surprised her. She missed marital shorthand and having all those joint memories and history. She especially missed everything she and Brad would never have.

She leaned against the dining room table. On the credenza, she noticed a pamphlet that seemed out of place atop the cards of congratulations. It was one of those public-service brochures passed out by the police department, usually to victims of crimes.

"Were you burglarized recently?" Charlotte asked, reading the pamphlet's title.

"Twice," Ed Muller said. "It's been an intense week."

"What was stolen?"

Husband and wife looked at each other; then Megan answered. "Nothing of much value, but certainly some peace of mind. That's why we're camping out down here. We were upstairs asleep while someone riffled through our things. Ed heard them and called 911. After the police came, we discovered our car had been broken into as well."

"How about your neighbors?" Charlotte asked. "Were any of them hit?"

"No, just us," Ed said, "and they didn't get anything besides some dirty clothes. I must have scared them off in time. Like I say, it's been a week of close calls and near misses."

"I'd say you've all come out clearly ahead," Charlotte said.

Megan stifled a yawn.

Charlotte stood to go. "What's your daughter's name?"

"Jane."

As in calamity, Charlotte thought. "Would you mind sharing your good news with a reporter? I think we can sell the human angle of the baby coming just in the nick of time to keep her daddy off a train that had an accident. They might want to take some photographs, too."

"Sounds like fun," Megan said. "Just please tell them to call ahead."

Charlotte assured them she would and that she would make sure the reporter was unobtrusive as possible. "Congratulations again," she told the proud parents as she left them for her next appointment.

It was eleven by the time she got to the medical examiner's office. The wind was blowing east to west, which meant that the nearby dairy farms were making their presence known. Charlotte didn't know how the people who lived out this way could stand it. She supposed that their noses simply stopped registering the stench after a while.

The parking lot was free of reporters, and she was early. A deputy escorted her to Dr. Donavon's office. The ME was on the phone and indicated that she should take a seat. The air-conditioning was set at seventy-two degrees, never higher or lower. Donavon was that kind of guy, very precise. He was also very careful. After twenty-five years on the job, he had never contracted a single disease from any of his clients.

He concluded his call and grabbed his suit jacket.

"I made reservations at the Mission Inn," he said. "I hope you don't mind the walk."

It was only a few blocks. "Not at all," she said.

He opened the door for them and indicated that she should go first.

"How's your wife? Has she gone back to work?"

Robin Donavon was a flight attendant with American Airlines, but had quit flying after 9/11. "She's staying busy locally. We've been redecorating."

They came to the intersection. The green walk signal was illuminated, but stale. Donavon eyed it critically and then held his arm out to block her path. "Let's wait."

While the light went through its full cycle, Charlotte asked, "How did the post go on Bob Peterson?"

"The autopsy on your engineer was inconclusive. His personal physician couldn't sign off on the death, because Mr. Peterson was in good health."

"When can we expect some answers?" she asked.

"That's a good question. I know a whole list of things that didn't kill him, but not what did. I put a rush on the tox report, but it showed nothing abnormal. We tested for alcohol, opiates, amphetamines, cannabis, cocaine, barbiturates, and muscle relaxers. None were found."

Charlotte breathed a small sigh of relief. "What else wasn't it?"

They crossed the street to Dr. Donavon's recitation of Bob Peterson's healthy and undamaged organs.

"What do you know for sure?" she asked, looking both ways.

"His heart stopped."

"Yeah, he probably stopped breathing, too. I guess the big question is, do you suspect foul play?"

"There is something . . . unnatural about this. Now Rachel Priest was fairly straightforward. Head trauma."

"What did she hit? Or should I ask, what hit her?"

"Near as I can figure, she slammed into the window when the train first jolted off the track. This led to edema, swelling in her brain cavity, and resulted in lost autonomic functions such as the ability to breathe or for her heart to pump blood." They reached the opposite curb.

Charlotte heard a siren wailing in the distance. "Sounds like the engineer's fate without the knock to his head."

Dr. Donavon turned in the direction of the approaching siren, a weary look on his face. "Or the brain swell. With him, it was as if his body just shut down. I've sent his blood out for additional and more detailed tests. A mass spectrograph might reveal more."

They went on to have a pleasant lunch, each of them chewing their food thoroughly and drinking plenty of water. As she left his parking lot, he stood outside her car, making sure she merged safely into traffic and told her, as always, to drive very carefully.

There was a guy, she thought as she waved good-bye, who had really seen it all.

Her next stop was in response to a call from Hank Nunzio from Iron Horse Technologies. "I'd like to discuss some findings with you," he'd said. "In person."

She told him she could be in Irvine in an hour. Fine, he said, but sooner might be better.

Charlotte didn't need to be hit on the head to pick up his hint. She postponed her update report with the staff of college students and headed over to the Irvine office of Iron Horse Technologies. Not wanting an unscheduled reunion with Dr. Donavon, she kept to the speed limit.

Hank escorted her into the firm's media room. A sixty-inch, flat-screen plasma television was centered on the wall and linked to his laptop. The show they were about to watch was titled *Sunliner Derailment*.

Hank sat her down and began the presentation. The screen showed footage of the countryside she had become so familiar with. They were seeing it as the engineer had, through the windshield of the cab with the control desk in front of him. It was eerily accurate, right down to the windshield wipers at rest, the reflections in the side mirrors, and the engineer's hand on the throttle.

"The train was traveling at fifty-eight miles per hour when the engineer initiated the emergency stop," Hank said. On screen, the hand moved to the red-handled control. The speedometer showed the speed as the scenery outside the window whizzed past. "Okay, see the mileage marker?" He froze the picture. "Five fifty-two." He advanced a few frames to a sign that read *1/4.*

"And this is significant?"

"He had a slow order for that section of rail." Hank stopped to fish out a computer printout from the papers on the table.

She looked it over, verifying the date and route. "And the engineer would have had a copy of this?"

Hank nodded. "When he checked in for the run. The readers were registering high temperatures and there was a danger of sun kinks, although a mile-long freight train passed by there an hour earlier with no problems."

"By readers, you mean what exactly?"

"The temperature gauges on either side of the tracks. Peterson shouldn't have been going faster than twenty-five miles per hour. Not if he had read the track bulletins."

"Is that why he put on the emergency brakes? You think he suddenly realized he was going too fast?"

"No, he could have slowed down just as efficiently by notching back the throttle and a light application of the brakes. He must have seen something that made him think he needed to stop immediately."

He resumed the presentation. Now there was a man on the tracks. The engineer's hand moved to the red lever and shoved it forward.

"Stop it again," she said. "He didn't sound his horn. If he saw someone on the track, wouldn't he have blown his Klaxon?"

Hank nodded. "Yes, that would follow. Maybe what he saw was inanimate, or he might have panicked and hit the brake first."

"And stopping that fast caused a derail?"

"No, it shouldn't. There had to be other factors."

"Such as a sun kink?" she asked.

"That would be one explanation. I'd like to present another theory."

He resumed the tape. Now they were viewing the consist from the side.

"You see the car carrier? According to the manifest, it was full of Range Rovers. The railroad was delivering them to a dealership in Rancho Mirage. All that weight in the back of the consist could very well have bumped the lighter cars off the tracks when the train came to a sudden stop. Especially since the front passenger car was almost empty."

"Would a few of those SUVs in the back make that much of a difference?"

"Not what you saw at the crash site."

"What are you telling me?"

"Nothing you couldn't figure out on your own, and certainly the other investigators will come to the same conclusion."

"Show me," she said.

He changed the image. "This is footage from news helicopters recorded right after the derailment."

"I have a tape of this, too," she said.

He played the footage, freezing the image when the shot included the two-tiered car carrier.

The video clearly showed eight new Range Rovers with protective tape still on their mirrors and door panels. She searched through the manifest until she found the cargo page. Yes, they were listed. Eight of them. The order countersigned by CEO Rayney himself.

"Okay," she said. "Eight Range Rovers."

"Now look at these." Hank showed her pictures taken by her when she first arrived at the wreck. By then, four hours had passed since the accident. In her pictures there were only four Range Rovers on the car carrier.

Not good. A critic might look at this information and accuse Sun Rail of not only misloading the consist, but trying to obscure that fact after the accident.

She thanked Hank for his work and waited until she was in the parking lot to call the car dealership in Rancho Mirage, the intended recipient. She went through the phone tree until she got an operator and asked to speak to the general manager. Four minutes later a woman with a French accent came on the line and identified herself as Susette Bourdon.

Charlotte described herself as a representative of Sun Rail. "I'm checking on the delivery of eight Range Rover Discovers that you were having shipped by rail."

"Yes, yes. They arrived. You are the third person to call about this."

"All from the company?" Charlotte asked.

"No, you are the second. The third was a reporter, following up on the derailment."

"And what exactly did the reporter ask?"

Charlotte heard Bourdon being paged. "One moment, please," the woman said without waiting for acknowledgment. Charlotte was treated to a two-minute recording extorting the virtues of the most rugged and safe SUV made. She wondered whatever happened to Muzak. And was this reporter on to something that could be perceived as a cover-up? There was nothing like a good conspiracy theory to juice up a story.

Bourdon returned to the line. "*Pardon.* You asked me something?"

"Who was the reporter with, and what did he want to know?"

"He asked when and how I took delivery. I explained to him that one of our salesmen was traveling on the train and called when he saw the delay. Four were for stock, three of the vehicles were already sold and the customers were ready to take delivery, and the last was for a promotion at the Agua Caliente Casino in Rancho Mirage. We called a flatbed tow company so our customers would get their orders on time."

"I'm glad everything worked out for you." *No sense in letting a little thing like a train wreck with fatalities slow you down.* "Do you remember the reporter's name?"

"A moment please. I had it written down on my desk."

Charlotte waited while papers rustled. Someone else was paged over the loud speaker; then Bourdon came back on the line. "Dennis O'Connor."

"Damn," Charlotte said. *Talk about your bad penny.* "Thank you for your time."

"Certainement."

"One more thing," Charlotte said. "How much does a Range Rover weigh?"

"Two thousand and one kilograms. With the enhancement package, closer to four thousand kilograms."

"Were any of the units equipped with enhancement packages?"

"They all were. That's what made them so expensive to transport."

"What's that in pounds?"

"Over five thousand each. They are very sturdy vehicles. The railroad gave us a much better rate than the company we usually use. They would have billed us for several trucks and both legs of the journey, the delivery and then the trip home with empty trucks."

So ten tons of cargo, reduced to five before the investigators arrived. "I'm preparing a news release. May I mention your name and dealership?" Charlotte asked.

"Absolutely," Bourdon said. "It is free publicity, no?"

"And the salesman?"

"Jeff Ammons, but he's not here today."

"No problem. And please, if any other reporters contact you, I'm here to help and answer questions."

Charlotte looked up the contact information she had for Jeff Ammons and called him at home.

She congratulated him on his quick thinking and learned that a mechanic from the railroad had assisted the tow truck driver in the unloading of the Range Rovers. She secured Ammon's permission to use his name and then drafted a quick update for the Web site.

She stuck to the facts, praising the ingenuity of the quick-thinking Range Rover salesman, the cooperation of Sun Rail employees, and hoping that all this was in time to take the "gotcha" factor out of whatever story Dennis O'Connor was scraping together.

On the drive over to the offices of Sun Rail, she called Hannigan and explained what she had learned.

"I'm sure we would have caught that," he said, "but I appreciate the heads-up."

"Just please remember to include in your report how cooperative we've been."

"Absolutely. I've found you very ... cooperative." There was something suggestive in his tone, and she didn't think it was all wishful thinking on her part. Her fluster and the big grin on her face were very real.

"All right, then," she said. "You're on my speed dial." Inwardly, she died a thousand deaths. *You're on my speed dial?* God, how lame was that? She was definitely out of practice with the whole boy–girl mating ritual thing.

She composed the press release in her head and then wrote it in one draft back at the office, thankful to immerse herself in the familiarity of work where she knew exactly what she was doing. She had the Web master add it to the company Web site as she briefed CEO Rayney on this latest development. God bless the Internet.

She almost got away with it.

CHAPTER 15

Dennis O'Connor, in a special report to CNBC, was the first to break the news.

"New evidence in the Sunliner derailment points to coverup" was the teaser. Dennis, looking earnest in a military-issue load-bearing vest (no doubt purchased at an army navy surplus store) with a press pass slung rakishly around his neck, filled one half of the screen. He was on some location somewhere, standing next to an empty car carrier. He needed little prompting for the reporter in the studio to tell his story. "This is what Sun Rail doesn't want you to know. The secret to their punctuality." He had it all: footage of the fully loaded car carrier at the time of the accident, and then the same car only half full hours later. He explained how the engineer was going too fast and that when he applied the brakes suddenly, the extra weight might have been responsible for bumping the passenger car off the tracks and ultimately resulting in the death of Rachel Priest.

Sherwood Priest's press conference followed soon after.

In a performance worthy of an Academy nomination, the "bereaved" son spoke to the cameras. "My mom meant everything to me," he said. "I wish I could have been with her. A day has never gone by that I haven't been reminded what an exceptional, loving, giving—" His voice faltered, and he pinched his eyes. He didn't go so far as to squeeze out actual tears, but he did manage to act overcome with grief. "For her to die needlessly, before her time because someone was trying to keep to a schedule . . ." He didn't finish his sentence. He didn't need to.

Charlotte felt a lump in her own throat, and she *knew* what an insincere louse he was. Think how this was playing to the folks in Peoria.

Sherwood went on to express his outrage at Sun Rail for its botched safety precautions, ticking-bomb employees, and alleged attempt to cover it all up.

Charlotte smelled a big stinky lawsuit coming.

She got on the phone to her contacts at CNBC. "I messengered over some footage this morning. Are you going to run that, too?" she asked.

"The producer is looking at it now," she was told.

"CNN got to it right away."

"I'll see if I can't hurry them along."

"You'll see that Dennis O'Connor failed to mention a few things in his report. We're having a press conference at the corporate offices in about ten minutes. I know you want to give a fair and unbiased account of this tragedy, and you can't do that with partial information. Credibility is everything in our business."

"We'll air your conference live. Thanks for the heads-up."

Ten minutes later, as promised, Charlotte faced a mob of reporters and introduced the CEO. Rayney handled himself well as he answered the accusing tone of the questions with calm, confirmable facts. That was all fine and good, but Charlotte was getting tired of this reactive stance. It was time to go proactive. She needed to do the one thing she thought she'd never do.

She waited until she was en route to her next appointment.

Her nemesis answered his phone with, "Dennis O'Connor."

"You left off 'the Great,'" she said.

"Charlotte? Hey, you," he said as if they were still the best of buddies, "how have you been?"

"I'm well, thank you. Listen, your name keeps popping up. You've been busy."

"Are you on a speakerphone?"

"I'm in the car. Dennis, you're killing me here."

"Ah, the derailment story. What can I say?"

"Actually, I'm calling to compliment you. Have you got a team helping you with research? I've only seen your name on the byline, and I know you always give credit where credit is due."

"And I don't make up facts."

"I know that." He considered himself very ethical. "I'm just wondering if we could help each other out. We both seem to have inside tracks on this thing. No pun intended."

"What are you offering?" he asked.

"When I determine who or what was at fault, I give you a half-hour lead on the news."

"And what do you want?"

"A half-hour lead on your next bombshell. You know I can't discredit you if your information is good, but in a way, it's too good."

"What are you saying?"

"Someone with his or her own agenda is helping you. I know you would hate to feel used."

"I have to admit," he said, "the juicy stuff has been falling in my lap. And here I thought it was good karma."

"I doubt it," she said dryly.

"You're not still mad about that other thing, are you?"

"Your personal betrayal that cost me my job? Not really. It actually propelled me to what I do now, so it all worked out for the best."

He laughed as if she had made a joke. "Okay, Char, you got a deal."

"Great. We'll be in touch." She wasn't mad at him, but she wasn't forgetting his nature. Better to deal with the devil you knew. And with that in mind, she arrived at the sports bar where Russell Grannis, so-called friend and neighbor of the Petersons, agreed to meet with her.

He was sitting at the bar when she walked in. She recognized him from his television interview. He was wearing the same faded denim coat and looked very at home with a mug of beer in front of him.

She introduced herself and suggested they grab a table. They took a booth in the corner, and she got right down to business.

"How long have you known the Petersons?"

He took a long draft of his beer, sneaked a look at the ball game playing on the television overhead, and then said, "Long time. I don't know, since the kid was in school."

"I met Dottie yesterday. She seemed like a very nice woman."

"Yeah, and she's been through the shits, too."

Charlotte signaled for another round. "How so?"

"You knew about her cancer, right?"

"I thought she had a stroke."

"The cancer came first. Surgery, chemo, radiation. She's lucky to be alive."

Yeah, Charlotte thought, people had all sorts of funny definitions of luck. *You're lucky*, one well-meaning lady told her when Char was a brand-new widow, *you're young*. The beer came and Charlotte put a five-dollar bill on the waitress's tray and waved off the change. "I don't think she's feeling very lucky right now."

"No, I expect not. Of course, Bob hasn't been much of a rock lately, with his troubles and all."

"You mentioned a fatal accident on the television."

"My wife gave me hell for that. She said it wasn't for me to air the neighbors' laundry. I told her it was a matter of public record. I figured if I broke the news first and told how broke up Bob was about it all, that it would look better for him."

Charlotte nodded sympathetically while wondering who had fed him this line of reasoning. None of it was public record by any stretch of the imagination. No doctor or medical institution would breach privacy laws to disclose any treatment of any patient. The railroad did not disclose the name of engineers and crews involved in fatalities. Reports were written, of course, and records were kept of what crews manned the trains on all the different shifts and routes.

"When was this accident? Do you remember?" she asked.

"Sure, it was the first week of business for that casino run. Young gal. He said she was his daughter's age. I think that's what hit him so hard."

Charlotte spent another ten minutes with Grannis before she felt she had exhausted his supply of useful information. She paid for his beer, but avoided shaking his hand.

Her next stop was Sun Rail's stockyard. It was in Anaheim, only a few miles away from the corporate offices. She had to cross tracks to enter the depot and then drive down a long paved road. No one challenged her business there, even after she parked in a visitor parking space. She changed into tennis shoes and walked toward the large outbuildings.

To her right, freight cars sat idle on one of the sidings. The company executive coach was pulled up parallel on its own piece of track. On her left, traffic on the Santa Ana Freeway maintained a low rumble. In the distance, the peak of Disneyland's Matterhorn rose white and fake. She smiled, remembering how when she was a child it had been like one of the seven wonders of the world. It used to be the tallest point around; now the surrounding office buildings, hotels, and even Disney's newer rides dwarfed it.

Two other sets of rails ran through a large hangar-size building, which she soon learned was a maintenance barn. She walked inside and discovered several train cars in varying states of repair. Wheel trucks and generators sat up on blocks, ready for overhaul and reinstallation, or perhaps they were just spare parts. A mechanic refitted a passenger coach with new brakes. Another ran a pneumatic sander over a dent in the sheet metal along the side of a locomotive. She looked for the guy who had been at the derailment, but didn't see him.

Away from the noise of the sander, she found a man her age doing something with an axle. "Excuse me," she said, "I'm looking for Stan."

The guy jumped back in surprise and smiled at her, flustered as a pubescent schoolboy who attended an all-male academy. "His office is through that door, to the left, and then the first right." He put down the tool he was holding and wiped his hands on a grease rag. "Here, it's easier if I show you."

She followed him past a lunchroom with vending machines. When she thanked the guy for his time, he almost blushed and didn't seem to know what to do with his hands as he walked away. Coming here was a definite boost to a girl's ego.

Stan's office was open. She entered and closed the door behind her. The train master jumped nervously. New lateral worry lines creased Stan's oily brow. Charlotte had seen her share of executives go gray over the course of a crisis. Of course, hair color was the easiest thing in the world to fix.

"Can we talk for a minute?" she asked.

He indicated a chair with the least possible enthusiasm. "What about?"

"What can you tell me about the fatality that took place in your first week of business?"

"I'm not sure I know what you're talking about." He looked at the door. Presumably, he was imagining her using it on her way out.

"I'll make it easy for you," she said, settling comfortably in her chair and crossing her legs. "I know Bob Peterson was the engineer and that a young woman died under his wheels."

"Not exactly." Stan lit a cigarette and took a deep drag. "Her name was Farrah Kent. She was twenty-four. She left her newborn at home with a neighbor. Her husband was at work. Mrs. Kent parked her car with the keys still in the ignition and took a walk on the tracks." He knocked the ash off his cigarette with a shaking hand.

"The train was traveling at forty-five miles per hour. If it had been moving at top speed, she would have been obliterated, and we would have been looking for chunks of tissue. These days you have to account for all the parts."

She nodded. "Biohazard." She actually knew quite a bit about that.

Stan clicked his lighter and studied the flame a moment before he let it go out. "As it was, she stuck to the front like a bug on a wind-shield. Bob told me he kept hoping she'd jumped free when he sounded his horn, but he heard the thump. When he looked out his mirrors, he didn't see any trace. Usually you would see blood, some body parts, something. So he goes out the front scoop and there she is. He pulls her inside. She's hurt, but still alive. They called ahead for an ambulance to meet them at the next stop. The assistant engineer took over the controls. Bob held the girl's hand, but she was hurt too bad."

"She died in his arms?" Charlotte asked.

Stan took another long, hard pull on his cigarette. "He sat right where you're sitting and cried as he told me about it. I offered him a three-day leave, no questions asked. He said he needed the work."

"So you offered him a few days off without pay?" Charlotte wrote herself a memo and marked it with two asterisks.

"That's policy," Stan said.

"Of course. Was Mrs. Kent's death ruled an accident or a suicide?"

"Suicide. The family didn't agree. They were superdevout Catholics and wanted to bury the kid in the church graveyard."

"But suicide is a mortal sin," Charlotte said, "and therefore she wouldn't be eligible to be interred in consecrated ground."

"Something like that," Stan said. "They pressured the coroner, the company, and then Bob to say it was an accident."

"Pressured him how?" Charlotte asked.

"They called him at home. Got pretty nasty about it, too. Said the girl was perfectly happy and at the peak of her life. No way was it suicide. The coroner wouldn't reverse his findings either, so the family is taking it to court, letting a jury decide. Bob was going to have to testify. He didn't want to, felt bad enough already. He told me the girl said two words before she died. They were, 'I'm sorry.' It was intentional, all right."

"Does this happen a lot?" she asked. "With the families, I mean?"

"Reactions are all over the board. I've had engineers get cards from family members. Nice cards. Telling them not to feel bad and even apologizing. Then there are the people who can't handle the fact that one of their own chose death."

"The ultimate rejection," Charlotte said, thinking how even if it was an accident, a family member, a wife, still felt rejected. Rejected and angry and sad and lost. All at the same time.

"I suppose." Stan rose and went to his filing cabinet. Moments later he returned with a form titled, "Unusual Occurrence Report." "Sometimes suicide is against the family's religion, like with the Kents, or there's insurance money involved."

Charlotte glanced quickly over the two pages. Stan was listed as the supervisor who had completed the form. He had filled in the fields for time, date, milepost marker, even the ambient temperature. Under number of crew members he had written three: one engineer/operator, one conductor, and one brakeman. The form did not have a space for the crew members' names, only the length of time they had been on duty.

The name and age of the victim were on the second page, and, according to the checked boxes, the engineer has done all he could to warn Farrah Kent with bells and horns.

"And I'll tell you another thing," Stan said, "Bob Peterson was a conscientious operator. He followed every safety protocol and then some."

"Then how do you explain him ignoring the slow-speed order on that section of track on the day of the derailment?"

"I guess I can't."

"Did he ever take those days off?" she asked.

"In a way—he was hospitalized for chest pains. Turns out they were caused by stress and exhaustion. Now they're saying on TV that he was self-committed to some loony bin. That's just not true."

The cell phone at her waist vibrated. The caller was Dennis O'Connor. "I better take this," she said.

She stepped into the hallway as she answered.

"I've got something for you," Dennis said.

"I'm all ears."

"I've been doing some background on Sherwood Priest. He's in debt to everyone. In fact, I was hard-pressed to find anyone who had anything good to say about the guy."

"Don't expect that from me," she said. "I've had the pleasure. So Mama wasn't picking up the bills?"

"No, she cut him off, not that that slowed his spending."

"I bet he resented the hell out of all her charity work," Charlotte mused out loud.

"I know what you're getting at," Dennis said. "The guy had good motive to want his mother dead."

"Big inheritance?"

"I know what you're implying," Dennis said. "But remember, he was in Switzerland when the train derailed."

"I'm implying nothing, just gathering the facts. But I will say something hypothetically. If there was a murder conspiracy, such as a murder for hire, an alibi would be pretty useless. It might even be construed as more evidence of guilt." Also, the existence of at least one inside man, and probably at least two.

She left him with that possibility to ponder and then returned to Stan's office. "I need you to walk me through the crew's morning prior to a run."

Stan pulled himself to his feet and guided her into the hallway. There were half a dozen offices, and all had their doors open. He took her to a room with a fax machine and copier. "The track warrants come in via fax. You know what a track warrant is?"

"Special orders, speed limits, positions of work crews."

"Right," he said, his face showed a grudging respect. "The warrants have the date and time on them. The dispatcher goes through them first and initials them. Then the assistant engineer picks up the orders and makes a second copy for the engineer. If it's been over four hours since they came in, he goes and checks with the dispatcher to make sure they're up to date."

"Where's the dispatcher?" she asked.

"In the control room. You wanna talk to him?"

"Yes, please." Charlotte felt her phone vibrate and checked the number. The caller ID showed that it was Dr. Trenbeth. Now what?

Charlotte let it go to voice mail. She was better off coping with one crisis at a time.

Stan led her into the dispatcher's lair. Monitors overhead showed the track routes, the various crossing points, and the state of the signals all along the line. The dispatcher was speaking into a microphone, giving an all clear to eastbound train number 3020. They waited until he had finished.

"Gorman, this is the troubleshooter the company hired. Charlotte Lyon. She has some questions for you."

Gorman had the build of a sedentary fifty-year-old man. His salt-and-pepper hair was cut short and close to his head. "What can I do for you, ma'am?"

"I'm interested in the morning of the derailment. Did Ed Muller check in with you before he left?"

Gorman thought for a moment. She suspected he was stalling. Surely he had gone over every action he had taken that morning numerous times. He probably dreamed about it. "No, ma'am, he didn't. But they only check with me when the warrants are expired. Everything must have seemed up to snuff to him."

"Were you aware of the slow order on that section of track?"

"Yes."

"Are you aware of Bob Peterson ever ignoring such a bulletin?"

This time Gorman didn't hesitate. "Never. Bob was very careful, very methodical. If he didn't follow the order, he didn't know about it."

Charlotte realized it was time to pay another visit to Ed Muller, but first she had a call to return.

CHAPTER 16

Something was going to have to be done about Ms. Charlotte Lyon. She was getting uncomfortably close. Why couldn't she just do her job and stick to writing press releases and handling the media? She should leave the accident investigation to the experts, and they would have no reason to find that the accident was any more than just that. They would also find as contributing factors the back-heavy consist and Bob Peterson's sloppiness. The dead engineer would not contradict those findings.

Even better, the engineer would be discredited, made the scapegoat, and the company would be liable for all sorts of damage. It was only right.

Now all those plans, all his preparation and research, were in jeopardy because some PR bitch thought she was Nancy Fucking Drew. If only she would stay in the office and not go gallivanting around the state speaking to God knew who all.

Her antics were using up lots of his valuable time. At least he was starting to build a picture of whom she loved. Everyone had or should have somebody about whom they cared enough to protect. It was only human.

He thought he heard a car pulling into the drive and turned down his radio, but whoever it was kept going. The last thing he needed was some nosy neighbor poking around. He left the radio turned down, but found himself humming as he worked. One of those inane advertizing jingles that gets in your head and refuses to leave.

We make it easy, easy on you.

He doused the long narrow-bore brush with protective lubricant and worked it into the barrel of his hunting rifle.

It was her own doing, he thought as he twirled the brush. She left him little choice. He would try to make it quick and painless. He'd make it easy, all right. He was not a monster. There was just too much at stake, not to mention his freedom.

Charlotte returned to her car but didn't start it until she had dialed Dr. Trenbeth's number.

"Has my mother been behaving herself?" Charlotte asked.

"I think we've reached an understanding," the doctor said.

Ha, Charlotte thought, *so you may think.* "So how is she?"

"Charlotte, I'm a straight shooter."

Charlotte steeled herself for what was coming. Doctors generally didn't warn you before dispensing good news.

"I got back the results of her labs. Her liver enzymes are abnormal and her proteins are low, plus she's exhibiting spider angiomas on her torso."

"What causes that?"

"I believe she has advanced liver disease. Probably a result of her lifestyle choices."

"That's putting it delicately," Charlotte said. "Is this a fatal condition?"

"Not necessarily. We can treat her symptomatically. One of the liver's functions is to control blood clotting. This would explain her prolonged bleed. Also, when the liver is compromised with scar tissue, the veins swell to accommodate the lack of flow through the liver. Sometimes these varicose clumps burst inside, near the esophagus. We'll need to check that out."

"So what's next?"

"A liver biopsy to confirm my diagnosis, but I'd be very surprised if I didn't find cirrhosis."

"What is the treatment for that?" Charlotte's voice was very calm, but her hands shook as she opened her notepad to write down this information.

"We'll see if we can't get her liver to compensate, grow new tissue to take over the damaged organ's functions. She's lucky. Livers regenerate. Of course, she'll have to stop drinking and using recreational drugs."

There goes that luck thing again. "She's not going to be happy about that," Charlotte said out loud. Secretly, Charlotte dared to hope. If her mom got sober, maybe they could yet have a true relationship.

"I can prescribe diuretics for the water retention, antidepressants, a regimen of vitamins, and a low-sodium diet. When she gets a little stronger, I'd like her to start exercising."

Charlotte thought of her mother on the couch, wrapped in an old blanket, eating chips and drinking beer while she watched her soaps.

"I'm not sure my mother is capable of making so many changes."

"Her life will depend on it. Try to get her to see that."

"And if her liver doesn't compensate?"

"I'd have her evaluated for a transplant. That is, providing she can change her lifestyle. But all this is way down the line. We'll take it one step at a time for now."

"Has she agreed to the biopsy?"

"I had to promise to sedate her."

"That's my mom. Consistent to the last. Thanks for calling me. When will you have the results?"

"Two days. Are you going to visit her later?"

"Sure." Charlotte started her car. She considered calling her sister and then decided to put that off until after she'd visited their mom. No sense in getting Jill all worked up until all the facts were in. She headed back to the corporate offices on Disney Way. On her way out the access road to the rail yard, she spotted the mechanic from the day of the wreck. Was it her imagination, or was he making a studied attempt to ignore her as their cars passed.

Ten minutes later, she was pulling into the office building's parking lot when she felt a sneeze coming on. She reached for a tissue and threw her head back. At that same moment, the world around her exploded. Glass struck her like shrapnel. Noise filled the air, temporarily disorienting her. The concussion made her ears ring. Instinctively, she threw herself down across the front seats.

Three more sharp, loud pops followed and echoed across the parking lot. Not an explosion, she realized, but gunfire. Hot air blew through the car, entering by the windows that no longer existed. Small sharp chunks of tempered glass covered the seat, floor, and her prone body.

She wondered if it was over; then another small burst of gunshots sent a second volley of bullets above her. A car alarm went off somewhere in the lot.

She cut the wheel and accelerated until her fender scraped against something unyielding. The car stayed there, idling in drive, its forward motion stopped by whatever she had hit.

Her purse was on the passenger floor. She found her phone between the seats. Without lifting her head above the dashboard, she turned her bag upside down, scattering the contents on the carpet. The Mercedes had a built-in SOS system that would summon police, but the button was on the rearview mirror and she didn't want to take the chance that the sniper still had her in his sights.

Her hands shook violently as she tried to pick up her phone. Glass nipped at her fingers, drawing blood. She forced herself to slow down, take a deep breath. She dialed 911 while she picked up her compact and flipped it open. She held the mirror so she could see outside without lifting her head. People were pouring out of the building. Her car was wedged against a large concrete planter.

"Nine one one," the operator said, "what is the nature of your emergency?"

"I need the police." Her voice was unrecognizable. It sounded childlike and an octave too high. "Someone's shooting at me."

"Are you injured, ma'am? Have you been hit?"

"No." Strange noises kept emanating from her throat, little squeaks of fear and adrenaline overload. "My car is shot up."

"What is your—?"

"I'm in the parking lot of the office building at one hundred Disney Way. I'm in a green Mercedes five hundred with a beige top." She gave the operator her name and license plate.

"The police are on their way, Charlotte. Stay on the line with me. Can you see who's shooting at you?"

"No, but I was looking forward, and the shots came from my left. They took out both front windows. I'm hoping they think they got me. Please hurry."

"Is he out there now?" the operator asked.

"I don't know. It's quiet. Maybe he's reloading or waiting for me to raise my head."

"Stay down, Charlotte."

"You think?" Charlotte noted that her voice had returned to normal.

A truck pulled alongside her, blocking the sun streaming in through her empty driver's side window frame.

"Someone just pulled up alongside me," she reported.

"Is it the gunman?" the operator asked.

"I don't know. It could be." A strange calm came over Charlotte. Her thoughts were crystal clear. She wasn't going down without a fight. Charlotte watched the passenger door of the truck open and a man emerge. She couldn't see his face. He crouched down, out of her sight. Her doors were locked, but with the windows gone, it was a simple matter for him to unlock and open her driver's door. She folded her legs in, ready to kick him.

He surprised her by wrenching the door open and jumping in on top of her. She squirmed, completely overwhelmed by his superior weight. The laminated badge hanging around his neck poked her ear.

"Are you all right?" Hannigan asked.

"What are you doing here?"

"Protecting you."

"Thanks, but I can't breathe." She pushed against his chest until he rolled off her.

"God, you scared the shit out of me. What's going on here? Why is your car wedged against the pylon?"

"I was playing dead," she said, brushing glass out of her hair and off her blazer. "But I'm done now."

Sheriff's deputies, fire engines, and an ambulance arrived in the next ten minutes. Charlotte showed them where she had been when the shots hit her. Glass from the shattered passenger window glittered on the blacktop. Units were dispatched to figure trajectory, but came up empty-handed, since her car had been in motion.

"How did you know to duck?" one of the cops asked her.

"A lucky sneeze, plus I grew up around gunplay. You learn real quick."

Hannigan, who had stayed by her side since gallantly body-slamming her against her seat, raised an eyebrow, clearly intrigued.

"Is there anyone who wants to hurt you?" the cop asked.

"Obviously," she said, finding another chunk of glass down her shirt.

"Have you received any specific threats?" he asked.

"No." She untucked her shirt and shook it out. A few more chunks fell to the ground. "This was the first one."

"Can you point us to anyone?" he asked.

She wondered if he wanted her to make a citizen's arrest while she was at it; maybe he'd give her her own set of handcuffs in case she found the shooter first. "No. If I was indeed the intended target, and this wasn't just a random anonymous shooting, then all I can think is that I'm making someone with a lot at stake uncomfortable."

"How so?" he asked, scribbling furiously in his notepad.

"I'm investigating a double fatality." She picked up the glass around her and threw it in the trash, lest some kid or dog walking by sustain a nasty cut. "Well, actually a train derailment that involved two deaths. Perhaps someone doesn't appreciate the direction my queries have taken."

"I'm sure the investigators assigned to this incident will want your notes."

Yeah, like that's going to happen. "I'd be happy to talk to them. Right now I have to make arrangements to get my car fixed."

"They might want to inspect it," the cop said uncomfortably. As he spoke, he looked wistfully toward the freeway, no doubt hoping that the investigators would arrive soon and relieve him of responsibility.

"There's nothing to see," she said. "And I've got appointments to keep." She excused herself to call the Mercedes dealership. They offered to bring her a replacement car while hers was being repaired. Ordinarily, this would be out of the question for Charlotte, especially if the loaner had mileage on it, which would mean multiple previous unknown occupants. But these were not normal times. Someone had made it personal. Charlotte was able to dismiss her hypervigilance regarding outside contaminants.

She had experienced this phenomenon before, most notably when she was fifteen and her life had been threatened by a modern-day Fagin. She'd stayed compulsion- and obsession-free for a month afterward. Kind of a good news–bad news situation.

So now, having a different car was just what the doctor ordered, especially one without a target painted on the side.

She turned to Hannigan. "And how's your day going?"

He chuckled. "You're pretty cool under pressure."

"So I've been told. God, I must look a mess." He grabbed her arm and guided her aside. The cop continued to take statements from the others who had gathered in the parking lot.

She and Hannigan kept walking until they were inside the building. "Give me a second," she said. "I want to go freshen up." She went into the ladies' room and barely made it to the stall in time to throw up. When she was done, she took careful inventory of her wounds. She always carried hydrogen peroxide. After cleaning the cuts, she applied antiseptic cream and sealed them shut with Band-Aids. The last thing she did was run a brush over her hair and freshen her lipstick. By the time she rejoined Hannigan, she had completely recovered her poise.

"Hey, you know the track warrants you retrieved from the cab?" she asked.

"What about them?"

"Did you notice anything hinky about them?"

"Hinky how?"

"Were they complete, legible, in the proper order? That kind of thing."

"I'm really not at liberty to discuss an ongoing investigation." His expression was apologetic.

She pressed her advantage. "Look, someone just tried to kill me. How about a little nod of your head?"

He nodded his head up and down as he repeated, "I really can't tell you anything at this stage."

"That's what I thought," she said. She didn't share her suspicions that there was an inside man or men. Obviously, there was a lot more to this so-called accident than fate and bad luck.

"I was thinking we could grab some dinner," he said. "If you're up to it."

Suddenly she was fourteen again and didn't know what to do with her hands. She felt a stammer coming on. "Sure. I'd like that. I mean, you gotta eat, right?" *You gotta eat? Shut up!* she screamed inside her head.

Hannigan didn't seem too put off. "There's a nice little continental restaurant on the ground floor."

"I know it. Can I join you there after I catch up around here?"

"Don't make me wait long," he said. His smile was not all business. She took off down the hall before she could embarrass herself any further. She also wanted to leave while she was ahead.

Andrew greeted her when she reached her office with a stack of messages balanced on his clipboard.

"What's all this?" she asked.

"For starters, we have interview requests and tips on the identity of our Good Samaritan. But it can wait. Are you all right?"

She finger-combed her hair, checking for glass, but she seemed to have gotten it all in the last nineteen passes. "I'm fine. He missed, remember?" She took the phone messages and stacked them neatly next to the phone.

"Thank God for that."

"If you tell me how lucky I am, I swear I'll scream."

"Wouldn't dream of it." Andrew handed her a fax. "Sherwood Priest's team has requested copies of the bill of lading for the Range Rover shipment, maintenance records—including the name of the mechanics who serviced the coach Rachel was in and the locomotive. They also want the name of the hostler who assembled the consist and a list of people who knew that Rachel Priest was aboard. And they want to examine the rails the NTSB investigators have at their facility."

Charlotte nodded as she perused the list. "Cooperate fully with them, but copy everything you give them to me and Hank Nunzio over at IHT. Anything else?"

"A guy from State Farm was here earlier, investigating a life insurance claim."

"Whose policy?" she asked.

"Bob Peterson's. The adjuster said it was a large policy, taken out six months ago. Apparently it pays double for an accident and nothing for suicide. The guy was very interested in our determination of the cause of the derailment. I said we were still looking into it, and he gave me his card." Andrew unclasped the business card from the top of his clipboard and handed it over.

She looked at it briefly and then stuck it in her card carrier. "What does the policy pay if it's murder?"

The clipboard clattered to the floor. Andrew, obviously flustered, bent down to retrieve it. "He didn't say."

"Don't worry," she said in an attempt to ease his distress, "we'll get to the bottom of this."

He smiled wanly, but didn't look reassured at all.

CHAPTER 17

Charlotte sat at her desk and went through the tips on the identity of their mystery Samaritan. She couldn't even say for a certainty that the object of their search was a man. The motorcyclist had been garbed from head to toe in black and red. The helmet and gloves had never come off. A word was never uttered. Some passengers remember seeing the biker coming from the front of the train. The motorcycle was parked out of view and left in a cloud of dust that obscured the make, color, and license plate.

The passengers he or she had helped to safety remembered only a strong, gloved helping hand pulling them through the popped-out windows.

So who the hell, she wondered, was this masked person? She was long past the assumption that he or she was one of the good guys. The timing of his or her appearance coupled with this person's continuing anonymity was very suspicious.

Charlotte decided she would squeeze in a visit with her mom tonight, after the traffic died down. The freeway into downtown was a nightmare and not to be faced on an empty stomach. Besides, the dealer hadn't arrived with her loaner. For now, she would take an early supper with Hannigan. She told one of the interns where she'd be in case the tow truck arrived and she somehow missed it. She left her keys with him.

Was this dinner with Hannigan really a date? she wondered. Her hands sweated. She laughed as she pictured the headline. PUBLICIST SURVIVES SNIPER ATTACK ONLY TO COLLAPSE FROM ANXIETY AT THE PROSPECT OF HER FIRST DATE WITH A MAN IN NINE MONTHS. She was still smiling when she took the elevator down to the ground floor.

Hannigan had secured them a booth in the corner with a view of the parking lot. He rose when she entered the restaurant, and gave her a welcoming smile that almost made her stumble into a busboy.

The waiter arrived and they both ordered wine.

"So," she said. "How'd you get into the train biz?"

"I got the bug early. Lived in a train town in Northern California, a little burg outside of Stockton. I worked my way up to engineer, then I worked with NTSB investigators on a head-on between a freight train and passenger train. I was offered a job as an investigator and here I am."

The wine arrived. They each took a sip and looked over the menu. The waiter announced the day's specials. Hannigan asked for the blackened trout; she ordered the portobello mushroom ravioli.

"So how about you?" he asked. "How does a girl who knows the difference between gunshots and backfires come to own her own company and get on the cover of *Forbes*?"

There were short answers and nonanswers. She was surprised to find herself giving him the long version. "I grew up with my younger sister and mom and a string of dads. My mom could barely keep a roof over our heads, much less food in the refrigerator. We did have about five good years when we were in the Witness Protection Program, but then the Feds lost interest in us and we were back on our own."

164

She paused to take another sip of wine, knowing she had Hanningan's full attention.

"You were in the Witness Protection Program?" he asked, wide-eyed.

She waved a dismissive hand. "Long story."

"You save that one for the second date?"

She smiled, pleased at his assumption. "Anyhow we settled in Venice for my high school years. I didn't know what I wanted to do, but I did know I wanted to make a lot of money. Both Jill and I knew we could do better than our mom."

"So Jill's the sister?"

"She's a stage actress in New York."

"Is your mom still alive?" he asked.

"Oh yeah. She's having a few problems right now. She's in USC Medical Center for some tests. I'll go visit her tonight."

"Long day for you," he said.

"Yeah, yeah. You know how it goes: Trouble breeds trouble."

The waiter brought the Caesar salad they had agreed to split. "My sister and I both did well in school." Valedictorians, in fact, but she didn't want to sound like she was bragging.

He buttered a roll. "School was your refuge."

"Exactly. We both went to college on scholarship. I got my degree and took a job with a congressman."

"Politics, huh? Going to change the world?"

"Or so I thought," she said.

"I wouldn't think there would be much money in it, not for support staff."

"No, but I liked it. Anyhow, that gave me a taste of how the press operated, the whole social science of image and perception. So I became a publicist and was enjoying a fair amount of success. Then I had a . . . something very sad happened." She paused, not used to talking about those times, and certainly not with a man she had only just met. Maybe it was the brush with death, but suddenly all her reticence, her reluctance to let someone know her, didn't seem so important. "My husband was killed."

Her eyes filled with tears. He covered her hand with his. His touch was warm and comforting and opened a floodgate of need for human contact, specifically male contact. It was all she could do not to jump across the table and into his arms.

"How did it happen?" Hannigan asked.

"He was a builder of green homes," she said. "Well insulated, solar powered, ambient heating, natural gas–run appliances, freeon-free refrigeration—that sort of thing. A crane tipped over and crushed him. It was quick, they said."

The waiter brought the entrées, and she paused until he left.

"Instead of apologizing or expressing condolences, the parent company sent a lawyer. He offered me a settlement if I agreed not to sue. I was planning a funeral, and this shark thought he'd take advantage of my grief."

"Terrible," Hannigan said, his eyes full of empathy.

"What he didn't know is who he was dealing with. I grew up in chaos—I'm comfortable there. He might have been a shark, but he was swimming in my ocean."

"And you served him his head on a platter," Hannigan said.

"Let's just say I didn't roll over and take it. I took their money and their apology." Half the money had gone to keep her mother from getting evicted and all the utilities shut off. Jill got enough to move to a safer part of town; the remainder Charlotte put in her savings. Her receiving the large settlement wasn't so much the point as was the idea of them paying. "That was nine months ago."

Charlotte and Hannigan spent the next twenty minutes sharing the personal statistics they thought the other would like to know—schools they attended, relatives still alive. Then they went on to books, movies, and sports—seeking common ground. The meal went by quickly.

"You asked me about the track warrants earlier," he said as he sopped up the last of his sauce with a crust of a sourdough roll. "Why?"

"From what I've learned about Bob Peterson, he wouldn't knowingly ignore one. I'm wondering if he ever saw it."

"I retrieved it from the cab myself," Hannigan said.

"But...," she prompted, sensing the word in his tone and body language.

He shrugged. "The warrants were all there and in order. Usually the engineer flips the pages as the journey progresses, so the next upcoming track condition would be on top. These seem untouched."

She nodded. "And remember how when we got there they were dust free?"

"You think someone pulled a switcheroo? You're suggesting a conspiracy."

"I know. Don't worry, I wouldn't go public unless I had more proof, more hard evidence. A confession would also be nice. Then we'd have the names of our bad guys."

He laughed. She liked the way his face relaxed and his eyes crinkled. He looked like the kind of guy who laughed often.

Andrew arrived while they were having coffee and brought the keys to her loaner. "I thought you could use some uninterrupted downtime." He smiled at Hannigan. She made the introductions and the men shook hands.

The waiter brought the bill and she reached for it.

"Don't be silly," Hannigan said. "I invited you."

"But I can expense it," she protested.

"As romantic as that sounds," he said, "I'm afraid I'll have to insist."

She backed down, grateful that the lights were dim enough to hide the glowing of her ears.

The loaner Mercedes was a white 320 model. Andrew had taken the liberty of transferring the contents from her trunk. He'd even thought to clip her remote control on her visor. She wondered if she could hire him away from Rayney, or had he made himself equally indispensable to the CEO?

"The tank is full," Andrew said.

"Good, I have to go downtown tonight, and I'd hate to have to stop for gas somewhere."

"You want me to go with you?" Hannigan asked.

"No, thanks, but it's easier if I go by myself." She stood. "Thank you for dinner. I guess I'll see you tomorrow."

"I'll be counting the minutes," Hannigan said.

"Yeah, right," she said, rolling her eyes. *There is such a thing as too good to be true.*

She took the 5 Freeway to downtown Los Angeles and made the trip in a little over half an hour. The USC Medical Center had recently been renovated, and for a hospital, it was downright inviting. She approached the concierge desk and said she was there to visit her mother. She filled out a time sheet with her name, the doctor's name, and the time she had arrived. Then she was directed to the fifth floor.

The sight of her mother in a hospital gown, gray hair fanned across the white pillowcase, made Charlotte pause. She hadn't expected to feel the sudden leap of grief that brought tears to her eyes. Her mom was a big pain in the ass, but she always seemed indestructible. Now, she was hooked up to an IV and different monitors that recorded blood pressure and heart rate. She wore her sixty-plus years hard on her face. Thin tubes full of oxygen fed her nose.

As usual, she was watching TV. One of those gory forensic shows.

It took Lisa a moment to notice her daughter standing there. "Whatcha waiting for? Pull up a chair and set your ass down."

"Are they treating you okay?" Charlotte asked.

"Is your sister here?"

Charlotte picked up the control and turned the volume down on the television. "I thought I'd wait to call her after we got more of your test results in."

"I want to see her, you know, before it's too late."

"Mom, you're not dying. You're sick, but it isn't hopeless. You need to start taking care of yourself." *For starters, no more booze and no more dope.* "It's time you start living for you." In her make-believe world, her mom pictured herself as a selfless giver. Charlotte had long since grown past the point where she used provable facts to convince her mother of anything.

Lisa turned from the television and gave Charlotte her full attention. "You look different. Calm-like, almost happy. What's wrong?"

"Nothing. It's been a long day. I've got a big job going. A train derailment. You might have seen it on the news."

Lisa waved a dismissive hand. "Oh, I never bother with the news. None of it is ever good. You know me: I try to stay positive."

In the reflection of the heart monitor screen, Charlotte watched a Hollywood recreation of a bullet entering a brain in slow motion. "Do you need me to do anything for you?"

"Oh, no, no. I know what an important schedule you have."

Charlotte detected only the tiniest hint of sarcasm—Mom must still be feeling the drugs they had given her for the biopsy.

"I wouldn't dream of putting you out. Jill can help me when she gets here."

"Sounds like a plan, Mom. Don't stay up too late. You need your rest."

Lisa laughed. It wasn't an easy laugh, more like a cackle. Her mouth flew open, and her small eyes disappeared into layers of fleshy white fat. "Now who's the mother?"

Charlotte smiled tightly and exited the Twilight Zone.

She drove home, amazed as always at the amount of traffic at any given hour in Los Angeles. *Who are all these people, and why aren't they home with their families?*

She pulled into her garage at ten thirty, feeling the effects of the long day and looking forward to bed. She unlocked the back door and reached for the light switch. It was already flipped to the up position. Unbelieving, she kept checking it over and over again. She would never leave it like that. Skin crawling, she crossed the room. The opposite switch was also in the up position. She stood very still and listened for any out-of-place noises. She stood that way for a full five minutes, until she was sure she was alone; then she turned the light on by flipping the switch down. The gesture felt as awkward as hitting the gas pedal when she meant to stop.

She wished she owned a gun or a large dog, just to hedge her bet. She walked backward into the garage and found a clawhammer. Then she waited. Sirens sounded in the distance. Her neighbor's phone rang. Nothing from inside the house.

She went back inside and walked down the hallway. The hammer rested on her shoulder, ready to strike. She noticed a nick in the paint on the hallway wall. Further evidence that someone had violated her domain. Her bedroom was untouched, as was the kitchen. In her office, she found more clues and called the police from there. She told the operator that she had a break-in and was promised a response within ten minutes. She turned on every light in the house and locked herself in her office.

She booted up her computer while waiting for the cops and searched her recent documents. Someone had opened the ongoing Sun

Rail file at 9 P.M. The file was not complete, so whoever it was wouldn't have gotten much. She kept her confidential notes and observations recorded on a flash drive that she carried with her. The component was the size of a matchbox and transferred easily from the computer she was using in Anaheim to the unit she had at home. She would never wonder again if she was being too paranoid.

She heard a car turn into her driveway and went to the front door to greet the officer. The cop was a she. Officer Mitsch, according to her name badge.

"How are you this evening, ma'am?" Mitsch said. She was a compactly built woman with short dark hair and a firm handshake.

"Not so good. Someone broke into my house while I was out." Charlotte invited the cop inside. They went to the kitchen. The cop sat at the table while Charlotte discreetly washed her hands. "Would you like some coffee?"

"No, thanks." Mitsch clipped an incident report onto her clipboard and took Charlotte's vital statistics. "Was anything taken?"

"No, they didn't go into my bedroom where I keep my jewelry and clothes, but I found evidence that they were in my office and on my computer."

"Do you keep your doors locked when you're not home?"

"Always."

"Do you have an alarm system?"

"No."

Mitsch made a note. "Was a window or a door pried open?"

"No, and I've checked them all."

Mitsch stopped writing. "What made you suspect that someone had broken in?"

"It was quite obvious the moment I entered the back door." Charlotte stood and gestured for Mitsch to follow her. Charlotte pointed to the light switch and explained how she had found it in the up position. "I never leave it like that."

"Perhaps you forgot?"

"Not likely." Charlotte took her down the hall and pointed to the nick on the wall. "And then there was this."

"What? That little mark?"

"Officer Mitsch, look around. Do you see an imperfection on any of my walls?"

Mitsch looked around, her expression betraying her thoughts. Kind of a now-I've-seen-it-all look around her mouth and eyes. Charlotte was used to it, but didn't let it detract her.

"And did I mention that someone shot at me today?"

The cop looked at her sharply, probably trying to assess how much of Charlotte's story to take seriously. Charlotte produced the officer's card who had responded to the scene of the shooting in Anaheim. "You're welcome to verify that."

"That won't be necessary, ma'am," Mitsch said even as she was copying the cop's name and number onto her form. She handed the card back to Charlotte. "You say your office showed signs of, uh, disruption?"

Charlotte didn't bother to point out that the stapler was misaligned or that the desk blotter was no longer parallel to the plane of the wall or that the photographs of Brad, her mother, her sister, and her aunt had all been turned at least five degrees. She showed the cop her recent document history and how someone had gone into her files before she got home.

"Do you usually arrive home this late?" Mitsch asked.

"My schedule varies."

"Who knew that you weren't going to be home?"

"That's a very good question, Officer. I'll have to give it some thought."

"Does anyone else have a key?"

"No. I live alone and I don't have very many visitors here."

Mitsch had her poker face back in place. "Maybe you would be more comfortable if you checked into a hotel tonight."

"No, I doubt that."

"I'll speak to my sergeant about increasing police visibility around your house."

"That would be great," Charlotte said.

Officer Mitsch left a pamphlet on home security and the direct number to Dispatch in case Charlotte had any more problems. After she left, Charlotte glanced at her pamphlet and started to put things together.

CHAPTER 18

Charlotte called the Mullers early, figuring the chances were good with a new baby that one of them would be awake. As it turned out, all three of them were.

She arrived on their doorstep at 8 A.M., carrying a tray of coffee and an assortment of doughnuts.

"Thank God," Megan said, falling on the doughnuts. "I couldn't face another fruit basket."

Charlotte pried the lid from her coffee. She hated drinking through plastic and harbored a secret suspicion that one day plastic food and water containers would prove to be carcinogens. This still didn't outweigh the risk of drinking tap water, so bottled water was still on the menu. "Did the reporter call?"

"Yes, we're all being featured in the 'Life' section on Sunday."

Ed Muller walked in the room, strapping on his cell phone and looking for his car keys. "Have they determined what caused the derail yet?"

"No, the NTSB is still studying the rails. We're thinking it was a result of many factors."

He picked up his sunglasses and cleaned the lenses. "I've been following the case on the news. They don't know what killed Bob?"

Charlotte wiped a crumb from the corner of her mouth. "The tests were inconclusive. The coroner is sending his blood out for a more detailed analysis. No drugs or alcohol were found in his system."

Ed took one of the coffees. "I'd have been very surprised if they had. He didn't even take aspirin. Weird that they can't figure it out."

"They will, eventually," Charlotte said. "There are too many eyes on this case, too much money at stake."

"So what can we do for you?" Megan asked. She put a cloth over one shoulder and prepared to breast-feed.

Charlotte addressed Ed. "Did you by any chance hold on to your copy of the track warrants from Tuesday's run?"

"I normally would have handed them over to my replacement, but I was a little stressed."

"So what did you do with your copies?"

Ed rolled his bloodshot eyes upward, trying to remember.

"Would they have been in your grip?" Megan asked.

"Probably."

"Would you mind looking for them?" Charlotte asked.

"If they were there," Ed said, "they're gone now."

"Let me guess," Charlotte said. "Your burglars made off with your grip."

"Yeah, and all it had in it was my shaving kit and a change of clothes."

And an important clue, Charlotte thought, *that has conveniently disappeared.* "When are you going back to work?"

Ed sneaked a guilty look at his wife. "As soon as they call me." As if on cue, the phone rang and Ed picked up the receiver before the ringing had stopped. "Hello . . . yeah . . . emmm . . . sure . . . I'll be there."

He picked up his new grip, which was already packed, bent down to kiss his wife and baby daughter. "You gonna be all right?"

Megan smiled wearily. "Sure. Go on."

"Are you heading out to Anaheim?" Charlotte asked.

"Yep."

"I'll see you there. I want to follow up on a few things."

Charlotte followed Ed Muller to the Sun Rail stockyard. Ed pulled into an employee parking spot, and she found a space on the far side of a shipping container. This also served to block the view from the yard and offices of her new vehicle.

Ed checked in with the dispatcher. Charlotte walked straight to the employee break room. There she spotted the mechanic she had first met at the scene of the derail.

"Can I talk to you a minute?" Charlotte asked.

"You have to go through the union. I got nothing to say to you."

"Who do you think I am?" she asked.

"You're from the company, looking for a fall guy, and I didn't do nothing I shouldn't have."

"First of all," she said, sitting down across from him, "I'm not with the company. I've been retained to help them through this crisis. The only way I know to do that is to find out what exactly went wrong so I can assure the public that it won't happen again."

"There was nothing wrong with that engine," he said, "or the couplers or the wheels or the controls."

"What do you think caused the derail?" she asked.

"Most likely it was a track problem."

"Would you mind taking me on board the locomotive?"

He glanced in the direction of Stan's office. "Well . . ."

"Don't worry. I have full access and authority. It'll just take a minute." She stuck out her hand. "Charlotte Lyon, by the way."

He clasped her hand briefly with his own callused one. "Tink Sawyer."

The locomotive was parked outside the mechanic's barn. It was still caked with dirt and sand, Charlotte was happy to see.

"We're going to clean her up today," Tink said. "Ordered a new chair, too."

There was a small stepping stool at the base of the stairs leading up to the nose of the cab. She grasped the side rails and followed Tink up. He swung the door open and propped it that way, allowing light into the cavelike space in front. They climbed the second flight of stairs to the cab. Charlotte bent over the controls and studied them carefully, noting how the small caged fan was pointed to drive air over the emergency brake control and into the operator's face. Something shiny, like tinfoil, caught her eye. It was wedged in the square slot in the very farthest forward position of the brake controls. The emergency position.

"What's this?" she asked.

Tink looked. "I don't know, gum wrapper maybe?"

"Hold on a minute." Charlotte went back down in the nose and retrieved the first aid kit she had noticed earlier. She returned to the cab and opened it. After a moment's rummaging, she found tweezers, sterile gauze, and cotton swabs. While Tink watched, she extracted the shard of metal from inside the controls and dropped it on the sterile white bandage.

They both studied it for a moment. "What do you think this is?" she asked.

"Looks like aluminum," he said.

"Where would it have come from?"

He reached down to pick it up, but she pulled it away. "Don't touch it. It might have chemicals on it." She swabbed the rest of the brake slot, folded the Q-tip and tiny snip of metal carefully inside the gauze, and then put them in an envelope, which she then sealed.

She wrote down the time and location and signed over the gummed flap. She then asked Tink to do the same.

"I would prefer you keep this to yourself for the time being," she told the mechanic. "I'm not sure who we can trust."

Tink Sawyer made a grunt deep in his throat, but seemed to stand a little taller. By including him in her circle, she suspected she had made an important ally.

She called Hank Nunzio at Iron Horse Technologies.

"I found something interesting in the locomotive," she said.

"You want to bring it by?" he asked.

"I think it would be more credible if I take it directly to the NTSB. I don't want to break the chain of custody and have anyone accuse me of manufacturing evidence."

"Sherwood Priest's people requested a chance to examine the steel tracks from the derail."

"Yeah, I know. We're doing that today?"

"At one. I suggest we all meet at the NTSB's Metallurgical Lab in Santa Ana."

"I'll be there." She programmed the lab's address into the Mercedes's never-lost system and reached for her phone to call Hannigan. It rang as she touched it. "Todd?"

"Who's Todd?" Jill asked.

"Oh, just some guy I met."

"I'm sorry, I was trying to reach my sister, but she never dates. She's too busy saving the world and making tons of money."

"Hey," Charlotte said, "even superheroes need some sugar now and then. Did you get the part?"

"I've gotten two callbacks, so I'm hopeful. What's up with Mom?"

"Apparently when you drink and use dope for almost fifty years, it can have an adverse effect on your liver."

"I can hear her now," Jill said. Then in a perfect mimicry of their mom's voice she said, " 'After all I've been through, now this. Can you believe it?' "

Charlotte laughed. "That's about the size of it. Oh, and she expects you to nurse her back to health."

"Yeah, right," Jill said. Then her tone changed. "How bad is she?"

"They've done a biopsy. I thought I'd wait and call you after we had the results."

"Let me know if you need me there."

"I sure will," Charlotte lied. She also suspected that Jill knew very well she was lying, but they were all playing the parts they'd chosen.

CHAPTER 19

Hank Nunzio met her in the parking lot. His Levi's, white dress shirt, and bolo tie completed her image of him as a Native American. Even though it was bright out, he eschewed sunglasses, preferring to squint.

A van pulled up with STILLWELL ACCIDENT INVESTIGATION stenciled on the side.

"Here they are," he said. "Stillwell himself. He rarely does the fieldwork anymore."

"It's probably not every day that he gets such a high-profile case." She realized she was already disposed not to like the man, not because he was the competition, but that he would work for a sleazeball like Sherwood Priest. Of course, he might have met an entirely different Sherwood than she had.

Fortunately, Sherwood did not see the need to make a presence at the lab. Instead he sent a sharp-faced attorney who arrived in a brand-new Jaguar, handed her his card, and waited for her to be impressed. She didn't oblige him, turning her attention to the guy laboring to exit his van.

Stillwell was a guy who carried his extra weight in his gut, but had never changed his pants size to accommodate the additional inches. She imagined there was a belt under there somewhere, holding up his low-riding pants as he heaved himself out from behind the steering wheel. He walked with the limp of a man who had blown out his knees playing football.

"Hank," Stillwell said with a nod of his head.

"Chip." Nunzio returned the nod. "This is Charlotte Lyon, representing Sun Rail."

Charlotte kept both arms wrapped around her folio as if it were a life preserver.

"Ma'am," Stillwell said, as if he hadn't noticed a thing amiss with her defensive posture.

Both men retrieved cameras and tape recorders from their vehicles. "Let's get this show on the road," Stillwell said.

Just a good ol' boy, Charlotte thought, imagining him giving interviews and testimony.

They all had to present picture IDs and have their names checked against the approved list. The security guard gave them clip-on visitor badges and asked them to wait for their escort. CJ Post arrived a moment later to take them inside his sanctum.

They walked down a long hallway, past open shower stalls and eyewash stations. Workers wearing full hazmat gear studied something on a table. "These are our negative flow rooms. The air pressure in the lab is kept five pounds below sea level."

They passed another room filled with computers and accompanying geeks. "Satellite imaging," CJ explained.

At last they arrived at a large open space. Sections of rail were assembled on the floor.

Nunzio stared at a piece of equipment not in use and said reverently, "It's a scanning microscope with energy dispersive spectroscopy capability for chemical analysis. The latest model."

"You're drooling, Hank," Charlotte said sotto voce.

Stillwell took out his camera, placed a twelve-inch ruler on top of the rail, and started taking pictures. Nunzio followed, taking his own pictures from the exact same angle.

"We've determined this area here," CJ said, pointing to a length of twisted rail, "to be the POD."

"That's point of derailment, darling," Stillwell volunteered.

"Thank you, sweetie," Charlotte responded without a hint of irony or resentment. She prayed that when and if they went to court, they would be assigned a young woman judge.

The experts continued to study the broken rail, and Charlotte took that opportunity to pull CJ aside. "I was at the yard earlier examining the cab." She pulled the envelope out of her purse and showed it to CJ. "I found this in an interesting spot, and I was hoping you could tell me what it is."

CJ reached for the envelope. She didn't let go. "Please note the signatures on the flap and the date."

"Who's the guy?"

"One of the mechanics."

"Can I open it now?" CJ asked.

"Be careful. It might have a toxic chemical on it. I'm hoping I found a smoking gun here."

He cut open one end of the envelope and pulled the folded gauze free. Charlotte took it from him and unwrapped it.

"Where was this?" he asked.

"Wedged in the brake controls."

CJ took the shard, still in its protective wrapping, over to the electron microscope. He tapped the flattened piece of metal onto a slide and inserted it into the machine. "Well," he said, looking through the viewfinder, "it's aluminum, and there is a chemical substance on it and inside it."

"Can you determine what that substance is?" she asked.

"I will in a moment." He continued to study the metal under his microscope.

Nunzio was looking their way with obvious yearning. Stillwell noticed, too.

The machine beeped and spat out an analysis. "Uh-huh," CJ said, "just as I suspected."

"Please don't tell me it's Diet Coke," Charlotte said.

"No. CO_2. My guess is that it charged an aluminum ampule carrying some other essence. I'll need more time to analyze it."

"Let me think out loud here," she said. "If this cartridge or ampule was lodged in the forward groove of the brake control, then when the engineer jammed the lever forward, the cartridge would be crushed."

"Setting off the CO_2 charge," CJ finished for her, "and releasing whatever substance it carried into the air above it."

"Perhaps killing Bob in the process."

"That seems like a lot of trouble to go to to kill one guy," CJ said.

"Oh, believe me, there's a lot more to it."

CJ picked up the cotton squab. "We have a mass spectrometer in one of the other departments. Let me get them to rush the analysis on this."

"Great. Give me a moment, and I'll come with you." She pulled Nunzio aside.

"What's going on?" he asked in a whisper.

"I'll let you know when I find out. How's it going here?"

"I'll brief you more fully later, but I'm not seeing a sun kink or any sign of thermal fatigue."

"Anything?"

He leaned forward to whisper in her ear. "There are some suspicious gouges in the side of the rail near the POD. I'd like to know what caused them."

"Okay, that's something anyway. We'll talk later and compare notes."

She left them to follow CJ to the negative flow lab they had passed on the way in. CJ tapped on the glass and pointed to the wall-mounted intercom. One of the techs lumbered over there in his bulky space suit.

CJ pushed the small black button under the speaker grille. "I need a chemical analysis. Stat."

"What you got?" the tech asked.

CJ held up the swab. "Possibly some sort of drug or toxin."

"Give me a second." The tech pointed to the anteroom. Charlotte and CJ entered. The tech placed a petri dish on a stainless steel chute, similar to what self-serve gas stations attendants or drive-through bank tellers used to pass cash and documents. CJ opened their side of the chute and placed the Q-tip on the petri dish.

Charlotte pointed to her watch and mouthed, "How long?"

The tech held up a gloved hand with fingers spread, then scraped the cotton off the swab and placed it in an impressive machine.

"Did he mean minutes or hours or days?" Charlotte asked.

"Minutes. This equipment is amazing."

Four minutes later, the spectrograph began spitting out data. The tech studied the readout, eliminating parts of it until coming to something that caused him to nod his helmeted head. Then he went to a computer and scanned in the data. Another minute later, he pointed to the intercom. "It's gamma hydroxybutyrate. Also known as GHB."

"Isn't that one of those date rape drugs?" Charlotte asked.

The tech nodded.

"Thanks," she said. "Can I get a copy of that analysis?"

The tech looked at CJ for approval. "Make four copies."

Charlotte knew she had to work fast now, before the Feds got back involved and she was shut out completely.

CHAPTER 20

Charlotte strode briskly to the elevator of the Sun Rail office building. She'd been coming here only four days, yet it was growing as familiar to her as her home, or at least one of the dozens she had lived in growing up. She credited her ability to travel light and adjust to changing situations to that same tumultuous childhood. Just as Jill's knack to assume whatever identity served her needs fed her acting.

She reached the seventh floor and went first to the conference room where her interns were hard at work on the phone banks. She had arranged for them to sort the messages into different baskets. One was for press requests, another for donation pledges, another for tips surrounding the accident—people who heard or saw anything on Tuesday before, during, or after the wreck. She picked up the slips in the Good Samaritan basket. She was interested in the identity of their mystery person now more than ever, but she didn't want to let on to anyone yet that she suspected the Samaritan was involved in the derailment itself, and by extension, either directly or indirectly responsible for the deaths of both victims. Then again, she could be way off base, so better to keep it to herself until she was sure.

The last basket was for the nut job tips. Any investigation with an open help line always got its share of those people claiming that God was smiting the unclean or that a hated neighbor/relative/coworker had been acting suspiciously or wanted to confess even though they knew none of the specifics of how the deed in question was done.

She went back to her office to make her calls in private. The first person she contacted was Dr. Donavon.

"Could gamma hydroxybutyrate have caused Bob Peterson's death?"

"Possibly," he said.

"Wouldn't it show up on a tox test?"

"Not in the blood. Gamma hyroxybutyrate or GHB occurs naturally in the body. It's a neural transmitter."

"Like serotonin?"

"Exactly."

Charlotte knew a lot about serotonin. She took Lexapro, a serotonin reuptake inhibitor, to help her fight the more extreme manifestations of her OCD. Her mother didn't understand why she "wanted to take that shit." Charlotte explained that it made her happier. "So you think," her mom had grumbled into her beer.

Dr. Donavon continued: "The first tox test we ran detected it, but didn't quantify amount."

"How do you quantify the levels?" she asked.

"Excessive measures would show up in the urine or in a GCMS."

"Which is?"

"Sorry," he said, "gas chromatography-mass spectroscopy."

"You got one of those?" she asked.

"We're on a state budget, remember. I'd have to send the sample to the Department of Justice, and no telling when they'd get to it. I'll try to put a rush on it. The urine might be a problem. Decedents lose bowel and bladder control. I could open the bladder and try to retrieve a sample, or possibly there's still some urine at the renal calyces. Don't worry, I'll figure something out. Anything else?"

"As a matter of fact, there is. Do you remember a train fatality in the beginning of the year? The decedent's name was Farrah Kent."

"Young woman? Left behind a husband and baby?"

"That's her."

"One of my doctors is testifying at the trial next month."

"What trial?"

"The family wants to reverse the ruling that her death was a suicide. We stood by our findings, so they're taking it to court and letting a jury decide."

She thanked him and asked him to please call her when and if he had further test results. She hung up the phone and spotted Dom in the hallway. He looked her way, and she gestured for him to join her.

"What do you need?" he asked.

"Close the door first."

He shut the door carefully behind him and sat. "This is either very good or very bad." His face was gaunt, as if he had lost a sudden five or ten pounds.

"Neither, really. I'm pursuing some lines of inquiry and would rather they not become common knowledge."

"Of course."

"What do you know about the jury trial to change the ruling on Farrah Kent's death?"

"I know the family is refusing to accept suicide as the cause. They really don't have much of a chance, but you never know where a jury's sympathy will fall."

"Would Bob Peterson have been testifying at that hearing?"

"Yes, but we do have sworn deposition from him."

"Still, a living witness makes a stronger case."

He looked at her warily. "Be very careful and very certain before you breathe a word of this to anyone."

"Don't worry, Dom. I know my job. Do you think you could scare up the Kent family's contact information for me?"

"I'll call you within the hour."

"How's it going with Sherwood Priest?"

Dom let his lawyer mask slip for a moment. "Oy. His attorney is subpoenaing our financial records, our maintenance reports, our roster of employees. I'm fighting him at every turn. No business can hold up to that much scrutiny. He'll find some janitor with sex offenses or that one of the engines suffered mechanical problems after being serviced. The guy's a bottom feeder."

"It's all about money with them. Between us, Rachel Priest's death has nothing but upsides for the son."

He indicated that he wouldn't argue that point and took his leave. She buzzed for Andrew and asked if he could come to her office. He arrived moments later, fresh faced and eager.

"I need you to do something for me, but I want you to be discreet about it."

"Absolutely." He practically saluted.

"I'd like you to go through the employee records and bring me a list of everyone hired since the first of the year. And anyone who quit or was let go since Tuesday."

"It might help if I knew why you wanted them."

"I'm compiling statistics to show what a good employer Sun Rail is."

"I could testify to that," Andrew said.

"You might need to."

Andrew fairly bounded out of the office. After taking a moment to grin at the young man's enthusiasm, Charlotte got to work sifting through the messages. Descriptions of the motorcyclist from the accident were all over the board. Most accounts agreed that the Samaritan was a man. Some said he was well over six feet tall; others put him at five-ten. No one could identify the dirt bike. Too much dust as it left, they said. She had learned from Hank Nunzio via the event recorder information that the locomotive's engine had been shut down three minutes after the emergency stop was initiated by the engineer.

No one else had ever admitted to shutting off the engine. That left three possibilities. One, someone was lying. Two, it was Bob Peterson. Unlikely, since by then he would have been under the effect of the gas. Or three, the so-called Good Samaritan had done it.

If it were him, then he probably had a working knowledge of trains and he was close enough at the exact time of the derail to be on board within three minutes. And what else had he done? Swapped the track warrants? Removed the spent CO_2 cartridge and finished off Bob? Climbed into the first passenger coach and made sure Rachel Priest was dead?

She tapped her pencil as she thought, then started to make a list, which soon turned into a flow chart. On a separate page, she began a time schedule of important events.

She was already fairly certain that the break-in at her house was related to the case. What had the cop asked her? Who knew she would be out late visiting her mom?

One name immediately popped into her head.

No, that was crazy. Hannigan was an NTSB investigator. He loved trains. That would be tantamount to a firefighter committing arson or a cop running a crime ring. . . . Both of which had happened in recent history. The more she tried to reason her way out of it, the more she convinced herself it could be true.

Or was she unconsciously trying to sabotage their relationship before it had a chance to get going? On the other hand, what better way to keep an investigator off her game than to flirt with her and take her out on dates?

Was there time on a motorcycle to get from the wreck in Riverside to his office in Anaheim and then take the call to investigate? What was his motive? Money?

Shit, she thought, she was really starting to like him, too. Had he shot at her, then come to her rescue? Had he been trying to kill her or just scare her off? Two people were already dead, why not one more?

She returned to her theory that there had to be at least two operatives at work. She was thinking an inside man at Sun Rail. Someone who would know enough to tamper with the track warrants, place the CO_2 cartridge in the locomotive's controls, and possibly have a hand in the orders to backload the consist with the heavy Range Rovers.

That someone would have had to be a man. A woman would have been too conspicuous at the Sun Rail train yard.

Well, she thought, *now I'm getting somewhere. I've certainly narrowed the field of suspects down to hundreds.*

She thought about motive. Why go to all the trouble of staging a train wreck when a simple drive-by would have sufficed? She considered the three victims. Bob Peterson, Rachel Priest, and Charlotte's client: Sun Rail.

No, there was at least one more.

She scratched out 3 and wrote 4. Now the list of either intended or ancillary victims read like this:

1. BOB PETERSON
2. RACHEL PRIEST
3. SUN RAIL
4. ME

CHAPTER 21

Charlotte booted up the computer she kept in her temporary Sun Rail office. She didn't insert her flash drive, but went online instead. She had a 2 P.M. briefing with Rayney and Dom in Rayney's office. She hoped to have some verifiable proof by then.

Her friends in the press and Mary Nightengale's follow-through had resulted in positive pieces all week. Charlotte had supplied safety stats, maintenance schedules, and the environmental impact of rail travel in lieu of all the single-occupant vehicles that now clogged the freeways. But of course, that was only half the job. Proving that the accident had been an act of sabotage would really tilt the scales, especially if she could also identify the saboteurs.

She did an Internet search on GHB and found, among other data, a recipe for do-it-yourselfers. Apparently all one needed to manufacture one's very own Liquid X was an inexpensive industrial solvent called gamma butyrolactone or GBL and 1,4-butanediol, which could be extracted from butane.

She watched the staff stroll by the window, often sneaking covert glances her way. She really couldn't trust anyone in the company, with the exception of Rayney, who had the most to lose. There was definitely a snake in the Sun Rail woodpile.

Dennis O'Connor chose that minute to call. She laughed when she realized it was him.

"What's so funny?" he wanted to know.

"Oh, I was just thinking of you. Sort of. What's up?"

"I want to show you something. Can we meet for a cup of coffee?"

She looked at her desk and all the work spread out across it in exasperation. Still, she didn't want Dennis inside her sanctum, so meeting him on neutral ground was her best option. "This better be good," she said as she loaded her charts and notes into her briefcase.

"Oh, it's good, all right. There's a Starbucks on the corner, right down the street from you."

"Which direction? There's a Starbucks on every corner."

"The one next to dry cleaners. I'll see you there in ten minutes."

Andrew met her in the hallway as she was going out. "I have those employee records for you," he said. "Should I put them on your desk?"

"Thanks, that would be great. I won't be long."

"The Mercedes dealer called. Your car will be ready in an hour. If you want, I'll call them back and ask them to deliver it."

"Do you cook, too?" she asked as she handed him the loaner keys. "I think I'm falling in love."

He blushed even though she was smiling to show that she was kidding. She liked her guys a little tougher, but maybe she could adopt him.

She walked to the coffee shop. Dennis was already there and waved her over to an outside table. There was a legal-size manila envelope on the table. She reached for it, but Dennis stopped her.

"Don't ask how I got this," he said. "And you can't keep it or make a copy. Just read it and tell me how good I done."

Intrigued, Charlotte opened the envelope and pulled out a copy of Rachel Priest's trust. Her estate was sizable, as Charlotte would have expected. Rachel left the bulk of it to various charities and scholarship fund. She also bequeathed a healthy endowment to the Actors' Guild Retirement Home. Sherwood was to receive a generous monthly stipend. Enough to take care of his needs for the rest of his life if he wasn't too greedy. On page three, the document got real interesting. In the event of his mother's death, Sherwood was granted an entitlement to all the royalties and use of her name and image.

Charlotte whistled and returned the documents. Knowing Dennis, his source was some female paralegal or office staffer who had put her job on the line for a dose of his Irish charm.

"This is good. Very helpful in filling in some blanks." She leaned forward and Dennis did likewise. "I'm going to hand you a huge story out of this. You've got my word you'll have first crack at it."

Dennis nodded. Charlotte's word meant a solid guarantee, and he knew that.

She stirred her coffee, hoping to convey a casual attitude about her next request. "I was wondering if you could help me with a little background first. I'm doing a fluff piece on the different emergency response teams. Red Cross I already know about, same with the police and fire department. The NTSB and how they operate are new to me."

"What do you need to know?" Dennis asked.

"How are the investigators assigned to which cases? Is it a rotation deal, or does everyone in the train department automatically check out every crash or problem? Do they keep regular office hours, or do they work off a beeper or cell phone?"

"Any one person in particular that you want me to focus on?"

"I suppose you should start with the top guy, the lead investigator in the Downey office. His name is Todd Hannigan." She wasn't sure Dennis was buying her smoke screen, but that didn't matter. What was important was whether he would do it or not.

"Just how meaty is this story?" Dennis asked.

"You won't be disappointed."

"I want a three-hour lead time when you're ready to break the full story," he said.

"Our deal was half an hour. I'm not sure how much I can control it beyond that."

"Oh, I think you're much more resourceful and clever than you let on. I'm sure you'll think of some way to keep to our deal."

"Okay, done. You'll get my best effort. You have my word."

"Good enough."

She returned to the office and made a list of everyone who gained from the derailment. It was longer than she would have liked. She really wanted it to be Sherwood Priest. He was a rude jerk, but was he twisted enough to want to kill his mother? The police always looked at family members first in a homicide. She couldn't discount the possibility that there was yet another player who hadn't even made it to her list. Someone or some entity who didn't want Sun Rail to succeed. Perhaps a rival casino of the Palm Springs—area gaming institutions. Or a freight shipper who felt that a passenger line needlessly clogged the rails. She was already focused on looking for someone with a knowledge of train operations or someone who could hire that someone.

She also knew from past investigations that if she could figure out the how and why, that would lead her to the who. In this case, though, the means of how the train was derailed was all she had to work with to lead her to the culprit. Then the person's motive would probably become clear.

The list of new hires since the beginning of the year had some eighty-plus names on it. Charlotte went through it with a highlighter, eliminating women and men hired before the date of Farrah Kent's death. She was still left with thirty names.

Three of those had quit or were laid off since Tuesday, and then there were the crew members on temporary leave so they could recuperate emotionally. She called the human resources office. A woman named Christina answered.

"Christina, this is Charlotte Lyon. I've been brought in by Mr. Rayney to get to the bottom of Tuesday's derail."

"How can I help you?"

"I have the names of three employees who've recently left." Charlotte read the names, spelling each one. "Can you tell me the circumstances of their terminations?"

"The first two gave two weeks' notice and helped train their replacements. One guy's wife got a job transfer. The other had medical problems. I can't disclose what they were."

"That's all right." Charlotte wrote the salient facts in her shorthand. "And the third man?"

"He just didn't show up for work Wednesday morning. The foreman called him at home but was unable to reach him."

"So no one knows what happened to him?"

"All I know is he doesn't work here anymore. If he wants his severance check, he's going to have to come pick it up."

Charlotte thanked Christina. It was one thirty, time to prepare for her briefing. The phone rang. She prayed that it wasn't Todd Hannigan. She wasn't ready to talk to him yet. Not until she could exonerate him. Caller ID identified the call as coming from USC Medical Center.

"Hello?" she croaked, then cleared her throat. "This is Charlotte Lyon. How can I help you?"

"The doctor says that I have hepatitis C. Turns out that the virus can stay dormant in your system for twenty-five to thirty years before you get symptoms."

"Hi, Mom."

"So anyway, I've been thinking I probably got it from a blood transfusion."

Charlotte rolled her eyes but kept her voice calm. "When did you have a transfusion?"

"Probably when I gave birth. One of those times. Do you think we can sue the hospital?"

"I don't know, Mom. What are the other ways it can be transmitted?"

"Tattoos. A lot of servicemen got it overseas. Body piercing, acupuncture—"

"So anything that involves needles?" Charlotte interrupted. "Think about it, Mom. You'd have a hell of a time proving how and when you got it. Did you get the biopsy results?"

"Maybe by the end of the day, but you know how these places are."

By *places*, Charlotte wondered if her mother meant teaching and research facilities, or a hospital that would take someone in who didn't have health insurance. Lisa even qualified for Medicare, but wasn't about to *do all the "bullshit" it took. The Man could fuck himself.* "When can you go home?"

"One more night, they said. They're getting my platelet count back where it should be. And there's this support group for hep C patients here this evening. I might go check it out."

"You should. Definitely. I've got a meeting right now, but let me know when they're letting you out, and I'll get you a ride home."

"You ain't coming yourself?"

"Probably not. Things have heated up around here."

"Ironic, isn't it?"

"What is?" Charlotte looked at her watch.

"Here I am going to a meeting about a disease that will kill me, and you're going to some meeting in a fancy boardroom."

"I'm not sure *ironic* is the word you mean, Mom." Irony was her mother confirming Charlotte's deep-seated needle phobia. A phobia that the older woman had often ridiculed. Now who had the last I-told-you-so? Yeah, it was almost funny in a tragic and morbid way, not that Charlotte was laughing.

"Well, far be it from me, Miss I'm-so-great, to keep you from *your* appointed fucking rounds." Lisa used her I've-gotten-a-raw-deal-again tone.

Charlotte wasn't sure if she was being called a mail carrier, as in "neither snow, nor rain, nor gloom of night," or if this was more of her mom's special brand of irony.

"And don't trouble yourself about me tomorrow," Lisa continued. "I'll just take a bus."

Wait for it, Char thought. Sure enough, the long-suffering sigh followed like thunder to the lightning barb.

Charlotte did a mental five-count. *They're trying to keep this woman alive. Why?*

"Suit yourself," Char said. "I've got to go." She hung up without hearing her mom's reaction, picked up her paperwork, and headed for the eighth floor. She realized she was smiling. Who knew that tough love could be so satisfying?

She kept the briefing on a need-to-know basis, limiting the attendees to Rayney and Dom. She explained what she had uncovered so far, her suspicions about the Good Samaritan's true intent, the spent fragment of the CO_2 cartridge, and the discrepancies in the track warrants and slow orders. Rayney's posture improved as she spoke. The slump left his back and, by the time she concluded her report, he had more color in his face.

"So who do you think is behind this?" he asked.

"I'd rather not start pointing fingers until I have the whole picture. If the names of any of the individuals who I'm looking at became public, we'd be opening ourselves for a libel suit."

"Do the police have any leads on who took the potshots on your car?" Dom asked.

"Not that they've shared with me. They don't have that much to work with."

"I want you to expense the repair bills on your car to us," Rayney said.

"Thank you," she said, having already done just that. What did he think she was gonna do?

"What now?" Dom asked.

"Just conduct business as usual."

Rayney seemed to approve of her answer. "Tomorrow, we're taking a junket of investors out to the casinos in the executive coach. We'll spend the night in Agua Caliente Hotel and return on Sunday."

"I have to warn you," she said, "there's a huge display of flowers and pictures and candles along the tracks where the derail happened."

"I know," Rayney said. "Our trains are still on orders to not exceed ten miles per hour on that section of new track."

"Bummer," she said.

"Not really," Rayney said. "We can't run enough trains to accommodate all the people who want to see it. I hear the locals are setting up lemonade stands for the procession of people and cars on Timoteo Road. It's actually been a big boon to the local economy."

"One man's rain cloud is another man's rainbow," Dom said.

Charlotte frowned. "I think it's sick that people are so stoked by death and disaster, but I guess it's human nature." Most humans anyway.

Dom slid her a piece of paper. "These are Farrah Kent's family's addresses and phone numbers. Her dad preceded her in death. The only local relatives are her mother and brother. I don't know if they'll want to talk to you."

"You just gotta know how to ask." She looked at the list. "Her husband took their baby and moved to Texas?"

"I think he had family there who would help him raise his daughter."

"So Farrah's mom lost a daughter and a granddaughter."

"Nobody's claiming the whole thing wasn't a tragedy," Dom said. He opened his briefcase and retrieved a document. "If you see Mrs. Reynolds and you can get her to sign this release of liability holding the railroad harmless, she'll have our written assurance that we won't give evidence against her on her daughter's manner-of-death trial."

"I might even be able to put in a word with the coroner," Charlotte said.

As the meeting concluded, Rayney and Dom both congratulated her on her good and quick work. She accepted their kudos graciously, as she would her check when she solved the case.

CHAPTER 22

The coroner called at three with disturbing news.

"We tested Bob Peterson's urine. I have the results."

"And?" Charlotte asked.

"No GHB, not in any excessive amounts. What made you suspect GHB in the first place? None was found in the thermos."

Charlotte explained about the CO_2 cartridge.

"Why didn't you say so?" Donavon said. "If a lethal dose was administered by airborne transmission, there wouldn't have been time for it to reach the urinary tract."

"I could kick myself," Charlotte said dryly. "So we're back to the—" She consulted her notes so that she would get it right. "—gas chromatography—mass spectroscopy?"

"Yes. I could put a rush on it, but you still might have to wait three weeks."

"Maybe I could do better than that."

"Probably, but it will cost you," Donavon said.

"That shouldn't be a problem."

"By the way, I released both bodies for burial."

"Do you know when the services are planned?" She hoped it wasn't Saturday or Rayney would have to change his plans. He needed to at least attend Bob Peterson's funeral, and really should be at both.

"No, I don't, but I can give you the names of the funeral homes."

She wrote down the information and thanked him. She'd talk to him about the suicide ruling when and if she got the release signed by Mrs. Reynolds.

After she hung up, she again perused the tip messages. In the "kook" pile she found something interesting. A woman named Dixie Lewis on Timoteo Road claimed that aliens had stolen her forklift. Ms. Lewis called the cops, but they wouldn't do anything because the aliens had put it back in the exact same place. Fortunately, whoever had taken the call had gotten the woman's address, which was actually directions via landmarks. Dixie didn't have a phone.

Charlotte called her newest and most unlikely partner, Dennis O'Connor.

"I need one more thing from you," she said.

"Just one?"

"I need you to arrange an interview with the mother of the young woman who was killed by a Sunliner train. A Margaret Reynolds. She lives in Costa Mesa." Charlotte provided him with the phone number.

"What's our angle?" he asked.

"The coroner ruled the death as a suicide, and the family is going to court to reverse that finding. If I went to them as a person connected with the rail company, they might be hostile. You, on the other hand . . ."

"But you want to be there?" he asked.

"I'll bring a camera, and you can introduce me as a freelance photographer."

"How uncharacteristically sneaky of you," he said.

"Yeah, but my heart is pure." Speaking of hearts. "Did you talk to the folks at the NTSB?"

"Sure did. You didn't tell me you had a fan there."

"Do I?"

"Yeah, that Hannigan guy. I think he's got a thing for you."

"I only met him last Tuesday," she said. She looked down at her pad of paper. She had written *Hannigan* in cursive, as if practicing the signature.

"I accessed his service records. He did two tours during the Gulf War, got some medals, and an honorable discharge."

"What branch of the service?" she asked. "Some sort of investigative unit?"

"No, actually he was in the marines. Their star sniper, as a matter of fact."

Charlotte got an instant buzzing in her ears, but managed to croak, "What else did you learn?"

"Nothing terribly exciting. At the NTSB, the different specialists in a given field, in this case train and rail, all respond as a team. The investigators carry special company-issued cell phones. When they get a call on one of those, they know they have a wreck to investigate."

"So they could be anywhere when they get the call?"

"Yeah, like a doctor."

"Did you happen to ask Hannigan where he was on Tuesday when he got the call?"

"Nothing so specific. I could do a follow-up," he said.

"That would be great," she said. She had to know. For the sake of their future children, if nothing else. She smiled at her fantasies and left for a brainstorming session at Iron Horse Technologies.

Based on the new information, Hank Nunzio had updated his reenactment video. She met him at his editing studio to see what it looked like. Nunzio had blown up the photographs of the broken rails and tacked them to the walls. She studied the pictures as he queued up his computer.

She pointed to the section of rail at what had been determined to be the POD. Overhead pictures showed grooves in the tracks where the train wheels had walked the rail. Some of the clips that anchored the rails to the cement ties were tweaked and bent. Others still maintained their structural integrity, as if they'd popped off.

"No spikes?" she asked.

Hank came to stand beside her and pointed to the photograph. "Not with concrete rails. They use these Safelok clips. Alloy spring steel rated at forty-seven hundred pounds. Properly installed, these babies never work loose. Not like spikes hammered through wooden ties."

"But they don't even go through the rail flange," she said.

"No, they're designed that way. The rails sort of float, makes for a better ride and less overall stress."

"Are the clips cast into the concrete?"

"Nope, they clip on. You can install and remove them with hand tools."

"I don't mean to tell you your job," she said. "But maybe somebody did just that."

Nunzio nodded his head thoughtfully, not in the least offended. "That certainly is a possibility, especially now that we changed our focus to look for tampering."

Emboldened, Charlotte moved on to the next picture, this one a side view of the grooved tracks where the wheels left the rail. "What made these scratches here?"

"We'd all like to know that. You ready to watch a movie?"

"You bet."

"Take a seat and I'll get this rolling." He dimmed the lights and started the video. Again the familiar scenery rolled by. The engineer's hand gripped the red-handled brake control and jammed it forward. This time, Nunzio had added the capsule exploding its lethal load into Bob Peterson's face, and Bob slumping back in his chair.

The scene then switched to an outside view of the consist. The locomotive stopped, the cars directly behind the locomotive stopped, but the heavily loaded car carrier full of Range Rovers kept up its forward momentum. The consist folded into itself, bumping the passenger cars off the tracks and onto their sides. At exactly three minutes and ten seconds after the brake was engaged, a figure in a black motorcycle helmet pushed the stop lever to shut off the engine with a gloved hand. The guy then boarded the locomotive.

Here, they had to make an educated guess on the sequence of events. The motorcyclist first checked Bob, either to ensure he was dead or to finish the job with a redosing. The film showed both versions. Dust and sand from the crash swirled in the air, providing a cover for his activities. Next, he loosened the brake controls enough to extract the spent capsule. The last thing he did was to swap out the track warrants, leaving his cleaner copy with the unturned pages on the clip next to the controls.

The scene switched to outside again. The biker exited the locomotive then pulled an emergency window free and climbed into the coach that Rachel Priest was aboard. He climbed out again less than a minute later empty-handed. Again, he had either seen that she was beyond help, or had made sure she was dead.

Without ever removing his helmet or gloves, the guy continued entering the cars on their sides, playing hero and helping passengers climb to safety. When everyone was free of the wreckage, but still reeling in stunned confusion, the no-so Good Samaritan hopped back on his bike and sped away.

"We still haven't addressed one important issue," she said.

"I know what you're going to say." Nunzio turned the lights back up. "Why did the engineer engage the emergency brake in the first place?"

"He obviously saw something up ahead."

"A pedestrian?"

"No, I don't think so." Charlotte thought back to her interview with Donna Moore. "Remember the no horn thing."

"Maybe he didn't have time before he was immobilized," Nunzio offered.

"But isn't the horn button right there?"

"All the controls were in front of him. He never used his intercom either."

"Maybe he saw the clips had been removed?"

"Not likely," Nunzio said. "He was too far away, and the curve in the tracks would have blocked his view."

"Well, something made him do it."

"I'm not arguing with you," he said, and returned to studying his photographs.

Her BlackBerry vibrated, and she saw that she had a text message: "TH was out of the office taking care of 'personal business' on Tues. morning.—Dennis." A chill flowed through her, and it was several seconds before she remembered to breathe.

"That must have been bad news," Nunzio said. "You just turned three shades of pale."

"The next time I see you, give me something to smile about," she said.

She left Nunzio to his puzzle. Hannigan called her just as she reached his car. She had a quick suspicion that he was watching her and waited to call when she would be alone. That was crazy, she knew. If he was tracking her, he could just shoot at her again. She doubted he would miss a second time.

"What's up?" she asked, trying to sound casual.

"I was hoping you'd agree to have dinner with me again."

That was the last thing she expected him to say. "Are you asking me out?"

"Unless you already had plans for tonight."

"I am pretty busy. I have a possible witness who called into our tip line who I want to interview. She lives off of Timoteo Road, near the derail, but she doesn't have a . . ." Charlotte wasn't sure how much she should reveal. "I have to go there in person. And I need to find out when the funeral services are planned." She also didn't tell him about the GCMS test that was needed to determine if Bob Peterson had been given a lethal dose of the drug. Although, she had been hoping to use the NTSB's lab.

"Why don't we go see her together and grab a bite afterward?"

"I'll let everyone at the office know, in case they needed to reach me. Cell phones don't work so well out there. Now I'll tell them that you'll be accompanying me."

"Okay," he said slowly. His accompanying tone was of consternation. "How's your mom, by the way?"

"They should be releasing her tomorrow. I'm not looking forward to that, believe me."

"Should I pick you up in Anaheim?"

"Actually, I'm on my way home to Laguna." She wanted to wash up, change her clothes, and put on some nice underwear. Not that she was planning anything, per se, but she did believe in being prepared. She gave him her address in Laguna Beach. "You weren't planning on going on your motorcycle, were you?" She didn't think she'd ever be ready for that.

"No, I'll bring a company truck since our business tonight will be semiprofessional."

"Get here as soon as you can," she said. "I'd like to speak to our possible witness in daylight. She also has something to show us."

"Give me an hour," he said. "Anyone ever tell you that you have a very suspicious mind?"

"It's a gift." *And a buzz kill.*

It was five o'clock when she pulled into her garage. This time her switches were in the proper positions and there were no further signs of foul play. She called the funeral homes and learned that Bob Peterson's service was set for Saturday at noon. Rachel Priest was going to have a much larger do, but in Los Angeles. That service was scheduled for the afternoon to give all the various dignitaries and celebrities a chance to arrive.

She called Mary Nightengale and asked her how much money had been raised in the Good Samaritan fund. Over six thousand dollars had been pledged, mostly in small sums. Charlotte instructed Mary to match the amount with Sun Rail money and cut a check for the Rachel Priest Foundation. "Send out a press release about the donation, and deliver it personally."

"Anything else?"

"Is Rayney in the building?"

"Yes, he is."

"Transfer me to his office." While Charlotte waited for Rayney to pick up, she booted up her computer and checked e-mail. She saved the various interview requests, deleted the spam, and opened an e-mail from Jill. Her sister's missive was mostly newsy. She didn't get the part. Her air-conditioning was on the fritz in her apartment. She was thinking of getting a cat. Not one question about how Charlotte or their mother was doing.

Charlotte forgave her sister a lot. To be an actor with any sort of success, a person needed to focused. And to be a survivor required a certain amount of selfishness. Sometimes, though, Jill pushed it too far. Charlotte saved the message. She never responded to e-mail as soon as she got it. She knew people who got in trouble that way, jotting off a quick reactionary reply, and then having those words in print. Better to wait and chose what you wanted to say with a cool head.

The CEO's voice interrupted her reverie. "Bernard Rayney."

"Hi, it's Charlotte. I just found out that Bob Peterson's funeral service is tomorrow. I think you should make an appearance."

"What time is it?"

"Noon. What time were you planning to take your people to the casino?"

"We depart from Anaheim at three in the afternoon. It's going to be tight."

"I really advise you be there. Got a pen?"

"Shoot."

She told him the names of Bob's wife and kids. She also gave him the number of the funeral home. "A very nice gesture would be if you paid for the funeral. Dottie Peterson is not in good health and doesn't work, so Bob's salary was their sole means of income. Eventually, she'll get his Social Security benefits and life insurance money, but all that takes time."

"I'll see to it personally. Bob was a member of the Sun Rail family. We won't let his survivors down."

"You won't regret it," she said. They said their good-byes, and Charlotte turned off her computer and went into her bedroom to disrobe. While the tub filled, she studied the clothes in her closet. She couldn't remember the last time it took her so long to figure out what she would wear. She settled on hip-hugging jeans, low-heeled boots, and a sheer blouse that required a pretty lacy bra. Over this she wore a light linen blazer for her interview with Dixie. The underpants were fresh out the package, feminine but not slutty, a subconscious desire to look good for whoever undressed her next. Whether that someone would be Hannigan, an emergency room doctor, or the coroner, it was too soon to say.

CHAPTER 23

Todd Hannigan rang her doorbell at 6:00 P.M. She checked her image in the mirror one last time, grabbed her purse, and opened the door. Hannigan also wore jeans, pressed and clean, she noted. Brown loafers matched his belt. His Hawaiian shirt was tucked in.

"I thought you would be the type who was ready on time," he said.

"And what else did you think you know about me?" she asked, not sure she liked being thought of as a "type."

"That's all I got," he said. "Otherwise you're an enigma wrapped in a mystery."

"Good save," she said. "You ready?"

"No tour?"

"I told you I wanted to get there in daylight." She didn't wait to catch his reaction.

The company truck turned out to be a brand-new Dodge pickup. It still had that new car smell in the cab, and the passenger side looked as if it had never been used. She suspected that Hannigan had her figured out a lot more than he claimed. With the help of the FasTrak toll road and car pool lanes, they reached Timoteo Road by seven thirty. There they came to an abrupt halt behind the procession of cars that had come to pay tribute to Rachel or gawk at the scene of her death.

Charlotte consulted her directions. "We're looking for a blue mailbox."

"I feel like we're on a scavenger hunt," he said.

"We are."

At the blue mailbox, they turned right. "Okay, now we're going to come to a fork in the road. There'll be a picture of a horse—go the way the nose is pointing."

"Now you're just putting me on," he said.

"No, I'm serious." They arrived at the horse picture. The horse was painted on a wooden sign and was grinning and winking. "You see? Can't get more serious than that."

"Okay," he said, "I stand corrected. What now?"

"Her ranch is called the Crazy D. It used to be the Lazy D," she said, "but somebody painted over the *L* and added the *CR*, so she left it like that."

"So what exactly did she see?" he asked.

"That's what I want to talk to her about. She claims aliens borrowed her forklift."

"I'm going to take a wild stab here," he said. "She reported it to the police and they didn't believe her?"

"Right. She must have seen one of our flyers. I think it's worth checking out."

They crossed under the Crazy D sign. Todd hummed the *Twilight Zone* tune and headed for a cluster of buildings where several geriatric horses sought shade under a green fiberglass awning. On closer inspection, the house, stable, and tack room were all patched with sheets of plywood of varying vintage, more fiberglass, and sheets of tin.

A pack of dogs, representing at least ten different breeds, surrounded the truck and barked at varying pitches according to their size and age.

"We'll just wait here," Hannigan said. "If she's home, she'll come out."

"Works for me," Charlotte said. Several of the bigger dogs were jumping up and slobbering on her window. Their claws made scraping noises on the door as they took turns throwing themselves against the truck.

An older woman emerged from the house, whistling and waving her arms. She was outfitted in old jeans, cowboy boots, and a Western shirt trimmed with leather fringe and silver buttons. The dogs ran to her. She petted each one, her long white braid hitting the dirt as she bent to accommodate the smaller animals. When she straightened, it wasn't all the way.

"Dixie Lewis?" Charlotte asked.

"The same," she said, smiling to show large horse teeth yellowed with age. "Who's asking?"

Charlotte opened her door, and Hannigan followed suit. Charlotte handed the woman a business card. "I'm here on behalf of Sun Rail. You called in to our tip line?"

"Took you long enough," Dixie said. She turned to Hannigan. "You with Sun Rail, too?"

"No, ma'am. I work for the National Transportation Safety Board."

"Government man, huh?"

"He's all right," Charlotte said.

Hannigan raised an eyebrow, but didn't respond.

"C'mon then." Dixie limped to one of the outbuildings. Hannigan and Charlotte followed, noticing the S-curve of her spine distinctive against the thin white cotton of her vintage shirt.

They found themselves in a tack room full of bridles and saddles and posters of cowboys riding bucking broncos. "This is me," Dixie said, pointing to one of the posters proudly. "I was the first woman to ride in the rodeo. Won three blue ribbons, one for riding a bull. Broke my back twice, each arm once, and shattered my right leg." She lifted her shirt and turned around. "You see those scars? Three different surgeries to put my spinal column back together."

Charlotte and Hannigan examined her scars, making the proper sounds of amazement and sympathy while smiling at each other.

"Been written up in magazines, too."

"You said something about your forklift disappearing on the day of the accident?" Charlotte prompted.

"Yeah, the alien took it. Right in the heat of the day. Me and the dogs were inside, having our siesta. That's about all we're good for when it gets that hot."

"And by alien, you mean—," Hannigan said.

"It looked like a big insect, its head was all black and shiny and round. I couldn't even see the sucker's eyes. And there was this bright light, almost blinded me. I tried to communicate with it, but it wasn't having none of it." Dixie pulled a yellowed framed photo off the wall. "This was me in '74. The horse was named . . . Let me think a minute—"

Charlotte interrupted. "You said that the forklift was returned. May we inspect it?"

Dixie hobbled back outside and to an adjoining barn. She swung the doors open and showed them her equipment. The forklift was stripped to its bare necessities. The simple black roll bar and frame, single seat, and exposed engine reminded Charlotte of a dune buggy. The part she was interested in, the fork blades, were chipped with age and service.

Dixie climbed aboard and started it up. There was no ignition key, only a button. The forklift was surprisingly quiet. Charlotte expected it to sound like a leaf blower or tractor, but the exhaust was well muffled.

"Bought it used from one of those rent-a-Dumpster outfits," Dixie explained.

Hannigan's eyes were riveted on the forks. "Excuse me a minute."

He ran out to the truck and returned moments later with a camera, tape measurer, and an evidence envelope. Charlotte held the tape while he measured the distance between the two blades. He also measured the width of each blade and the distance they were from the ground at the lift's lowest position. Charlotte held a ruler next to them to give the shot dimension while Hannigan took photographs. The last thing he did was to take scrapings off the tips of the blades.

"So is there some kind of reward for all this?" Dixie asked.

"You bet," Charlotte said. "I'll take care of it personally. Thank you so much for calling this in."

"I wanted to call NASA, but it was a toll call."

"Can I use your bathroom before we go?" Charlotte asked.

"Sure, help yourself." Dixie pointed to her house. "The door's open."

Charlotte left Hannigan to entertain Dixie and went into the house. She was tempted to ask Dixie if she had perhaps been dropped on her head during one of her rides, but thought it might be rude. The dogs stayed with their mistress and didn't seem the least concerned about Charlotte's trespass into their domain. The first thing Charlotte noticed about the house was the wall-to-wall dog beds with bowls of water next to each one. The next thing that caught her attention was the curtains. They were heavy and double layered, blackout curtains. Much like the kind found in Las Vegas hotels that completely shut out the neon lights of the city that never slept. Charlotte imagined the shock to the eyes and senses of leaving this dark cocoon and stepping directly into the bright sun of a July summer day. She went into the bathroom and washed her hands using her own soap. The medicine cabinet was ajar, so she nudged it open the rest of the way with her elbow. The shelves were filled with prescription medication. Vicodin,

Percocet, Soma, codeine, and Valium. If Charlotte were taking any or all of these, she'd be taking regular siestas, too. She took a photograph of the pharmaceuticals and then put the cabinet door back the way she'd found it.

Hannigan was speaking slowly and carefully to Dixie when Charlotte joined them outside. "I'd like to come back tomorrow and visit you again. I'm going to bring some other men and a big truck if that's all right with you."

"You gonna call NASA?" Dixie asked.

"If we find evidence of aliens, they'll be the first people we contact."

"Now you're talking. Sure, bring all the scientists you want. We'll just see what's what." Dixie was still smiling smugly as she waved good-bye.

When they were alone again in the truck and heading back down the hill, Charlotte told Hannigan about what she had discovered in the house.

"What a great witness she'll make," he said.

"Hopefully, the evidence will speak for itself."

He maneuvered the truck down the rutted dirt road. Dust swirled around the windows like smoke. "We'll bring out a length of rail, anchor it on some ties, and then ram the forklift blades into the side of it." He looked at her sideways. "You do know that if the tool marks match, we're going to have to call the FBI back in."

"I'm fine with that. They won't get in my way at all."

Hannigan grinned. "Where to now, Sherlock?"

"Let's eat."

"On one condition," he said.

"What's that?"

"No shop talk at dinner. I want to hear more about the Witness Protection thing."

"That's only fair, I suppose."

Hannigan found them a home-style Mexican restaurant. Telemundo played on the television over the counter, and mostly Mexicans filled the seats. "That's a good sign," he said. "If they're eating here, then you know the food is going to be good and authentic."

"You're some kind of detective," she said.

The waitress was a surly, raven-haired thirty-something with heavy eye makeup and a definite attitude against tourists or gringos or both. Hannigan ordered them beers. Charlotte conversed with the waitress in Spanish. Not school Spanish, but as Hannigan would say "authentic" Mexican Spanish. It was the language of her mother's family, though now her mother spoke only English. Charlotte had kept her Spanish tuned, recognizing at an early age the advantage of being bilingual, especially in Southern California.

The waitress, Carmen, defrosted as they bantered. When the busboy arrived with the chips and salsa, Carmen pointed to the inferior canned sauce in the small white dish and told him to bring the fresh stuff. She left them menus and tips on what was best to order.

Hannigan watched the exchange with awe. "You're just full of surprises."

"I should hope so." She dipped a chip in the homemade salsa the busboy had returned with and savored the bite of fresh cilantro.

Hannigan handed her an envelope. "You could have just asked me yourself."

"What are you talking about?"

"Our receptionist couldn't help but notice the pointed nature of your friend Dennis O'Connor's questions."

"He's no friend of mine," she said truthfully.

"Was he asking questions at your behest?" Hannigan persisted.

She had no choice but to be honest. "Yes, he was."

"And you thought I needed an alibi established?" He handed her an envelope.

"What's this?"

"Open it."

There were two things inside the envelope: A strip of X-ray film that was dated and labeled HANNIGAN. There was also a letter that was written on the stationery of Dr. Kerr, DDS. "To whom it may concern," it read, "Todd Hannigan spent the morning of Tuesday, July 13, in my office. He had a cleaning, X-rays, and a filling in one of his back molars replaced." The dentist signed the note and included his home and cell phone numbers.

"You brought me a note from your doctor?" Her ears were probably the color of an ambulance beacon.

"It seemed important to you, and I didn't want you to waste your time suspecting me." He smiled. "And because I like you."

Again she stuck with the truth. "The feeling's mutual."

She felt herself grinning like a madwoman. Her relief was palpable, and she had to struggle to regain control over herself.

He dipped another tortilla chip.

She briefly reflected on the PR friend of hers who had come up with the phrase *restaurant-style*. He said he'd been in the shower when it came to him. That got her thinking about men taking showers, and how you could make out their silhouettes through the glass with the water running down their bodies—running everywhere—forming tiny waterfalls, like drinking fountains. . . .

"So, you were going to tell me about your childhood," Hannigan said.

She had to clear her throat and take a sip of water before she spoke. She ran a hand over her hair, half-expecting it to be as damp as the rest of her.

"You mean the Witness Protection thing? Not much to tell. My mom helped the Feds with a case against some bad guys. In exchange, they relocated us."

"So is Charlotte even your real name?"

220

"Actually it's Charles, but they can do amazing things with surgery and hormone therapy."

Hannigan started to react, but then caught himself. "Okay, so you all get new identities and a new home. Isn't that supposed to be a permanent thing?"

"The bad guys ended up dead, or in prison, or living on the streets and really weren't a threat anymore. Then my mom asked for more money from our FBI handlers, and they responded by turning us out. After that, we were on our own." Later, Charlotte learned from her aunt that her mom had claimed one of the guys she ratted out was stalking the family. The guy she named was an unfortunate choice since he had been killed six months earlier. The Feds were touchy about attempted extortion, and completely heartless when it came to the impact on Jill and Charlotte.

"So then what happened?" he asked, obviously sensing that there was much more to the story than she was revealing.

"We went back to living in Los Angeles so my mother could pursue her interests."

"Which were?"

"Dope, sex, and rock and roll."

"Must have been groovy."

"That was one word for it."

Carmen returned and they ordered.

Charlotte checked out the Spanish soap opera going on above them. Kohl-eyed vamps sneered at each other. Cleavage abounded. "It wasn't all bad," she conceded. "I had a lot of freedom. My mom or one of her friends would give me and my sister money to blow on candy and junk food as we roamed the streets. I didn't know what she doing then. Later I figured out that she was partying. When I was a teenager, I used to hide her stash and try to get her to get a job or at least to exercise a little."

Hannigan hadn't touched the chips or his beer since she began talking. "How did your sister handle it?"

"Jill was smarter. She saw that my screaming and yelling wasn't getting us anywhere, so she went the sweet route. People were always taking her on trips, letting her stay with them when we were between apartments. One family even gave her a car when she turned sixteen."

"And now she lives far away," he observed.

"I don't begrudge her that. She's doing what she has to do." *And she still managed to be Mom's favorite.* Charlotte didn't say the last out loud. She wasn't looking for pity, and besides, showing jealousy would tarnish her halo. *And who asked me to put it on in the first place?*

"What now, Sherlock?" he asked.

"Two things." She told him about the GHB and how she needed to use his lab equipment to verify her suspicions.

"No problem," he said. "I'll set it up tomorrow. What was the other thing?"

For a long moment, the only thing that came to mind was her clean underwear. "I was hoping we could swing by an apartment in Orange."

"Whose apartment?"

"One of the maintenance people from the stockyard in Anaheim. He didn't show up for work on Wednesday, and no one's been able to get a hold of him since."

"All right," he said, "but can I pick the third thing?"

"That's only fair."

They devoured their food when it arrived. It was good. So good that they kept eating even after they were full. They didn't speak until they had cleaned their plates. Hannigan again picked up the check, leaving Carmen a generous tip. All in all, it was a perfect second date until they found the body.

CHAPTER 24

The ride back to Orange County was uneventful. Between the glow of the good meal and the warm satisfaction of feeling that they were really getting somewhere on the case, they lapsed into an easy silence. Hannigan turned on the radio and tuned it to a classic rock station.

Lorrin Wood, the man they hoped to interview, lived in a ground-floor condo. The place had probably been an apartment building at one time and then converted. Each unit had a separate street address, but were all part of the same three-story building. There were five units to each floor. The upper levels had balconies. Their quarry, the maintenance man who had not showed up for work since Tuesday, had a small plot of grass and some fledgling impatiens in pots by the front door. The flowers drooped and had shed most of their leaves.

Three days of newspapers littered the front steps.

The front units shared a thigh-high picket fence. Identical aluminum mailboxes stood on four-by-fours by the gates. Hannigan opened the one belonging to the AWOL employee and found it stuffed with three days of mail.

They proceeded up the walkway. The porch light flicked on. "Motion activated," Hannigan said, pointing to the sensors.

Charlotte looked at the soil in the flowerpots and saw that it was dry. "I'm getting a bad feeling about this."

Hannigan put his nose to the front window, hands cupped over his eyes to block out the bright porch light. "I think he's home, and it looks like he's dead."

Charlotte wiped the glass with a tissue and looked for herself. There was a man inside. He had a noose wrapped around his neck and was hanging from the ceiling. He was also naked and bloated. The mode of death and the fact that he was naked were both classic signs of suicide.

"I hope he left a note," Charlotte said.

Hannigan was already on his cell phone. "Let's find out."

Charlotte listened as he explained to the police dispatcher that they had discovered a dead body. He gave the address and his name, then hung up.

"What did they say?" she asked.

"To wait for the police and not to touch anything." They sat down on the step to wait. After a moment, the porch light switched off. "So what do you want to do for our third date?"

Obviously, the personal part of the evening had come to an abrupt end. She knew she should be feeling sadder about the dead guy inside instead of the interruption of her social life, but in truth she didn't know the deceased and it had been a long dry spell between hookups.

"Maybe a movie," she said.

"Works for me. You gonna come out tomorrow and watch the test?"

"No, I have a funeral to attend. Sorry."

"Bob Peterson's?" he asked.

"Yeah." They sat side by side in the dark. The evening was warm, except where Hannigan's leg casually brushed her own. There it was hot. He was making it very difficult to shift back to work mode. "Can my investigator Hank Nunzio come and observe the demonstration?"

"Sure." Hannigan reached over and took her hand in his. The gesture seemed as natural as the moon overhead breaking through a cloud.

"I guess we better notify Chip Stillwell, too."

"Charlotte?"

"Hmm?"

He leaned toward her. She was finding it difficult to breathe, and then she realized it was because she was holding her breath. She giggled at her own awkwardness. He wasn't deterred.

"Shut up, will you?"

She didn't answer him with words. His lips were warm and surprisingly soft. They lingered that way for a few seconds; then they heard the approaching sirens.

He broke away smiling. "It's showtime."

"Just when I was enjoying the halftime show." She stood to await the authorities.

In addition to the police, a fire engine and a paramedic responded. The first cop on the scene told Charlotte and Hannigan to wait on the sidewalk. After shining his flashlight through the window, the cop called over his shoulder to the paramedics. "Don't rush. He looks pretty ripe. Been dead for a couple of days at least." He radioed for a coroner and the homicide inspectors on duty. Then he tilted back the flowerpots, finding a rusted key under the second one he tried.

Not such a secret hiding place, Charlotte thought. She would never hide her spare key in such an obvious spot. Not that that had stopped whoever had broken in the other night.

When the officer opened the door, the pungent fetid aroma of decay wafted out. He swept the room with his flashlight.

"Did he leave a note?" Charlotte asked.

The cop left the door ajar and walked back to where Hannigan and Charlotte waited. "I'll leave that for the coroner to investigate. Are you relatives? Friends?"

"Actually, we never met," Charlotte said. "He hadn't shown up for work since Tuesday, and I was in the neighborhood so I thought I'd check on him."

"But you never met?"

"No, but we work for the same company and I've been looking into some improprieties. That's why I asked if there was a note. Maybe he was worried he was going to get caught, or maybe feeling bad about what he did. If he made a confession, that would really make my job a lot simpler."

"You got a name for the guy?" the cop asked.

"Lorrin Wood."

"And who are you?" the cop asked Hannigan.

"The boyfriend."

The cops ended up keeping them for another two hours, but Charlotte was rewarded in the end with a quick peek at Lorrin Wood's suicide note.

I'M SORRY, it read, I NEVER MEANT TO HURT SO MANY PEOPLE.

Great, Charlotte thought, would it have been too much to ask for him to be a tiny bit more specific or to add a line telling her who his accomplices were?

"What do you think?" Hannigan asked as they drove back to her house.

"I suspected there was an inside man. His suicide doesn't prove he was involved in the derailment, and it certainly doesn't let Sun Rail off the hook."

"You know I can't make my investigation come out any certain way," he said.

"Who asked you to? God, is that what you think?" She pulled away from him.

"No. Wait. I'm an idiot. I'm sorry."

She was too pissed to consider his lame handoff. "Tell you what, stud. Let's just put whatever's happening between us on hold until the case is done. I would hate to taint either of our reputations with bullshit accusations of favoritism."

Hannigan sighed. "I'm sure you're right. Damn it."

They didn't speak again until he dropped her off at her house and saw her safely inside her door.

"Thank you for running those tests tomorrow," she said.

"Don't mention it. I'm very motivated to close this case."

She surprised both of them by stealing one last kiss.

SATURDAY

CHAPTER 25

Dennis O'Connor called at 8 A.M. "I'm not waking you, am I?"

"Emm, a little bit. But that's okay." Charlotte rubbed her eyes and took a sip of water from the bottle by her bed.

"Hot date last night?"

"Why are you calling?" she asked.

"I got an interview with Farrah Kent's mother. She agreed to meet with us at her home this afternoon."

"What time? I'm going to the Peterson funeral at noon."

"Two thirty. Where's the funeral?"

"Fullerton." She told him the streets.

"You should have time to make an appearance and then hop on the Five. Farrah Kent's family lives about thirty minutes from there. Traffic should be lighter on a Saturday."

"Does Farrah's mother know that today is the day of Bob Peterson's funeral? The man who last saw her daughter alive?"

"That's one of the questions I'll be asking her. Don't forget to bring your camera."

"I never do."

She got out of bed and stretched, feeling happier than normal. She knew just whom to thank for that.

Just to keep some balance in the universe, her mom called at ten.

"They're letting me go home today."

"Well, that's good. Did you get your biopsy results?"

"Oh yeah, didn't I mention it? Stage four cirrhosis and my hep C viral count is off the charts." Charlotte knew from her research on the Internet that stage four was the worst.

"Oh, Mom," Charlotte said, sitting down. She knew they were expecting this, but to hear it confirmed . . . "I'm so sorry."

"Are you crying?"

Charlotte sniffled. "Yes. I'm sorry. I didn't expect to be so shocked. I guess I was holding out some hope that they were wrong."

"I'm not dead yet, kiddo." Lisa's voice was soft, even tender.

"What can I do for you?" Charlotte asked, ready in that moment to blow off everything else.

"You said something about sending a car for me?" Lisa said.

"Or I can come myself. I just have to make some calls, cancel a few things."

"No, don't do that. I know you have a big case going on. They said I could go home anytime. I'll just wait until the car gets here."

Charlotte looked outside for other signs of the apocalypse, but the rest of the world still seemed to be obeying the laws of gravity. The ocean and sky were still blue. Birds still flew right side up, and so forth. "Okay, thanks. I'll come see you later." She gripped the phone tightly, struggling to say exactly the right thing. "I love you, Mom."

"I love you, too, baby."

As soon as Charlotte hung up, she called a livery service that she used often enough to have a corporate account.

"I need a sedan to pick up my mother and take her home." She gave the dispatcher the addresses and her mom's name. "She probably doesn't have any food at home, so if the driver could pick up some deli sandwiches, orange juice, milk, and a fruit tray."

"Certainly, Ms. Lyon, anything else?"

"Give the driver an extra twenty-dollar tip, and have him or her call me when my mom is safely home."

"You've got it."

The funeral for Bob Peterson was held in small chapel on a hill overlooking the north end of Orange County. The cityscape was laced with storm drains and railroad tracks. The warning knells of train horns periodically punctured the quiet, but also seemed entirely fitting. Some seventy mourners lined the pews. Among them, she was happy to see, were CEO Rayney, Mary Nightengale, and the ever-faithful Andrew. She also recognized Stanley Mack, the train master, but it took her a second. Not only was he out of context, but he was wearing a dark suit, his hair was clean and styled, and a beautiful redheaded woman hung on his arm.

The widow was in the front row. Sam Ricketts sat beside her, his arm around her shoulder in a protective, almost proprietary manner. If Charlotte didn't know better, she would have pegged them as husband and wife. Sam had also gone to great lengths with his appearance. Dottie's daughter, Stacie, sat on his other side. In profile, Charlotte realized with a jolt, Stacie Peterson and Sam Ricketts shared a nose.

Mary Nightengale caught Charlotte's eyes and gestured to the door. The service wasn't going to begin for another fifteen minutes, so Charlotte met the woman outside. Andrew watched anxiously as they departed, probably wondering if he was needed. Charlotte mouthed to him that they would be right back.

Mary's cheeks were flushed and her eyes sparkled. Charlotte wondered what sort of news she had that was so urgent.

Mary spoke softly but quickly. "I delivered the check to the Rachel Priest Foundation."

"Good. How was it received?"

"Gratefully. I met with the chairman of the board, and she had some interesting things to say about Sherwood."

Mary waited to be prompted. Charlotte played along. "Tell me everything."

"Sherwood used to be on the board. He even drew a small stipend. But then funds started disappearing, especially cash donations. They kept it quiet, but the upshot was that instead of prosecuting him for embezzlement, he was kicked off the board. There were a lot of hard feelings from everyone. The people who truly loved Rachel wanted to press charges. Apparently, she was very wounded by his double-dealings and blamed herself for not being a good enough mother. Out of respect for her wishes, Sherwood escaped prosecution. He was also cut off from the cash cow he'd been milking."

"Do they want to press charges now?" Charlotte asked.

"Even better. They've offered us the evidence against him. They figured that any damage they did to his lawsuit would hit him where it hurt."

"Are they proposing we blackmail Sherwood into backing off?" Charlotte didn't like it. Blackmail had a way of hurting everyone.

"Dom said it was more like leverage," Mary said, obviously a little hurt by Charlotte's less-than-ecstatic reaction.

"You went to Dom first?"

"I figured it fell within his domain," Mary said. "Was I wrong?"

"You're a team player and a company woman," Charlotte said tactfully, ducking a direct answer. Scruples and ethics were between Mary and her conscience.

The service was over by two. Sam Ricketts stood with Dottie and

Stacy to receive the mourners. Charlotte spoke to Dottie while some-one else was holding her hand. "I'm so sorry for your loss."

"Are you coming over to the house after?" Ricketts asked.

"No, thank you. I have an appointment."

He didn't seem that disappointed. In fact, he seemed very comfort-able stepping into the shoes of his dead friend.

CHAPTER 26

Farrah Kent's mother lived in an older home in Costa Mesa, on the kind of residential street where people raised their children, took pride in their yards, and knew their neighbors. Or so Charlotte imagined, having never had the experience of living in such a place.

The street was lined with fifteen-year-old cars and the economy models at that. She realized how out of place she was here with her shiny new Mercedes. She parked half a block away and joined Dennis on foot, her camera in hand, the release form in her purse.

"There you are," he said, giving her a full up-and-down with his eyes, then a slow, seductive smile to demonstrate how pleasing he found her.

"Live and in person," she replied, not at all swayed by his charm.

"Shall we do this?" Dennis opened the front gate and invited Charlotte to precede him.

"You lead," she said. "I want to watch the master at work." They walked past a statue of Saint Francis and onto the front porch. The figure of Saint Mary resided in an alcove by the front door.

Dennis knocked. There was no answer. He rang the bell. They

heard the chimes echo through the house, but still got no response. The curtains were drawn, but there was a small triangle left open where they had caught on what looked like a couch in the front room.

Charlotte peeked through it. The interior of the living room was lit by several flickering votive candles. Head shots of Jesus—appearing cleaner, better groomed, and more Caucasian than she imagined he ever had in real life—looked down benevolently from the walls.

Charlotte cupped her hands over her eyes to block out the day's bright sunshine and after some seconds, she was able to make out more details in the room. A woman in a bathrobe rocked in a wooden rocking chair. She clutched a framed photograph to her chest and stared straight ahead. Occasionally she would wipe at her eyes with a tissue. The rocking reminded Charlotte of autistic children, lost in their own world. Margaret Reynolds's private world didn't look as if it were a happy place.

Charlotte straightened and faced Dennis. "You spoke to this woman on the phone?"

"Yes. She said she'd be home all day."

"Well, I'd say she's home and she's not."

"You saw her in there?"

"Yeah. She's sitting in the front room with the lights off."

Dennis tried the doorbell again, this time yelling, "Mrs. Reynolds? It's Dennis O'Connor. We spoke on the phone yesterday. We have an appointment."

They waited a few more long minutes. Dennis knocked once more and repeated his message through the mail slot in the front door.

"She's probably having one of her days," a voice called out from behind them.

They turned.

An elderly man in a cardigan was standing on the sidewalk. His obviously male Scottish terrier marked a tree.

"Do you know Mrs. Reynolds?" Charlotte asked.

"We've been neighbors for nigh on forty years." The dog moved on to the gate and marked that as well.

They left the front porch to join him on the sidewalk. "What do you mean by one of her days?" Charlotte asked. "Is she ill?"

"Sick at heart is more like it. Ever since she lost her girl."

Charlotte studied the freshly mowed lawn and the weed-free flower beds. "Is someone taking care of her?"

"Oh yeah. Her son lives with her. He's a good boy. Quiet, but I guess that's to be expected." The dog waddled over to Dennis's car and blessed the tire with a few drops of urine. Charlotte was now very glad she had parked down the street.

"Should we leave a note?" Dennis asked.

"Who'd you say you were with?" the old man asked.

Dennis handed him a business card. "She wanted to talk to me about her daughter."

The old guy didn't ask if Charlotte was also with the newspaper. She had been ready to lift her camera by way of explanation.

"Might do her some good," the old guy said. "Come back tomorrow. She never misses morning Mass. The church ladies bring her home around eleven. That would be your best bet."

The old man moseyed on, his prolific dog at his heels.

"What do you think?" Dennis asked. "You want to try again tomorrow?"

"Absolutely. I'll see you at eleven."

"It's a date," Dennis said.

It most certainly is not, Charlotte thought even as she smiled at him with lowered eyelids. Two could play the old charm game.

They parted.

She had turned off her phone and now she saw that she had a message. It was the limo driver, telling her that her mom had gotten home safely. Charlotte stopped at a Ralphs and bought yellow rubber gloves, sponges, 409, Lysol, various scrub brushes, and a mop.

It was one thing to tell someone you loved them, another to show it.

She found her mom swaddled in a blanket on the couch, eating a sandwich and watching television. "What are you doing here?" she asked when Charlotte came through the door with her cleaning supplies.

"Nice to see you, too."

"Didn't you have a meeting or something?"

"I got stood up. How are you feeling?"

"They gave me some pills to keep down my water weight and told me to go off salt."

Charlotte went into the bathroom and changed into jeans, a T-shirt, and tennis shoes. After folding her good clothes carefully and sealing them in plastic bags, she ripped open the packaging on her supplies and put on the elbow-length yellow gloves.

"Where do you keep your bucket, Mom?"

"My bucket? What in the world? . . ." She stopped talking when Charlotte reentered the room.

"I'll start in the kitchen."

"You don't have to do this," Lisa said.

"I wanted to. Nothing like getting a clean start." Charlotte started in the kitchen. Throwing out moldy food in the refrigerator and cleaning it as thoroughly as only the obsessed can. While she worked, she thought about the many different relationships people had with their mothers. That brought her back to the case and all the messy lives she had uncovered.

At the sound of the moldy bread hitting the trash can, Lisa called out, "What are you doing in there? Don't go throwing a bunch of my stuff away."

"I'll buy you another loaf of bread, Mom."

"And don't go moving my shit around. I know where everything is."

"I don't know how," Charlotte said, wiping a lock of hair from her eye.

"It might seem a big mess to you, but it's my mess."

Charlotte almost laughed. Those were probably the truest words her mother had ever spoken. Charlotte could get the place tip-top, and in a week it would be back to unwashed dishes in the sink, overflowing wastepaper baskets, and seven days' worth of dirty underwear on the bathroom floor.

"Okay, Mom, you win. I'll just make a pass at the bathroom and run a load of laundry for you."

"You want to watch some TV? There's some good old movies on." She patted the couch cushion next to her, dislodging crumbs and sending dust and cat hair swirling in the air above it.

"We'll see," Charlotte said.

She thought about Hannigan as she stripped her mother's bed and remade it with clean floral printed sheets. Would he like her as much when he got to know her better? Would he be willing to indulge her idiosyncrasies? He could do a lot worse than a neat freak. Wait till he met her mom. On second thought, he didn't need to meet her mom for a least a year. Charlotte might be obsessive and compulsive, but she wasn't stupid.

She fluffed the pillows and turned to leave. That's when she spotted them. A collage of posters and photographs were tacked to the wall above the dresser. It made Charlotte think of a teenager's room, the walls filled with rock idols and posters. There were playbills from some, probably all, of Jill's plays, and newspaper clippings. Charlotte at first thought these were reviews, but on closer inspection discovered they were articles written of crises she had unwound. And next to all these, the *Forbes* magazine piece. Her mother must have bought two copies of the magazine, because every page (including the double-backed ones) that her profile was on, appeared in order on the wall. The pages were then bookended by two of the cover photos of Charlotte.

Lisa was asleep on the couch when Charlotte returned to the front room. She tucked the blanket around her mom's ample shoulders and kissed her lightly on the cheek. Then she let herself out.

CHAPTER 27

Charlotte watched Rachel Priest's funeral extravaganza on the TV in her bedroom. She had taken a hot bath, made a cup of chamomile tea, and wrapped herself in a soft white terry cloth robe. Her tea cooled on the nightstand as a blue facial mask dried on her face. The procession wound through the streets of Hollywood. Tourists lined the street, taking photographs. She concentrated on the red polish she was applying to her toenails.

Hannigan called halfway through.

"So, what are you wearing?" he asked.

She laughed. "How was your date with Dixie?"

"Nunzio and Stillwell were there, too, with sections of rail to perform field tests. Dixie charged us twenty bucks a pop to ram her forklift into the sides of them."

"Good for her."

"CJ has the day off, but he said he'd come in tomorrow to compare tool marks."

"What do you think?"

"I think it's a distinct possibility that we'll find a match."

She screwed the cap back on the polish. "If the Safelok clips had been removed and the rail rammed from the side, would the engineer have spotted it?"

"If he were looking close, he probably would have noticed the narrower gauge."

"Would it have alarmed him enough to engage the emergency brake?"

"I should think, but that's only a guess. He would have been expecting a rail problem to appear as a warping of the rail outward, not inward. If that slowed his reaction or make him overreact, I can't say. I'm inclined to give any engineer the benefit of the doubt, especially one with Bob Peterson's safety record, and say that he acted in an entirely appropriate manner."

"That's good to know. I'm not sure if it will be much consolation to his wife and kid, but it sure beats finding him at fault."

"Did you go to the funeral today?" he asked.

"Yeah. There was a good turnout."

"How about your mom?"

"Well, she's home. She was in good spirits when I left her."

"You must be exhausted," he said.

"Tomorrow will be a light day. I just have one interview scheduled. By Monday I'll be ready to slay dragons again." Actually, she was feeling very positive. She now had the complete scenario of how exactly the train came to derail. All she needed now was the identities and motives of the bad guys, and she was closing in on those. When she had all those last few pieces in place, she could sell it to the public.

SUNDAY

CHAPTER 28

Charlotte wrote Jill a long e-mail explaining their mother's condition and wishing her sister well. She did some housecleaning and laundry, watered her houseplants, and painted the spot where the nick had been. She had spackled the night before. It would be dry enough for a second coat by the time she got back from her meeting with Margaret Reynolds.

The autopsy on Lorrin Wood, the apparent suicide victim she and Hannigan had discovered, was scheduled for early Monday morning. Charlotte told the Orange County medical examiner to be sure to test for excessive amounts of GHB in the man's system.

She dressed conservatively and then headed for Costa Mesa. She allowed an hour for beach traffic and took the Coast Highway north. The next town up the coast was Corona del Mar. It had a villagelike atmosphere. Dolphin topiaries danced in the center meridian and were decorated according to holidays. On the Fourth of July, they sported Uncle Sam hats and carried small flags in their fins. At Christmas, they cavorted in white-trimmed red Santa caps.

The streets of Corona del Mar were named after flowers and arranged alphabetically going from north to south: Acacia, Begonia,

Carnation, and so on. Addresses on the flower roads were so desirable that residents were willing to brave the impossible parking on narrow streets to live in upstairs garage apartments with addresses measured in fractions. Almost every beach cottage had a second unit behind it, and some an apartment above that.

She appreciated the charm but preferred less crowded conditions.

The next town north was Newport Beach. Mercedes, Porche, and Rolls-Royce dealerships lined the highway. The discerning buyer also had his or her pick of yacht shops to browse. It was widely held to be the unofficial breast augmentation and Pamela Anderson–look-alike capital of the world. Plastic surgery was also not for Charlotte. She couldn't imagine undergoing elective surgery.

On Newport Boulevard she turned right, heading inland for Costa Mesa. She was early, but Dennis had still arrived at the Reynolds's home first. She parked up the street again and walked back to his car.

"She's not home from church yet," he said.

"So we bushwhack her before she gets inside?" Charlotte asked.

"But gently."

"Of course."

"How goes your investigation?" he asked.

"You'll have your story soon," she promised. "But I'm hoping to identify who was behind the sabotage before we break the story."

He raised his eyebrows. "You sure it was sabotage?"

"Absolutely. You're looking at a scoop that will get you a segment on *Sixty Minutes.*"

Dennis all but licked his lips.

A twenty-year-old but well-maintained four-door Buick sedan pulled into the Reynolds's driveway. Margaret Reynolds got out of the backseat and waved good-bye to her escorts. She was wearing a black dress that hung on her bones. Her shoes were scuffed, and her purse didn't quite match. A lace doily was pinned to the top of her head.

The woman walked slowly to her front gate, taking each step as if lifting her feet were a monumental effort.

"Margaret Reynolds?" Dennis asked.

She turned. "What is it?" Terror showed on her face as if she were expecting more bad news.

"Nothing's wrong," Charlotte said quickly.

Dennis opened her gate and offered her his arm. "I'm Dennis. Dennis O'Connor. We had an appointment for an interview."

She let him lead her to her door. "Was that today?"

"We won't take much of your time, ma'am."

Charlotte trailed behind. Dennis was smooth; there was no disputing that.

Mrs. Reynolds opened the door and led them inside. "My son isn't home right now. Did you want to talk to him, too?"

"Eventually," Dennis said.

They sat in the living room. "Do you mind if I draw the curtains?" Charlotte asked. "It's such a beautiful day."

Mrs. Reynolds scratched at a stain she discovered on her dress. "Is it?"

Charlotte took that as a yes and allowed some sunshine into the room. A shaft of light seemed to spotlight a shrine on the coffee table dedicated to Farrah. The wax from many spent candles covered the glass surface, creating a topographical map of grief.

The woman was obviously drowning. She needed help, possibly medication. Before they left, Charlotte would get the work number of the son and talk him into getting his mother into counseling. This wasn't fair to him either.

"Would it bother you to talk about your daughter?" Dennis asked.

"She was a happy child. I have pictures of her birthday parties, pony rides, Christmases." Mrs. Reynolds pulled out a photo album from the bookshelf and put it in Dennis's lap. She turned the pages with trembling hands. "See? See how she's smiling and laughing. She had the most beautiful smile."

Charlotte heard the desperation in the woman's voice. Desperation and guilt, as she feverishly presented the evidence of her daughter's happy but too-short life.

"I'm very sorry for your loss," Charlotte said.

"That's why I know it was an accident. I don't know why the railroad is doing this to us. We don't want their money."

"What about your son-in-law?" Dennis asked.

"Lance? He's no kin of mine. He took my grandbaby away. The truth didn't matter to him. He didn't believe in mortal sin. Now, he won't even talk to me anymore; he says we're all nutty. Blames me for Farrah's postpartum depression. She loved her little baby. She loved her life. She had no reason to be depressed."

"What does your son think?" Charlotte asked.

"My son is the only one I have left. The only one who understands."

"And he lives here with you?" Dennis asked.

"Yes. He would never abandon me." Tears leaked down her face, but she didn't seem to be aware of them.

"Can I get you some water?" Charlotte asked.

"Thank you, dear. I'm not much of a hostess, am I?"

"Don't give it a thought," Dennis said. "Charlotte is happy to help. We all want to help you."

Charlotte found the kitchen easily. The son had left his mother Post-it Notes on the pantry door and the refrigerator, urging her to eat. Charlotte opened the refrigerator and found he had filled it with cups of pudding, halves of sandwiches, cut-up fruit, and raw vegetables. On each, there was a note that read EAT ME.

She filled a glass with water and brought it back to Mrs. Reynolds.

Dennis looked at her expectantly. She took the cue.

"Mrs. Reynolds. Are you aware that the engineer of the train that collided with your daughter passed away this week?"

"Yes, my son told me."

"I have a document with me. You don't have to sign it now. Wait and discuss it with your son."

"What sort of document?"

"It's an agreement between you and Sun Rail. If you sign a release of liability, they will not present any argument that your daughter's tragic death was anything but a horrible accident. I'm also a personal friend of the Riverside coroner. I believe I can convince him to reverse his ruling of suicide." There were times, and this was one of them, when Charlotte's rule of uncompromising honesty could be relaxed a little.

A small spark of life flickered in Margaret Reynolds's eyes. "I'll sign it now."

"No. I don't want you to act without your son's approval. Besides, it will have to be notarized. I'll just leave it on the table here along with my card. Have him call me when he gets home."

"All right."

Charlotte was skeptical that the woman had it together enough to deliver the message correctly. "Can I use your restroom?"

"It's down the hall."

Dennis resumed his questions after Charlotte excused herself. When she was out of eyeshot, she wrote a note to the son explaining who she was and what she was offering. She asked him to call her at his earliest convenience and clipped one of her cards to the note. Then she opened doors until she found the son's bedroom.

"Oh, my God," she said out loud. Over the son's bed were motorcycle posters, specifically dirt bikes. Four dusty, smiling guys in protective gear smiled at the camera from a framed photo on the dresser. She had no trouble picking out the familiar face among them. It was Andrew.

She grabbed the photo and ran into the living room. "Mrs. Reynolds," she said as she fought to get her breathing under control, "is this your son?"

"Yes. Where did you get that?"

"I went into his room by mistake and found it," she said.

Dennis stared at her sharply, sensing that something big was up. His instincts weren't wrong.

"Where is your son now?" Charlotte asked.

"He might be on his motorcycle today. You can check the garage and see if it's in there."

"I'll come with you," Dennis said.

They walked outside, picking up their pace when they hit the yard. Dennis lifted the garage door. Charlotte found the light switch on the wall.

The motorcycle wasn't there. Charlotte spotted a workbench and moved in for a closer look. Without a word, she slid her camera shutter open and starting documenting. There were many fine tools for small intricate jobs. Awls, drill bits the diameter of pencil lead, a tiny funnel, syringes. Tacked to the wall was a wiring schematic for railroad signal lights, track switches, and the wires that ran inside the rails. He'd been doing something with alligator clips, solder, and a soldering gun. Small rubber cylindrical husks of wiring insulation littered the area under the vise.

"Look at this," Dennis said. He held open a cabinet full of industrial cleaning solvents, beakers, Bunsen burners, and butane.

She photographed those as well.

Dennis studied the debris on the workbench. "What do you suppose he was making?"

"A shunt to fool the signal light and give the engineer false information. I need to make some calls before we have another derail on our hands."

CHAPTER 29

Charlotte ran to her car. Dennis followed, and she reluctantly let him in. She called Stanley Mack first. He wasn't in his office, so she tried his cell. She knew he kept it on and charged in case of an emergency. The news she had certainly qualified.

"What trains are running today?" she asked.

"Just the one. Mr. Rayney and his party are returning from their casino jaunt."

She quickly outlined what she had discovered. "We need to stop that train until we can locate Andrew and find out what he's been up to."

"Call Rayney on his cell, and I'll get word to the dispatcher to halt the train."

"Where are we going?" Dennis asked.

"To the desert." She called Rayney, but his phone either wasn't on or he was out of the service area. She left a message for him to call her immediately. She hopped on the 55 Freeway, which would connect with the 91 to Riverside. If she pushed it, she would be in the Calimesa area within an hour. "Keep an eye out for cops," she told Dennis, "and buckle up. We're going to catch this son of a bitch in the act."

Charlotte realized that all the answers had been staring her in the face. Andrew had been so solicitous, and almost invisible. What better way to track the investigation than to attach himself to the investigator. Andrew had been the one to supply her with the list of new hires: a list he made sure he wasn't on. Andrew also had access to her house keys. It would have been a simple matter for him to make copies while she had dinner with Hannigan. And the bill of lading for the Range Rovers. He had probably slipped them in with other papers for Rayney to sign. He had it all—access, means, and in his mind: motive.

"Who are you calling now?" Dennis asked, both hands gripping the handholds.

The Mercedes wheels screeched but kept traction as they negotiated the toll road turn off. "Todd Hannigan."

"That guy you had me check out?"

She glared at him. "You know, for a reporter, you have a big mouth."

"Sorry, I didn't know it was a big secret."

"Thank God for that or you would have really embarrassed me."

Hannigan answered his phone. She quickly filled him in on where she was and what she had discovered.

"So you think he's tampering with the track again?" Hannigan asked.

"Something to do with the lights or the switches—or both."

"Okay," he said, "let me get my hands on some schematics, and I'll have Search and Rescue take me on a flyby of the tracks, see if I can spot anything."

"The only passenger train we have running today is the CEO of the company and some investors. They're in the company's executive coach car. They were coming back from the casino today. I haven't been able to reach Rayney on his cell." Two beeps sounded. "Hold on a second. I've got another call."

She flashed to the waiting call.

It was Stanley Mack. "We've got communication problems on our end. Our radios are out."

"Do what you can. I'm on my way out there now."

She flashed back to Hannigan and relayed the latest twist. "The train master just told me that the radio is out."

"We've got to get out there now," he said.

"No kidding. If this guy has it out for the company, what better way than to cut off its head?"

Charlotte hung up with Hannigan then filled Dennis in on the entire story. He took feverish notes. "When can I break this?"

"If we can catch Andrew, you can run it this evening."

"So kick it," Dennis said.

She drove past the site of the first derail without turning off the freeway. Her logic being that there were too many witnesses for him to try anything there and that he would want the train going as fast as possible when it reached the point of whatever he had done to the tracks this time.

Rayney was still not answering his cell, and with the radio down, there was no way she could communicate with anyone on the train. Her only hope was to get there first and physically flag the train down. This was further complicated by the fact that the railroad tracks didn't always run parallel to a paved road. Andrew had a distinct advantage of accessibility on his dirt bike.

She turned to Dennis. "Can you drive a motorcycle?"

"I never have, but I'm willing to learn."

A helicopter flew low overhead; Charlotte watched it follow the track. Hannigan hung out the open bay door with binoculars pressed to his face. She couldn't bear to watch him for fear he'd fall. He swooped ahead just as the train tracks went out of view of the freeway.

She pulled over at a roadside fruit stand and tried to reach him by phone. A moment later, the helicopter reappeared. To the gawking amazement of the other drivers on the freeway, it landed on a dirt plateau across the street. Hannigan jumped out of the craft and ran down the hillside on the other side of the street. Charlotte crossed the freeway after him with Dennis on her heels. Honking horns, screeching tires, and yelled insults issued from the unforgiving motorists that had been caused to slow down, swerve, or stop.

Hannigan came roaring up the hill on a dirt bike, borrowed with or without the permission from one of the enthusiasts jumping the nearby verts and moguls of De Anza Motorcycle Park.

He slid to a stop beside her. "I think I spotted something about a hundred yards ahead. You can't get there by car."

Charlotte, hardly believing what she was doing but not taking the time to think about it, climbed on the back of the bike and yelled, "Let's go!"

She clung to him tightly as they flew full speed across the rocky terrain. He slid to a stop when he got to a frog, the mechanism of electrically controlled switches for open-track turnouts. The nearest signal light showed green. She slid off the back of the bike, taking care not to touch the exhaust pipe. Hannigan hunkered down and inspected the switches.

"What is it?" she asked.

"They're stuck halfway between open and closed."

"Can you fix them?"

"No, we'll need to get an electrician out here and a switch man with the keys to the control box."

"If there's an open circuit, shouldn't the signal light be red?" she asked.

"He must have tampered with that, too."

Charlotte spotted a small dump site. She picked her way through old clothes, a used car battery, empty paint cans, and then she hit pay dirt: an old rusted charcoal barbecue with a broken tripod of hollow steel legs. She twisted two of the legs off and held them up triumphantly.

"Let's see how fast we can get to the next signal."

Hannigan smiled and restarted the bike. She could only hold on to him with one hand, but she felt perfectly secure. They arrived at the next signal down the line. The ancient earthquake fissure yawned wide and deep several yards north of the rails. A locomotive tumbling into this crevasse meant certain death for all aboard.

Charlotte shunted the rails with the barbecue stand, and the signal light turned red. She turned to Hannigan. "I'll wait here and explain what's going on when the train comes."

"I don't want to leave you."

"I'll be fine, but you've got to get the other end of the line shut down in case any freight trains are running today. They'll need to be warned."

"Okay, keep your head down. I'll be back as soon as possible."

"Good," she said, "now go."

Hannigan was a cloud of dust in the distance when the first bullet struck the track at her feet.

CHAPTER 30

She ducked behind the concrete base of the signal.

"It's over, Andrew!" she yelled. "We know everything. You don't want to hurt anybody else."

The second shot pinged off the steel tubes, sending them spinning off the rails. Seconds passed, and then the signal turned back to green.

"I went to see your mother!" she yelled.

A helmeted figure holding a rifle appeared on the other side of the fissure. She realized he was reloading.

"I know you just wanted to help her. I told her we would help get the suicide ruling reversed. I put it in writing. You have my word."

He lifted the visor of his helmet. Anger contorted his features. "Too little and way too late, bitch. They ruined my family. Nothing's bringing it back."

"You won't help her by getting yourself killed or sent to jail for the rest of your life. Stop this now."

"I can't," he said. "Even if I wanted to, it's already too late." He raised his rifle again. "Where were you six months ago?"

She rolled behind the cement base of the signal light. A bullet pinged against the pole a foot above her head.

She heard a train whistle and knew she was running out of time. "Andrew, I can't let you do this. I know you don't want to hurt me." She peeked over the top of the barrier.

He adjusted his aim and fired at her head. She felt the wind of the lethal pieces of lead part her hair. Okay, so maybe she was wrong about the not-hurting-her part.

She belly-crawled down the embankment to retrieve the metal tubing. It had landed next to an old broom. She took off her shirt and pulled it over the bristle end of the broom, then lifted it in the air.

Three quick shots ventilated the shirt before the broomstick was knocked from her hand.

She vaulted up the hillside with the metal tubing and dressed only in her bra and pants. Andrew was reloading.

On the rise behind him, a figure dressed in desert camouflage raised his own rifle. The calvary had arrived. Charlotte made out two more snipers, all drawing down on Andrew. Their bullets would drive the final spike through his mother's heart. But if CEO Rayney's train were allowed to blow through this signal, many more innocents were at risk.

"Andrew, drop your gun now and raise your hands. Don't break your mother's heart any worse. I'm begging you." She felt a vibration on the tracks. The train was coming. They had all run out of time.

She dived for the tracks. The ground shook beneath her. She reached over the concrete tie and wedged the pipe between the two sizzling-hot rails. The steel branded her arm, but her shunt wasn't coming loose this time. She rolled back down the hillside, covering her head with her arms as if that would ward off bullets. The signal turned red just as the locomotive came into view. The brakes hissed, and the two-car consist came to an abrupt stop amidst much groaning of steel on steel.

If shots were fired on the opposite side of the chasm, she couldn't hear them. She ran ahead to where the train had stopped. The engineer met her on the ground.

"What's going on?" he asked.

"The switch is out up ahead. I had to stop you."

"Who are you?"

She looked down at what was left of her clothing, now dirty and full of leaves and roadside weeds. The knee of her pants was ripped, and she had lost some skin. "CEO Rayney will vouch for me."

The assistant engineer found her a shirt, and they walked back to the executive coach. Charlotte did her best to tidy herself before climbing aboard. A helicopter swooped low overhead. Rayney met her on the platform.

"What's going on?"

"Plenty." She pushed past him and looked out across the valley. Andrew was on the ground facefirst. One of the men in camouflage was securing Andrew's hands behind him with PlastiCuffs strips. She watched for a long minute; then Andrew raised his head. He was alive.

She brought the executive up to speed.

"It was Andrew," he said. "I can't believe it. I really liked that kid."

"How long has he worked for you?"

"Since March, but he seemed so eager to learn."

"Now we know why," Charlotte said.

Rayney looked down at the steep drop of the crevice running parallel to the tracks. "You want to hold another press conference?"

"It can wait. If I were you, I'd tell your engineer to put it in reverse and push you back to the first casino available. Today is your lucky day."

CHAPTER 31

Hannigan returned for her on his borrowed dirt bike. He hugged her long and hard once he determined her injuries were only superficial.

She climbed on the back of the bike, thinking it wasn't so bad to feel the wind in her hair. An electrician was already on his way to reverse whatever Andrew had done to override the system's safety features.

Dennis O'Connor flagged them down. Keeping up her end of the bargain, Char told the whole story while Dennis absorbed. "I'm going to stay here for a while," he said, hugging his notes to his chest as if they were the lost Ark of the Covenant. "I'll catch a ride back to the city with someone, so don't worry about me."

"I never do," Charlotte said. "You're a survivor." He probably wanted to do a live feed.

Hannigan delivered her to her Mercedes and waited while she opened her trunk and opened the plastic box that held her extensive first aid kit. She kneaded a cold pack, mixing the chemicals inside to create an instant ice pack, and applied it to the burn on her arm. Then she doused her scrapes with disinfectant and wrapped them in bandages. When that was done, she peeled off the assistant engineer's shirt and put on one of her own.

Hannigan used the time to make calls to his team and explain what had happened.

Charlotte put away her first aid supplies and grabbed a thin plastic tarp to cover the driver's seat before she got in.

"You saved the day," Hannigan said.

She started the car, rolled down the window, buckled her seat belt, and turned the AC to its coldest position. "We did it together."

His knelt outside her open window, a hand on the doorpost. "So what now?"

"How about I cook you dinner tonight?" she asked.

"I'd like that a lot. Is breakfast on the menu, too?"

"Eventually. You might have noticed, I'm the cautious type."

"Six, then?" he asked.

"I'll see you then."

When he kissed her that time, he didn't need to warn her. She saw it coming a mile off.

In the days that followed, the test results poured in that confirmed Charlotte's theories. The spectrograph identified the fatal dose of GHB in Bob Peterson's system. The tool marks from Dixie's forklift matched perfectly with the scratches detected on the rails.

A search of Andrew's garage and room recovered the tool used to remove Safelok clips.

Dennis had his big story, which earned him a segment on the show *48 Hours*. A producer approached him about hosting his own show. The money was too good to pass up.

Sun Rail would come out all right, too. Charlotte recommended some modifications to their employee screening, and an overhaul of their policy regarding employees involved in fatal accidents. The new rules would include a mandatory paid leave and counseling.

The odds were good that Mrs. Reynolds would have the ruling of her daughter's death changed. Charlotte spoke to the woman's priest about the need to get her into therapy for her depression.

Andrew went straight to jail. He didn't fight the charges against him and provided investigators with a full confession. He had never meant to kill Rachel Priest. His paid accomplice, Lorrin Wood, had been horrified by the result of their actions. Andrew told him he was playing a joke on Bob Peterson, for his birthday. Later, he ensured Wood's silence by convincing him he would go to prison for murder if he breathed a word of their activities to anyone.

Sherwood Priest quietly dropped his lawsuit and moved to Thailand, where the value of his American dollars would be more than enough to provide him with the lifestyle to which he felt entitled.

Charlotte's mom qualified to participate in an all-expense-paid drug trial to fight her hepatitis. If the drug was successful, Lisa would get the cure a good five years ahead of when the new treatment would be available to the public. The trick would be getting her to adhere to the strict protocol of the treatment.

Meanwhile, Charlotte took full advantage of her own condition's temporary reprieve. She hoped her OCD would return gradually so her new boyfriend would have a chance to adjust.

For the moment, she felt anything was possible.

HLOOW MYST
SERAN

SERANELLA, BARBARA
DEADMAN'S SWITCH

LOOSCAN
08/07